Never Con a Corgi

by Edie Claire

Book Six of the
Leigh Koslow Mystery Series

M
Claire

Dedication

For my friends in Novelists, Inc. (NINC), whose support and encouragement kept me writing through the dry years, and without whose optimism, professionalism, and cutting-edge business savvy the Leigh Koslow series would have ended forever in 2002.

Thanks, guys.

Chapter 1

"Chewie!" Leigh called, struck by the absence of the tawny mammal that generally remained within six inches of her ankles. "Where did you go?"

A tan and white ball of fluff burst promptly from the undergrowth, resumed its normal orbit for about five seconds, then scurried off the opposite direction.

Leigh chuckled. The dog was enjoying himself. No matter how big a yard he had at home, it was always fun to explore (and plot to destroy) new territory. She looked out at the rambling forest around her with appreciation. The woods were thick enough here, on all sides, to obscure any signs of civilization—even though the animal shelter was just a few minutes' walk away. The trail could use some work, and some new ones should be added, but overall, Warren's idea was a good one. The unused acres behind the shelter would make a fabulous off-leash dog park.

The shelter would have to charge admission, of course. But if the fence was donated (and she was quite certain her cousin Cara would help with that), they needn't charge much to make a profit, and the attraction would bring more people to the shelter, increasing its visibility and—hopefully—its donor list.

Leigh, who had joined the animal shelter board only a month ago, smiled to herself smugly. Her husband was a genius.

The corgi reappeared, his pink tongue lolling haphazardly from his oversized head as he misjudged her pace and crashed clumsily into her shins. Leigh recovered from the stumble with ease—heaven knew she had plenty of practice. Like most others of the breed, the two-year-old pup was sweet, lovable, child-tolerant, and unswervingly loyal. Unlike most others of the breed, he had the intelligence of a coat hanger.

"Personal space, Chewie," Leigh chastised. "You have this whole woods to run around in. Why don't you go dig something? Get it out of your system here instead of attacking my raspberries—"

But the dog was already gone again. Leigh continued her traipse toward the pond, keeping one ear open for the crackling of brush that indicated the dog's position. He was unlikely to go very far. He never did.

In the distance, she could hear cars driving down Nicholson Road, the occasional one going way too fast as it sped by the animal shelter and her Aunt Bess's church. Nicholson had once been a country lane, but with all the new housing plans, its character had changed dramatically. Bess's cozy hideaway, which was nestled on the other side of these same woods, had seemed to be protected from all that, being located on a private road and surrounded by only a few other residences. Until now.

Leigh cast her gaze toward the Church of the Horizon, which she was moving steadily closer to, but was unable to see through the thick summer foliage. In winter, she knew that the back of the church, its rear parking lot, and the bare foundation on which its parsonage once stood would be clearly visible from the trail on which she walked.

In winter, she would avoid looking at it.

The church was perfectly functional and above-board now, as it had been for over a decade. But there were some things, memories of certain... unsavory events, that Leigh preferred not to recall.

Actually, there were quite a few of them.

But life was different now. She was happily married, she was a mother, she was almost middle-aged (the numeric definition of "middle-aged" having gradually increased over her lifetime), and she was — all things considered — perfectly, wonderfully content.

Woof!

The single, short bark drew Leigh's attention. Chewie had his vices, but barking was not among them. The dog almost never barked, except, of course, when it came to the all-important job of alerting the family to a ringing doorbell.

"Chewie?" she called. "What's up?"

The sound had come from ahead, in the direction of the pond, but within seconds the corgi was back at her feet again. He had no tail to wag, but his bright eyes assured her that the bark was of no consequence — all was well.

Leigh pressed on toward the water. She knew the pond ahead to be a small one, and not particularly picturesque. But surely, with a little brush clearing and a few well-placed benches, it could make a nice resting spot for the dog park.

If there was a dog park.

She cast another nervous glance in the direction of the church. Last night's meeting had ended as her Aunt Bess had hoped, that much she had learned from her cousin Cara's rather animated phone call last evening. No one in the congregation wanted to sell — it was too much hassle to move, even if the money offered would cover the costs of relocation and rebuilding, which was an open question. And if the church refused to sell, and if the woman who owned the rest of the property fronting Nicholson (and leased most of it to the animal shelter), refused to sell, then the huge tract of woods on the other side of Aunt Bess's house — already bought up en masse by a speculator — could not be developed.

And Chewie could dig holes to his little heart's content.

The dog paced back and forth on the path in front of her, too excited to walk straight. "Want to dig, boy?" she prompted. "Wait till we get to the pond. There'll be softer ground there, fewer roots to stall you."

Chewie took off into the brush again — in the opposite direction.

Leigh sighed.

The trees thinned immediately ahead of her, and she stepped out into the small clearing that bordered the shallow pond. It was definitely not much to look at. Just a low spot among the slightly rolling hills that otherwise drained off to the nearby creek. Her Aunt Bess dearly loved that creek. The fact that it routinely flooded out the private road that led to her house was entirely forgivable — given that it also made said road unusable for new development. The only way to reach Nicholson from the land the speculator had already bought would be to level a new access road right through the church, her Aunt Bess's house, and/or the land on which Leigh was standing.

Her aunt had no intention of letting that happen.

The corgi reappeared, circled Leigh's ankles a few times, then trotted off along the bank of the pond toward the church. Leigh followed, her mind drifting to the mundane. She had no idea what she would fix for dinner, and the laundry was already a day behind. Never mind that pesky leak in the half bath she kept meaning to ask her Aunt Lydie about —

A man in a suit was lying on the ground beside the pond.

Chewie sniffed at him perfunctorily, then trotted on.

Leigh stood still for a moment, her pulse pounding in her ears. Then she rushed forward, hoping against hope for drunkenness, dizziness, or disease. Anything, anything at all, so long as the man wasn't lying there because —

Dead.

She broke her run so abruptly she nearly fell forward.

The man was dressed in an expensive suit, complete with dress shoes. He was lying on his stomach in the dirt, face twisted to one side, eyes open and staring. His mouth gaped — as if in surprise. Leigh did not bend down to take a pulse, but instead, stepped back. She knew death when she saw it. She had grown up seeing it as a matter of course in her father's veterinary clinic.

Among other places.

No.

Beads of sweat broke out on her brow. It was a cool day, for Pittsburgh in July, but her insides were boiling.

This could NOT be happening.

It was a trick.

She whipped her head to either side, looking for the prankster, the television cameras... the anything. There was no one else around.

She breathed in heavily. She breathed out. She extended one tentative, sneaker-clad foot. Her toe nudged one of the man's outstretched hands, still decorated with an impressive array of gold rings.

The fingers were stiff as wood.

Leigh dropped back a few more paces.

This was no trick. Of all the people on this vast, overpopulated planet — all the policemen, all the firefighters, all the doctors, pathologists, ambulance drivers, and morticians — she, Leigh Koslow the advertising copywriter, had found another body.

It was starting all over again.

Chapter 2

Leigh corralled her dog, took his lead out of her pocket, and clipped it back on his collar.

To the extent possible in a dog with no tail, he pouted.

"Sorry, Chewie," she said distractedly. "We've got to—"

Got to what? Her cell phone, naturally, was safely stashed in her purse, which was safely stashed in her car, which was back at the animal shelter. She could walk either back there or to her Aunt Bess's, but the church was closer. It was midmorning. Someone should be there.

She took one more hopeful look in the direction of the body— hoping that in the last few seconds it might magically have disappeared.

It had not.

She let out a breath, then set off with a determined stride. The corgi raced back and forth across her path and around her ankles like a spinning spider, but Leigh, long-practiced in the art, switched the lead from hand to hand, whirled, and uncoiled herself as she moved, all without conscious thought. They reached the church all too quickly, and in the parking lot outside its office, she stopped a moment to collect herself.

There were three cars in the lot. Surely not everyone inside would think she was crazy. Maybe they wouldn't even know who she was.

That would help.

She slipped Chewie's lead over the newel post on the wrought-iron stair rail, then jogged up the side steps to the office door and walked in.

Two women looked up from their desks with smiles.

"Leigh!" said the secretary closest to her, a tiny, rail-thin woman of about fifty. "Whatever brings you here?" The woman's once ash-blonde hair was now perfectly white, but it was as devoid of style as ever, and her blue eyes gleamed at her visitor through the same overlarge plastic frames she'd been wearing as long as Leigh could remember.

"Hi, Shannon," Leigh stammered, wondering how she could have forgotten the fact that Warren's uncle—and his second wife—had rejoined the new church some years ago. She didn't know that Shannon was volunteering in the office again, but given the woman's dedication to charity work, that was no surprise.

"This is Michelle," Shannon said politely, gesturing to the younger employee who sat behind the main desk. "She's the new office manager here. Michelle, this is my niece, Leigh."

The strangers exchanged nods, but Shannon was perceptive enough to spare them further niceties. "What on earth is wrong?" she asked, studying Leigh with concern. "Do you want to sit down?"

Leigh shook her head. "I just need to use the phone, please. I've... found something in the woods behind the animal shelter, and I need to call the police."

The phone on the main desk rang, making all three jump. After a beat, Michelle hastened to pick it up. Shannon looked at Leigh intently, her pale face growing paler. She started to say something, but stifled the impulse. Silently, she led Leigh around the corner of her desk to the other phone. "Here," she said gently. "But sit down first, okay?"

Leigh complied. Her limbs felt like lead.

"You want me to dial 911?" Shannon asked, her fingers poised.

"No thanks," Leigh replied, taking the handset. "I'll just call Maura."

Maura.

A shiver ran down Leigh's spine. She had last seen Maura, her former college roommate, less than twelve hours ago, when they had waved goodbye to each other on Leigh's front porch, both Maura's and her husband Gerry's hands full of plastic containers of pierogie casserole and pickled beets. Maura, who just happened to investigate homicides for a living, was one of her dearest, best friends in the entire world.

Perhaps she should call 911.

Leigh shook her shoulders, attempting to regroup. This was not her fault. She hadn't done anything wrong.

Since when had that ever mattered?

Her hand hovered over the phone. She couldn't remember Maura's number—she couldn't remember anybody's number. They were all in her cell. With a sigh, she dialed information, eventually getting herself routed to the Allegheny County detectives unit.

"Homicide, Polanski here."

Leigh shifted her weight in the chair. "Hi, Maura. It's me."

"Koslow!" the cheerful voice boomed merrily. "What's up? I had your beets for breakfast. Good stuff, there. You may learn to cook, yet."

"This is..." *Stop spluttering!* "Kind of an official call. I was walking Chewie in the woods behind the animal shelter just now, and we found a body."

Leigh winced as Shannon, beside her, drew in a sharp breath. Maura, on the other hand, exploded into a loud guffaw of laughter.

"Yeah, right, Koslow. What'd he find, a squirrel? Spare me. I'm too old for this."

Leigh pictured her solid, six-foot two-inch, two-hundred-forty pound, notoriously short-fused policewoman friend leaning casually back in her department-issue swivel chair. Age and marriage had mellowed her.

But not that much.

Leigh swallowed. "No, Maura, listen to me. I'm serious. It was a person. A dead man. Lying beside a little pond out here. And before you say—"

Too late. With a sigh, Leigh held the phone away from her ear, waiting for the expected string of exclamations, curses, and linguistically colorful references to certain previous, perhaps ill-advised actions on Leigh's part to diminish. It took a while.

"She's upset?" Shannon asked weakly, listening to the only partially muted tirade from several feet away.

Leigh nodded grimly. "She has a thing about how often my name shows up in her police reports. Petty, really."

When the noise from the receiver quieted, Leigh returned the phone tentatively to her ear. "At least I gave you a break for a while, right?"

She winced and moved it back out again.

Shannon's eyes widened.

After a suitable pause, Leigh tried again.

"Koslow!" the voice barked. "Are you listening to me?"

"Of course."

"Then listen to this. Stay right were you are. Don't go anywhere

near that body again. And don't let anyone else go near it, either."
The detective let out a breath. "Hellfire, Koslow! You know my
heart can't take this."

"The doctor said your heart is perfectly fine. Besides, this really
isn't something I chose—"

"I suppose I should just be thankful it's not someone you're
personally involved with!" Maura continued gruffly. "At least *this*
time, since you don't know the victim—"

Leigh's heart skipped a beat. "Um... did I say that?"

Silence.

"Maura? You there?"

The brusque voice weakened to a groan. "Just spill it, Koslow."

Leigh cleared her throat. Both Shannon and Michelle, who was
now off the other phone and looking as pale as her coworker, stood
staring at Leigh with bugged eyes.

"It's... Brandon Lyle," she began hesitantly.

Michelle and Shannon shrieked in unison, their hands flying to
their mouths.

"What was that?" Maura demanded. "Who's there? And who the
hell is Brandon Lyle?"

The women slumped onto nearby desks.

"We were talking about him last night, remember? He's... I mean,
he *was*, a client down at the agency. But more importantly, he was
the real estate developer who wanted to buy Aunt Bess's land—and
the church's. I'm at the church now, because it was the closest phone
I could get to. The office manager is here. And Warren's aunt."

Maura's voice rose. "Then this is the same church that—"

"Yep."

Leigh could hear muffled sounds: a chair squeak, a drawer
sliding.

"Maura?"

"Just getting my meds," the policewoman returned. "I'll be there
in twenty—sending out a black and white now. And Leigh?"

She braced. "Yes?"

"Don't. Do. Anything. Stupid!"

Leigh's jaws clenched. "Now seriously, when have I ever—"

The phone line clicked off.

"Brandon Lyle!" Shannon exclaimed, her voice barely above a
whisper. "But he was here last night..."

"That must be his car in the lot!" Michelle interjected. She turned to Leigh. "I wondered whose it could be; I don't know anyone in the church with a BMW convertible."

"But he *left* last night," Shannon insisted, her voice growing steadily stronger. "I know he did. A bunch of people saw him drive away. Right after the argument with Gil March."

"You mean the fist fight?" Michelle queried.

Leigh's stomach twisted uncomfortably. She hadn't told Maura the half of her—and her extended family's—rather unpleasant entanglement with the late Mr. Lyle. If she knew anything about police interrogations (and sadly, she did) the process was likely to take a while.

She considered, then rose with a jerk. "Shannon," she said earnestly, "I need to take my dog back to the animal shelter and let the manager know where I'll be. I'm going to walk him over by the road, but—well, if there's any suspicion that I've sneaked back to the pond, Maura really will have that coronary she's always talking about. So could you—both of you—watch me go? I'll be back in five minutes."

The women looked at each other anxiously. "Of course, Leigh," Shannon said firmly, walking with her to the door. "We'll park ourselves right here on the steps until the police come."

Leigh looked thankfully at her aunt-by-marriage, who despite looking like she could blow away on a strong wind, often showed surprising strength. Nice lady, always had been. Still, Leigh could never quite shake the feeling that there was something a little... well... *odd* about her.

"The police are coming, aren't they?" Shannon added tentatively.

The question was answered by the high, thin wail of a distant siren.

"Gotta run!" Leigh exclaimed. She hurried down the stairs, grabbed the lead, clucked to her eager-looking corgi, and took off at a jog. The animal shelter was only a short distance down the road, at least for a healthy human. To a thirty pound dog with six-inch legs, it probably seemed longer, but Chewie was not one to complain. He charged off beside her at a full gallop, his short strides bunching up his long body like an inchworm.

Not daring to slow, Leigh swerved around the parking lot and headed for the back of the building.

"Hey, mom!" A young voice called with amusement. "Why are you running?"

Leigh halted at the gate to one of the empty play yards. The fact that the sight of her running would elicit such a question was evidence of the shape she was in.

After several long moments, she caught her breath.

"I've got to get back to the church," she answered, locking Chewie securely in the run, where he made a beeline for the automatic waterer. "I'm meeting your Aunt Maura there — it may take a while. You just stay put till I get back, okay?"

The boy, who was walking a lab mix with one hand and some chow-looking beast with the other and making little progress in any direction, tossed his head to see from under the sheaf of bright red hair that fell across his eyes. "Whatever," he said cheerfully. "I'm not going anywhere. With these two, I may never go anywhere!"

Leigh paused just long enough to smile. Ten-year-old Ethan loved hanging out at the animal shelter — walking the dogs no one else wanted to walk. His clothes were already laced with slobber and his shoes would have to be scraped before she'd let him back in the car, but she was terribly proud of him. Besides being a hard worker, the boy had her love of animals and his father's cheerful disposition... what more could a parent ask for?

She hurried through the back door and passed through the hallway by the cat room. She would have to let Angie know she might be late in returning —

"Mom?"

Leigh halted in her tracks and back-stepped. "Yes?"

A petite, dark-haired girl sat cross-legged on the floor, a litter of kittens mewling as it tumbled across her bony lap. "Grandpa needs to take a look at these," the girl said determinedly. "They were all fine yesterday, but today this one's kind of sluggish, and I don't like the look of that eye discharge at all. They may have to be quarantined."

Leigh fought back an indulgent grin. If ever a pair of siblings were twins in birth only, it was hers. Her brainy, solemn daughter made quite a contrast to her easy-going, extroverted son. Even physically, while Ethan seemed an even blend of her own features and Warren's, Allison resembled neither of them. Rather, the poor thing was the spitting image of her grandfather Randall. "Do you think I should call him?" the girl asked, wrinkling her nose to adjust her glasses.

"Sure, honey," Leigh answered, bemused at how her daughter seemed to have inherited her grandfather's mannerisms as well. "Go ahead. I may be late getting back today. Just please, don't get scratched again."

"I'll be fine," the girl answered, not looking up. "I have my antiseptic spray."

The sound of a second siren wailed on the road outside, and Leigh hastened her steps through the building and up to the reception desk. "I may be back late, Angie," she said to the young manager at the desk as she moved, "there's been... a problem at the church next door. Just keep the kids here—don't let them wander around the woods today, okay? Call me if you need me!"

"All right, but what—" the front door closed behind Leigh before she could hear the end of the question, which was just as well, because she knew she couldn't answer it. She raced to the car, grabbed her purse and phone, and took off down the road at a jog. Her fingers itched to text her husband, but she had no idea what to write. *Found body; please sympathize? Client dead; not my fault?* Either way, it would hardly make his morning.

She arrived back at the church parking lot, panting, to find not one but two black and whites in residence, their occupants already questioning a visibly flustered Shannon and Michelle. "She's back now," Leigh heard Shannon say as she came into range. "She'll tell you."

The three policemen turned to face her.

"Sorry," Leigh said weakly, still trying to catch her breath. "I got back as fast as I could, but I had to check on my kids and make sure they stayed at the shelter."

"She ran right there and back," Shannon chimed in. "Michelle and I have both been watching—she hasn't been gone five minutes."

Leigh resisted the urge to throw Shannon a thankful smile. At least one person understood her paranoia where law enforcement was concerned.

"You say you found a body?" one of the township policemen questioned, his skeptical tone making clear that either (1) her full name hadn't been mentioned, or (2) he had never spent quality time with anyone on the county detectives' squad.

Both points were in her favor.

She nodded.

"Supposing you show us where?" he prompted.

Leigh looked in the direction of the woods, took another steadying breath, and started walking.

She really wished she could develop another hobby.

Chapter 3

Maura dropped her solid frame down onto the wooden picnic table that sat in the shady grove behind the church. She settled herself next to Leigh, who had been effectively chained there for the last half hour, and sighed.

The two women stared at one another.

"I don't do it on purpose, you know," Leigh offered.

Maura's eyebrows puckered. "Debatable."

"How could I?" Leigh argued. "You think I have some cosmic attraction for the marked to die, or the recently deceased?"

The detective considered a moment. "Let's hope not. Sure as hell wouldn't bode well for me."

Leigh frowned.

The ghost of a smile crossed Maura's otherwise sober face. "Sorry. Couldn't resist. Now let's get this damned thing over with, shall we? You know the drill. You tell me absolutely everything about how you happened to be the first one to stumble onto Brandon Lyle's body, and then you move on to everything else you know that you're planning *not* to tell me unless I ask you about it specifically. And so help me, Koslow, if I find out later that there was one shred of evidence you didn't tell me, one little detail you thought it would be better for your cousin's in-law's daughter's pet turtle if I didn't know, I will—"

"Yes, yes," Leigh cut in. "Thumbscrews, honey and ants, partial decapitation with a dull razor, yada, yada. Why would I hide anything from the authorities? I want nothing to do with this mess. I'm a mother now, remember?"

"Yes," Maura said hopefully. "There is that." She tapped her pen impatiently on her notebook. "Start talking."

Maura lifted a hand to massage her temple. Her short, dark hair was limp; her dimpled baby face (which had always made an interesting contrast to her otherwise intimidating appearance) was beaded with sweat. "Koslow," she said wearily, "when you say 'he practically blew up, right there in my office,' do you mean that he raised his voice, or do you mean—"

"I had to threaten to call security before he would leave."

Maura sighed.

Leigh's description of how she had found the body had gone well enough. Explaining her personal association with Brandon Lyle was proving more problematic.

"It wasn't the first time an ad agency ever had a business argument cross the line," Leigh defended. "I've seen it happen other places. At Hook, we work hard to keep our clients from getting irate in the first place, but when you're dealing with a guy like Lyle, who was a total—"

"Koslow!" Maura barked, "Will you watch what you say to me, please?"

"Oh, right," Leigh retreated. "What I meant to say is, when an agency has a client with a volatile personality who's risking large sums of money, meetings can get emotional, no matter how professional we are. Brandon was a problem from day one, but Jeff Hulsey and I were able to manage him. Until yesterday, that is."

The sweat on Maura's brow had coalesced into droplets, and she pulled a handkerchief from her pocket and dabbed. Maura was the only woman Leigh had ever known who carried a handkerchief. Then again, she was the only woman Leigh had ever known who did a lot of things.

"Just start at day one," the detective said tiredly.

"His development company has been with Hook for a couple of years now," Leigh explained. "We did two other projects for him before this one; we produced brochures and presentations to help him recruit investors and then later to sell the properties. Things went fine on our end, but rumor has it those two previous developments ran into major problems. Exactly what, I don't know—we had nothing to do with the financials. But it was clear he was banking on this current project to bail him out somehow."

"You mean the deal where he needed to buy your aunt's land, or the church's, in order to connect his other properties with the road?" Maura questioned, clearly remembering at least some of the conversation they had enjoyed so casually over pierogie casserole last night. Leigh had given her guests a quick overview of the situation after she had excused herself to take Cara's anxious call about the church meeting. But she hadn't told them everything. When you had a family like hers and you were friends with two married detectives—both of whom had a thing about not showing favoritism in official matters—you learned certain editing skills.

"Either both of those properties, or the land where the animal shelter is, or maybe both the church and Bess's neighbor Clem's place," Leigh explained. "It's a little complicated, but Lyle had several options. Two months ago, when he hired us to do the investment piece, he wasn't even worried about the access. I had no idea Aunt Bess's place was even involved until Cara showed me the mockups for the brochures."

Leigh's cousin Cara, a graphic designer of some repute, had for years now been doing high-profile jobs for Hook, the ad agency Leigh had helped to create. Cara didn't ordinarily work on brochures, and she hadn't been working on Lyle's. The woman was just plain nosy.

"When I saw the architect's drawings, I almost lost my lunch," Leigh continued. "These things never turn out as grandiose as the original plans, of course, but Lyle wanted more than just a fancy entryway with brick gateposts and a waterfall. He had a whole neighborhood shopping square laid out, with a coffee shop, boutiques, even a grocery market! In order to do even half of that, he'd have to buy *all* the land on that side of the road. It was awkward, under the circumstances, but Cara and I decided to warn him, right up front, that we didn't think our Aunt Bess would ever sell. Lyle just blew us off, saying that everyone had their price, and that he had surveyed those houses already and he was sure none of them were worth anything."

The detective issued a low, growling sound. "So," she asked gruffly. "What did you two do then?"

Leigh widened her eyes innocently. "*Do?* What do you mean?"

Maura growled again.

"We didn't do anything!" Leigh protested. "Aunt Bess already knew about it; she had ignored umpteen letters and phone calls already. Like we suspected, she had no intention of selling to the man at any price, and furthermore, she planned to see to it that the church didn't either. She's been dead set against development on Nicholson all along, and now those acres around her are about all that's left of the original woods. You know how Bess is...once she takes up a cause and digs her heels in—"

Maura raised a hand. "I'm familiar with the family trait, Koslow. Believe me. Now, proceed. What exactly led up to Lyle's outburst yesterday?"

Leigh took a breath. Now her own forehead was sweating. "Lyle paid for his brochures, and that was that. I didn't see him again until about two weeks ago, when Gil sent him to me for PR advice."

"Whoa, wait a minute!" Maura exclaimed. "Gil as in Gil March, Cara's husband, the county's highest-priced business consultant? Do *not* tell me he's involved in this, too!"

Leigh nibbled on a fingernail. Or at least, she started to. But her fingers smelled like corgi slobber. She put her hands at her sides instead, bracing herself.

"Would nearly getting in a fist fight with Lyle behind the church last night qualify as 'involved?'"

Maura's face turned an unpleasant purplish shade.

"I'll take that as a yes," Leigh said carefully. "But you'll be delighted to hear that I wasn't present for that particular event. All I know about their argument is what Cara told me over the phone, that—"

Maura raised another hand. Speaking calmly appeared to be an effort for her. "Don't tell me what Cara said. I'll deal with the two of them personally. Just tell me what happened when you saw Lyle two weeks ago. He hired you to do what?"

Leigh chose her words with care. The more she thought about it, the more she realized just how deeply her family *was* entangled with the affairs of one Brandon Lyle.

And not in a good way, either.

"Gil's known him a long time," she began. "They've done business before. But you'd have to ask Gil about that. All I know is that Brandon wanted Gil to help him save this housing development, and Gil—despite the obvious risks to family harmony—was trying to do his best. He sent Brandon to Hook because he thought we could put our best PR person on it—have them try to persuade the church, and maybe this guy Clem, to sell. I think Brandon had given up on Aunt Bess by that point, as well as the woman who leases land to the animal shelter, Anna Krull. If Brandon had her on board he could get his access road, at least, but she's even more of a tree-hugger than Aunt Bess is, and just as obstinate."

Leigh stopped and took a breath. Maura tapped her pen aggressively on her notepad, waiting for Leigh to go on.

"I don't want to see those hills leveled to make way for yet another crop of mushroom mansions any more than my Aunt Bess does," Leigh continued, wondering if the stab of guilt she felt at having worked with a scumbag like Lyle in the first place was showing. "But business is business. We do have a really good PR person, Geralyn Toms, so I put her on it. Who was I to say the development was a lost cause? As long as Lyle wasn't lying to people, I figured the other landholders had a right to make up their own minds. Geralyn is honest; she doesn't mislead people. But she is skilled at maintaining goodwill in tense situations."

"So what happened?" Maura prompted. The detective was still a little too purple for Leigh's tastes, but at least steam wasn't coming out of her ears.

"Geralyn set up an open meeting at the church for last night. She was also supposed to be meeting privately with Clem, Bess, and Anna—but that end of things wasn't going well. Anna and Bess politely refused her, and Clem wouldn't meet with her at all. Yesterday Geralyn told me that she'd finally caught up with him that morning—and he'd threatened her with a shotgun."

Maura turned her head to the side and muttered a string of words Leigh didn't often hear anymore, seeing as how Maura generally managed to control her mouth around the children.

Yet another benefit of being a parent.

"Geralyn was still willing to do the church meeting," Leigh continued, "but she refused to deal with Clem again. Lyle was furious. Started yelling, blaming Geralyn, calling her incompetent, among other things. He went totally off the rails. Sweet, mild-mannered Geralyn finally told the—"

"Watch it, Koslow," Maura warned again.

"Right. What I mean to say is, Geralyn told the fine, upstanding gentleman exactly what location he could place his job into and at what velocity he could place it there—"

"Yeah, I got it," Maura interrupted again. "Keep going."

"There's not much else to say," Leigh finished. "When she walked out, Lyle asked me if I could run the meeting myself, and I refused.

I told him I wasn't trained as a negotiator, and that—despite what he seemed to think—I had no personal clout with the Church of the Horizon. He got furious all over again, cursed at me, cursed at everyone else in the office, and told us we were all incompetent and he would never do business with any of us ever again. I told him to leave or I would call security, and he cursed a little more, and then he left. That was about three o'clock in the afternoon, and that was the last I heard from him."

The detective did some more cursing of her own. "So you didn't go to the church meeting?"

"You know I didn't!"

"Well, where were—"

Leigh's raised eyebrows stopped her.

"Oh, right!" Maura exclaimed, her pained face erupting, albeit briefly, into a genuine smile. "You were with me and Gerry!"

Leigh smiled back. "A county detective and a city police lieutenant. Best alibi ever, eh?"

Maura snapped her notebook shut and slid off the picnic table. "The situation's bad enough, Koslow," she commented wryly. "But I suppose it could be worse. At least we won't have to scrounge up bail money this time."

Maura's mouth twisted suddenly into a frown, and Leigh could sense her next, unspoken thought. *At least not for you.*

"Look, Leigh," Maura continued soberly. "The department's been cracking down on personal involvement in cases lately—we've had some problems. With my being friends with the person who found the body, as well as knowing Gil and Cara and your Aunt—there's no doubt I'll be off this case by tomorrow. But I can at least get it started right. I'm going to pull in our best guy, pronto, and as soon as I do, he and I will question Gil and Cara, and Bess. And until we get there, I don't want you telling any of them jack. Do you understand me? *Not. One. Word.*"

Leigh offered her best, most sincere salute. This was one promise she would have no trouble keeping. The list of things she would rather do than tell either Gil March or his doting wife that the man he'd publicly brawled with had been murdered later the same night was very long indeed.

That was, if Lyle *had* been murdered. Leigh was pretty sure she had seen at least one dark spot on his suit jacket, but she hadn't looked all that closely.

"Maura?" she asked, daring to be hopeful. "We wouldn't be having this conversation if you thought Lyle died of natural causes, obviously, but... is there any chance it was suicide?"

The detective offered a stern look. For a moment she seemed disinclined to answer. "I'll say this, Koslow," she said finally. "I've seen people find all kinds of creative ways to kill themselves. But I've never seen any man shoot himself in the back."

Chapter 4

Leigh sat in her car in the animal shelter parking lot, staring at her phone. She had deleted three unfinished text messages to her husband already. She started a fourth, which made no mention of corpses, but simply asked him if he could come home for lunch.

She deleted that, too. Warren had appointments downtown all day long. She could wait until dinner.

She looked toward the shelter, where her children were still happily walking, petting, feeding, and scooping. Maura's interrogation hadn't lasted nearly as long as Leigh thought it would; the kids' volunteer shift didn't end for another hour.

She nibbled on a fingernail—which smelled liked vanilla now, thanks to the soap in the church bathroom—and wondered what on earth she would tell the children. Even if the family did have detective friends, murder was hardly an ordinary topic for dinner conversation. How could she explain in a non-frightening way that not only had their mother stumbled upon a corpse in the middle of their favorite woods, but that their uncle was almost certainly going to be—

Leigh's phone buzzed in her hand. She looked down, hoping to see Warren's name, but seeing instead a call from Aunt Bess.

Her heart skipped a beat. The woman couldn't know already, could she? Unless Shannon or Michelle had called her...

"Hi, Aunt Bess," Leigh said tentatively, bracing for a maelstrom of rapid-fire questions. Her mother's older sister, always the dark sheep of the family, was the nosiest of the bunch. She was also impossible to say no to, reckless as a teenager, spirited as a polo pony, prone to involvement in every kind of natural and human disaster... and tremendous fun to be around.

"Hey there, kiddo!" Bess chirped merrily. "Listen, I was wondering, are your offspring working up at the shelter this morning? If so, why don't you swing by here after you pick them up? I've got the coolest new toy; I can't wait to show you all!"

Leigh let out her breath in a rush. Bess didn't know a thing. *Yet.*

But she could at any moment, which meant the sooner Leigh accepted her invitation, the better. And *without* the kids. "A toy for whom?" she questioned.

"For me, of course!" Bess said with a chuckle. "Can you come?"

Leigh glanced at the time. At least seeing her Aunt Bess would give her something to do while she waited—besides worry about the coming nightmare for her normally straight-arrow cousin-in-law.

"I'll be right there," she agreed.

Leigh tried not to rubberneck as she passed the church, but it was difficult, seeing as how the parking lot was now packed with official-looking vehicles, and every other car on the road was stopping to look as well. If the Ivey sisters were still living in the house across the street they would be plastered to their picture window like flies; but according to Bess, the two were now wreaking equivalent havoc at a nearby assisted living facility, where they spent most of each day sitting comfortably in the lobby making mental notes of the comings and goings of the other residents and their visitors—much to the chagrin of at least one wandering husband.

Leigh drove on, then turned onto the unmarked private drive to Bess's house. In contrast to her mood, the road was peacefully picturesque as it meandered through mature oak and maple trees along the now-trickling creek. In the woods opposite the creek stood the trim, modest cottage which Anna Krull had built and moved into some twenty years before, when her family's ancient farmhouse at the end of the road had literally begun to crumple over her head. Anna, being no fool, had placed her own new drive on the near side of the spring flood zone, an option unfortunately unavailable to Aunt Bess and the road's other residents.

Another house soon loomed up on the right, this one considerably larger and more grandiose than Anna's. Leigh knew that until quite recently it had been owned by a family named Morrison, whom Bess now spoke of only as "those traitors," lumping them in with every other neighbor who'd taken Brandon Lyle's money and skedaddled. Leigh suspected that the Morrisons, like herself, probably preferred to live someplace where the only access road was neither riddled with manatee-sized potholes nor, at times, completely underwater. But there was no point in arguing such trivialities with her Aunt Bess, whose only response to the road's gradually deteriorating condition had been to purchase a Jeep with bigger wheels.

As the road turned and crooked through the particularly thick woods obscuring the home of Bess's longtime neighbor Clem, Leigh's brow furrowed. The man had never caused her aunt any trouble, but his threats to Geralyn had been unsettling, to say the least. His house, which was set well off the road and back in the trees, was a rambling, ramshackle affair that had not seen a coat of paint since Leigh had been a size six. She caught only a glimpse of wheel-less vehicles, rusted oil drums, one brand-new pup tent, two wandering goats, and a hand-lettered sign reading "no trezpassing hear" before her attention was drawn back to the road, lest she wreck the van's suspension.

She would have to talk to her Aunt Bess about him.

One more bend in the road and she at last reached her Aunt's place, a well kept, white frame, one and a half story farmhouse. Though nowhere near as showy as the ex-Morrison's, the house's wide, inviting front porch, prominent chimney, and large windows made it by far the coziest dwelling in the neighborhood. Leigh parked, hopped out, and strode quickly to the front door, behind which she could already hear the yapping of Bess's primarily Pekingese, Chester.

"Come in, come in," Bess called gaily, swinging the door open wide as the geriatric pooch spilled out and hastened to sniff at Leigh's ankles, spinning like a top as he did so. "Calm down, Chester!" Bess corrected gently. "You know perfectly well it's only Miss Leigh." She turned to her niece. "He may not see too well anymore, but he certainly isn't deaf, is he? Still lets me know every time a car passes. Which is practically never, since the neighbors all did their deals with the devil. So, where are the kids?"

Leigh hesitated. Her Aunt Bess looked the same as she always looked, which was to say, ageless. The woman was in her late sixties, but you couldn't tell it by her choice in fashions. She had worn her hair in a modified beehive well into the twenty-first century, changing it only when—after a long-awaited vacation to London—she decided that she really must do a little neon pink highlighting. Since then, her hairstyle had changed almost weekly. Today, Leigh was being treated to an off-the-shoulder flip that could be right out of the sixties, if it weren't for the fact that Bess's dyed-brown hair was also sporting feather extensions. Never one to confine herself to the fashion of a single decade, Bess's outfit of the day consisted of a staunchly conservative-looking cotton wool cardigan matched with modern capris (both filled to capacity by their wearer's bounteous curves), and bare feet adorned with dark blue nail polish.

"They're still at the shelter," Leigh said hesitantly, entering. Why exactly had she thought it was a good idea to see Bess now, before she could say anything about the murder? She couldn't ask about Clem yet, either—she would have to stay off the topic of the development altogether. "I was waiting for them anyway, so I thought I'd just pop over," she explained truthfully. "What's this about a new toy?"

Bess gave a little hop on her feet and whirled back toward the big-screen television that graced the center of her living room. She grabbed a remote and moved to sit on the couch, an action which caused a mad scurrying of the three cats currently occupying that space. Bess had, at any given time, at least seven felines in residence. Ever since she had lost Punkster, the diabolical attack cat that had once inadvertently saved four people's lives (and who had remained ornery as sin throughout the entirety of his nineteen years), Bess was the shelter's most reliable sucker when it came to accepting hard-to-place cats.

"Sit here," the older woman ordered, waving to a spot already taken by a one-eyed ginger tom who showed no inclination to scurry anywhere. "Ralph!" she chastised. "Go eat something! There's plenty of kibble left in the kitchen. Shoo!"

The cat shot her a sulky look, but then stretched his legs, rose, and obediently plodded toward the kitchen.

"Sit!" Bess ordered again, patting the cushions. Leigh sat. "Now," Bess continued gleefully, "look at this!"

She pushed some buttons on the remote, and Leigh found herself looking at a dark background with a date and time stamp—and not much else.

"Wait for it," Bess urged. "The camera is motion-activated, so the DVR only kicks in when something is happening. Look!"

Leigh studied what appeared to be a night-vision video of a pile of wood. A blur that might have been an animal flashed briefly across one corner.

"Can you tell where it is?" Bess asked excitedly.

Leigh considered a moment. "Is it out back, the woodpile by your shed?"

Bess clapped her hands. "Right-O! I have two cameras, but this is the one that hit pay dirt. Keep watching!"

As Leigh stared at the pile of wood, the animal, now clearly identifiable as a black and white tomcat, jumped up and perched itself at an awkward angle, its attention keenly focused at a particular point on the ground. After several seconds of intent tail flicking, the cat launched himself onto what Leigh could only guess was an emerging field mouse, catching it neatly between his paws.

Bess squealed with delight. "It's just like *National Geographic!* Isn't that amazing? And it's real! Talk about ideas to raise money for the shelter! Well, what do you think?"

Leigh blinked. "Raise money?"

Bess paused the video just as the cat lifted a paw and the mouse made a break for it. "Of course! You know how fascinated people are with feral cats. My Ferdinand could be a rock star! He could have his own website. I could get more cameras, film the females, too. Fans would tune in to watch, and of course, they could donate to the shelter through the site. Brilliant, eh?"

Leigh's eyebrows rose. She was no stranger to the tale of Ferdinand, a tough and scrappy tom who had been wandering the woods for years now, resistant to all manner of tricks and traps, until her Aunt Bess had finally cajoled him into a carrier just this past winter. At one point, the woods behind the shelter had been crawling with feral cats and kittens, and although Bess and the staff had managed to reduce the population significantly through live trapping and adoption, there was a core of particularly wily felines they could never manage to capture. When Bess at last caught Ferdinand, the patriarch of the colony, Leigh's father had decided to try a different form of birth control: instead of neutering the tom, he had given Ferdinand a vasectomy. The cat was released back to his colony, vaccinated and otherwise healthy, but the usual crop of spring and summer kittens never came. The scrappy tom was still king of the woods... and evidently, sole master of his harem.

But an internet sensation?

"Maybe," Leigh offered. "You really think people would tune in just to see things cats do every day?"

Bess's forehead creased. "You think people with indoor cats see *this* everyday?"

She pressed the play button, and Leigh watched as the cat recaptured the mouse, let it squiggle out between his paws again, then pounced upon it once more.

"I would rate it PG," Bess said thoughtfully, as the cat tired of the game and stopped the mouse's antics once and for all. "But it's highly educational. Not to mention good publicity for your father's methods of handling feral cats. Just think, if we could actually catch them breeding—"

Leigh ceased listening. Something in the video had caught her attention, and it wasn't the animals. "Aunt Bess," she interrupted. "Can you replay that? Just the last few seconds?"

Bess complied, and Leigh leaned in closer, her heart beating rapidly. It was faint, but there was light shining in the woods in the background. Just a tiny beam flickering, then it was gone. Then another. Almost like fireflies... but not.

"Aunt Bess," Leigh said uneasily. "Did you notice those lights?"

Bess leaned in beside her. "Oh... that. Looks like flashlights in the woods. Kids getting ready for their fireworks, probably. They were at it last weekend, too."

"Fireworks?" Leigh asked, perking up. "Where?"

Bess shrugged. "Depends. Sometimes in the parking lot behind the church. Sometimes at the pond. That pond's always been a popular hangout, you know. Drinking, smoking, whatever."

"Did you call the police?"

Bess's eyebrows rose. "Why would I do that?"

"Well, I mean..." Leigh stammered, "if they were trespassing... they could start a fire."

Bess chuckled ruefully. "If anyone sets my woods on fire, they'll have me to contend with. As for the rest, they're just teenagers, for heaven's sake! Where are they supposed to drink and smoke? The mall? I certainly spent some quality time in the great outdoors in my—"

"Aunt Bess!" Leigh interrupted, looking over her shoulder reflexively to make sure no impressionable ears were listening. The exploits of Bess's youth had made great entertainment when she and Cara were kids, but she would prefer to keep the youngest generation unaware of them.

Bess looked at her and sighed. "Ah, poor kiddo. I didn't think it would happen. Not even after the twins were born. But it is. You're turning into your—"

"I am not!" Leigh snapped.

"Are too," Bess said smugly.

Leigh groaned. "Can we just watch this part of the tape again?"

Bess pursed her lips and rewound. As they watched the faint, dancing light appear again, Leigh decided she agreed with her aunt. It looked like a distant flashlight.

But whose? The time stamp on the DVR had said 9:24 PM. The meeting at the church had been over long before then.

"Did you hear anything?" Leigh asked. "I mean, when this was happening?"

Bess considered, then shook her head. "I don't really remember. The kids themselves aren't usually loud, but I have been hearing a lot of fireworks lately—always do around the Fourth. I might have heard a crack or two last night, but I'm not sure. I was on the phone quite a bit, you know, debriefing from the meeting. Wait—there's one. You can just see the light from it. Look."

Bess rewound the video a bit, then hit play. Leigh leaned forward again and stared at the screen, breath held, as a quick flash—distinct from the bobbing light—lit up the woods behind the woodpile. In the same instant, Ferdinand—who had considerately turned his backside to the camera while devouring his prey— visibly startled.

"Definitely some kind of firework," Bess confirmed. "Probably a bottle rocket. You could tell he heard it, couldn't you? I really should spring for audio, once we get the show going."

Leigh's stomach churned. Maybe there had been some teenagers messing around in the woods last evening; maybe the flash in the distance had come from a bottle rocket. Maybe Brandon Lyle hadn't been in those woods until much later, and she was overreacting to what was probably a coincidence.

Or maybe she had just seen the flash of a gunshot.

And her Aunt Bess had inadvertently time-stamped a murder.

Chapter 5

Leigh pulled her van into the private drive shared between her house and her cousin Cara's farm. She drew in a sharp breath. Maura's car was ahead on the same lane, coming toward her.

Leigh pulled off into her own driveway. She considered rolling down her window, but refrained. What could she say anyway, with the kids in the back? Maura pulled up level and offered a wave; a man Leigh didn't recognize sat in the detective's passenger seat.

Leigh waved back without enthusiasm.

"Was that Aunt Mo?" Allison asked immediately. "Who was with her? And why was she at Aunt Cara's?"

Leigh bit her lip. It never failed. Whenever she or Warren made a concerted effort to hide some age-inappropriate issue from the children, Allison was on it like sonar. Having the uncanny ability to detect information she had no business knowing in the first place was, Leigh noted ruefully, just about the only trait the child did *not* share with her socially oblivious grandfather.

Ethan's attention remained on his handheld game.

"She told me she had to see Cara this morning about something," Leigh answered, keeping her voice matter-of-fact. "I don't know who the man was. Probably another detective."

She pulled the van into the garage, and she, two kids, and one dog piled out. Within seconds, the children had multiplied to four.

"We've been waiting for you!" came a sing-song female voice.

"Hope you're hungry!" came a young tenor. "We made a power lunch. You've got to come see it!"

"Mom let us cook whatever we wanted, and she said you could come!"

"Can we, Mom?" a smiling Ethan and Allison asked in unison.

Leigh looked from her own offspring to those of her cousin: the cherubic, sensitive ten-year-old Melanie and the commanding, confident twelve-year-old Mathias. "The Pack," as the foursome were affectionately called, had been inseparable ever since she and Warren had decided to buy the house next to Cara and Gil's six acre farm five years ago. It hadn't exactly been their dream house, but the appeal of having readymade access to both playmates and babysitters had been too enticing to pass up.

"Are your sure it's okay with your mom?" Leigh asked, noticing as she did so that Cara herself was approaching up the driveway.

"Of course!" Mathias insisted. "It was her idea in the first place!"

Leigh looked over her young "nephew's" shoulder to survey her cousin, whose pale face and artificial smile did not bode well for the outcome of Maura's interview. Most likely, Cara had released the children in her kitchen along with the ordinarily forbidden stores of tortilla chips, cheese dip, pepperoni, and frozen nuggets in order to keep them out of earshot of the detectives' questions.

It looked like it had worked.

"Sure, then," Leigh answered. "You guys run along and eat. But *don't* forget to help clean up the mess afterwards — "

The children were already gone.

Leigh stood silently as her cousin approached. No sooner had the throng of children run past her than Cara's fake smile morphed into an anxious grimace. "I *cannot* believe this," she proclaimed, patches of red now inflaming the cheeks of her ordinarily peaches-and-cream complexion. "I just can't. It's so unfair!"

Leigh reserved comment. She could interpret the statement as sympathy for Brandon Lyle, but she knew better. Although her cousin was a kind, tolerant, and good-hearted soul who wouldn't ordinarily squash a fruit fly, when anyone or anything threatened one of her brood, the woman was downright scary.

"That man!" Cara continued, "has been nothing but trouble for Gil since the day they met. And now... *this!*"

Leigh reached down and released Chewie from his lead, against which he was straining in a vain effort to follow the children. Given the dog's proclivity for treating cars (and trucks, and motorcycles, and armed bandits) as friends, he was limited to his own yard by an electronic fence. But he nevertheless dashed off as soon as he was freed, determined to keep vigil as close to the property line as possible.

"I'm sure it won't be a problem," Leigh lied. "People saw Brandon leaving the church after the fight. Someone must have seen Gil leave too, right?"

Cara pushed a lock of her still long, still strawberry-blond hair over one shoulder. Leigh's always prettier cousin, who was two years younger, had somehow managed to emerge from their decade of mutual motherhood looking a full ten years younger. Fortunately, since they had grown up next door to each other feeling more like sisters than cousins, Leigh loved her enough to get over it.

Mostly.

"Of course he left the church," Cara responded, her voice cracking a bit. "But he didn't come home. At least not right away. He was really angry—he didn't want the kids to see him that way. So he drove to North Park and walked it off. He didn't get back here until around ten, and I have no idea when Brandon— Well, when it happened, but..." Her voice wavered; her beautiful blue-green eyes grew misty. "Leigh, what if no one saw Gil at the park?"

Leigh's own stomach gave a flutter of panic, but she stifled it by gathering her cousin up in a hug. Her own bad luck in matters of police record was epic; but there was no reason to fear it had rubbed off on Gil. The man practically had Lady Luck grafted on his shoulder. He was blond, hazel-eyed, tall, gorgeous, and a self-made millionaire; *and* he was married to Cara and had two wonderful children. He might not have the sense of humor God gave a vacuum bag, but no one else seemed to notice that.

"They're not going to find any evidence against Gil," Leigh assured. "Someone else murdered Brandon, and that's who the evidence is going to point to. Maura and the other detectives know their stuff. Don't worry."

Cara drew back and smiled slightly, her eyes a mixed bag of gratitude and sympathy. The topic of false arrest was a touchy one in present company.

"Come and sit down a minute," Leigh urged, leading Cara over to her patio, where they settled on a gliding loveseat offering a good view of the family's conjoined yards. "The Pack will be gorging themselves for a good half hour, at least."

Cara complied, and Chewie, seeing an opportunity for immediate attention, promptly returned and hopped up into her lap. Cara stroked his tawny fur absently, her mind far away.

Leigh studied her expression. "I know it doesn't look good that Gil and Brandon had that fight," she said carefully. "But I'm getting the idea that there's something else, here. Am I right?"

Cara's eyes began to mist again, and she swiped at them with the back of her hand. "There is," she said miserably. "Nothing real. Nothing that would ever make Gil hate Brandon enough to hurt him—Gil could never hate anybody like that. But I'm worried, Leigh. Because if the detectives start digging back into their ancient history together... well... it's complicated."

Leigh cast a glance toward her cousin's house. "Did you let The Pack into the marshmallows and the ice cream toppings?"

Cara nodded guiltily.

"Then we have time," Leigh responded. "So talk. When Gil first sent Brandon to Hook, he told me they went to college together. Brandon made it sound like they were old chums, but frankly, I didn't get that from Gil. He didn't even seem to like the guy."

"Couldn't stand him," Cara confirmed. "Never could."

Leigh started to ask, "So why did he work for him?" but bit off the question. She already knew the answer: the same reason *she* worked for him. It was business, and business paid the bills. Refusing to deal with criminals was one thing, but if you started turning clients away just because they were arrogant jerkwads, you'd best prepare to starve.

"They met when they were fraternity brothers at Bucknell," Cara explained. "Brandon was one of those guys who was born with money and figured all he had to do to get more of it was snap his fingers. He wasn't stupid, but he was reckless and overbearing and just generally obnoxious. After college, several of the guys ended up in Philadelphia, where Gil was in grad school, and they pulled in some others and shared a house together. Gil hardly ever saw Brandon or the others he knew, but the rent was cheap and he was buried in student loans, so it worked out. But then..."

Cara's voice trailed off. She pulled a perfectly manicured nail to her perfectly shaped, rosy mouth and proceeded to nibble.

Leigh's eyed widened. Her cousin didn't nibble for nothing.

"Cara," she said with concern, "what happened?"

Cara gave her head a shake, as if to break an unwelcome reverie. "Once Gil got his MBA, he left Philadelphia. He didn't have any real contact with Brandon for over a decade, except for running into him at reunions. But apparently, several years ago, Brandon inherited a huge pile of money from his father. He tried to start up some retail venture with it, but he failed miserably. So when he decided to try again with real estate development, he looked up Gil, whom he knew was a business whiz. Once Gil set him up with the right people, Brandon finally started making some money for himself. But being the reckless oaf that he was, he eventually got greedy and started taking on too much risk. When he went ahead with two deals in a row that Gil had specifically warned him off of, Gil dissolved the relationship."

Leigh nodded. "And that's when Lyle started getting into financial trouble."

"Exactly," Cara agreed. "You know the rest. He got into this last development mess all on his own, but when he realized Gil had family ties to Aunt Bess and her church Brandon tried to pull him back in, the same way he tried to use you at Hook. Gil didn't want anything to do with him, but he didn't want him to fail, either—it never looks good for a client to go bankrupt, former or otherwise. So he did what he could, but all the while holding his nose, if you know what I mean."

Leigh knew.

Color rose again in Cara's cheeks. "Gil didn't go to that church meeting because Brandon was paying him!" she said defensively. "He wouldn't take another dime from the man; the last thing he needed was to have Lyle's soon-to-be-sullied name back on his client roster. You know why he went—he went because he was afraid things might get ugly, and he was concerned about Aunt Bess."

Leigh's own cheeks reddened. In her case, out of guilt. Cara wasn't saying so, but it was Leigh's own fault her cousin-in-law had been in attendance at the church last night. She had told Gil about Brandon firing Geralyn and storming out of her office, specifically hoping that Gil might offer to referee. It wasn't either of their jobs to keep Lyle in line anymore, but she knew that Gil, like her, still felt somewhat responsible for the havoc Lyle's development plans were wreaking on Aunt's Bess's neighborhood.

"You told me the meeting went badly," Leigh asked soberly, "but you never said exactly how."

Cara shook her head. "According to Gil, it started off fine. Brandon made his presentation; the church members listened. The Council Chair, Sid Kendig, could have opened it up for discussion then, but instead he chose to do a preliminary vote, to see if there was any interest in selling before the meeting went any further. The vote went something like twenty to one in favor of 'Hell, no.' There was applause, and people started to leave. That's when Brandon got upset. He started yelling, telling people that they were fools not to take whatever money was offered, because if they didn't, they would lose the land anyway, by eminent domain."

Leigh's eyes widened. "I hadn't heard that part. Can he do that?"

"Gil doesn't think so," Cara answered. "But no one knew that for sure at the time, and some of the church members got really upset. A couple of them raised their voices back at Brandon, which is when Gil hustled him outside—you know, to cool off."

Leigh's pulse quickened. She was feeling guiltier by the minute. Chewie, perhaps sensing the rise in tension, hopped off and disappeared behind the raspberry bushes.

"Of course," Cara continued, "then Brandon got mad at Gil. Told him it was all *his* fault, that Gil should have been on the project from the beginning, that he shouldn't have let Brandon's other ventures fail. The guy was completely irrational. He started going on about how he was going to ruin Gil's business over this—how he would tell everyone what a fraud Gil's consulting firm was. Of course, there were any number of witnesses listening, which set Gil off as well."

Cara's fingernail took another hit. She cast a glance at Leigh. "Gil's never been in a fist fight in his life," she insisted. "And he wasn't last night, either. All he did was threaten that if Brandon didn't calm down and shut up, he would call the police. And, well..." She moved to a fresh nail. "I take it there was a bit of name calling. That was when Brandon took a swing at him. Gil ducked it, and Brandon practically fell over."

"All that was bad enough," Cara continued, his tone increasingly miserable. "But the worst was what happened *after* the swing. A couple of other men closed in around Brandon—and when he looked around and saw how things stood, he lowered his fists. But then he said something else."

Leigh waited.

Cara took a breath. "He made a reference to something that happened decades ago—back in Philadelphia. He couched it as a threat. Along the lines of: 'You're no better than me. You weren't back then, and you sure as hell aren't now. If these people knew what *I* know about you, we'd both be put away, wouldn't we?'"

Leigh made a choking sound. "Holy — "

"Yes," Cara said faintly. "That's what he said. In front of a dozen witnesses, no less. Last night it was merely aggravating. But now, it's..."

Motive.

Leigh cleared her suddenly parched throat. "What on earth was Lyle talking about?" Not for a second did she believe that Cara's Dudley Do-Right of a husband had ever done anything extortion-worthy, no matter how young he was at the time. The man was born square.

Cara hesitated. "Leigh," she said tentatively, her voice dropping to a near-whisper. "You know how well I know Gil. If I told you that he had told me something unbelievable, but that I believed it... would you?"

Leigh hesitated. Then she thought about it. Cara and Gil were as close as she and Warren; and her cousin, despite being desperately in love, had never been anybody's fool. "Yes," she answered.

Cara offered the slightest of smiles. "Something did happen in Philadelphia," she admitted. "Something illegal, involving the murder of a street thug, who was also a drug dealer. Brandon and a couple of the other guys who were sharing the house with Gil were either involved in it themselves, or knew who was. The police came and questioned them all, but no arrests were ever made." She paused and faced Leigh squarely. "There was some kind of cover-up. People lying about where everyone else was. Brandon seems to remember that Gil was a part of that — that he lied to the police along with the rest of them. But the crazy truth is, Leigh, that Gil never *did* know what happened. He wasn't there at the time, and none of the guys would tell him anything! Probably because they didn't trust him not to rat them out. They all broke the lease after that, and the group split up. To this day, Gil has no idea what the others were hiding. But Brandon seems to think — "

Her voice broke off. "I mean, *thought.*" She rose from the loveseat and let out a heavy breath. "I didn't say much to Maura; I just told her I thought Gil should call a lawyer before she questioned him, and she agreed. The detectives were on their way to talk to Bess first, then meet him downtown. Gil's probably talking to an attorney even as we speak."

Her composure crumpled. "Oh, Leigh!" she cried. "Now do you see why I'm so worried? All those witnesses heard Lyle's threat. What does it matter if there's nothing to it?"

Leigh rose and offered her cousin another sympathetic hug. "Maura will get to the bottom of it," she said firmly, "or she'll make sure the other detectives do. Innocence always wins out, you know. Aren't I living proof?"

The crunching sound of wheels on gravel drew both their attentions to the drive, and Leigh's heart did a little leap. Warren was home.

"I'd better go check on The Pack," Cara said quickly, wiping her eyes again. "I heard Mathias saying something about smoothies when he was running past, and they are *not* allowed to use the blender..." she was already walking away.

"Make them clean up!" Leigh called, watching her ordinarily strong cousin drift away like a specter. The unwelcome vision of Brandon Lyle's staring, sightless eyes jumped suddenly into her mind, and another sick feeling surged in her stomach.

A car door slammed.

Leigh whirled around and walked toward her husband, having no idea how she would explain everything that had happened to her that morning. But when her anxious eyes met his soft brown ones, she realized she didn't have to say a word. He already knew.

"How did you—" she stammered.

"Mo called me," Warren answered, using the nickname that only he, among all living adults, was allowed to call Maura. In college, the trio had been inseparable. They were the Three Musketeers: the Creative Genius, the WonderCop, and the Future President of the United States.

Leigh smiled. "She did?"

Warren nodded. "She was concerned about you. So am I."

He opened his arms, and Leigh walked into them.

Chapter 6

"So you see," Warren explained calmly, "there's nothing for any of us to worry about. The police will figure out who killed the man, and they'll put that person in jail. Your Aunt Mo's working on it right now, and she's very good at her job, so it shouldn't be long. But in the meantime, she does have to talk to everyone who knew him, and that means your mom and your Uncle Gil will have to answer a lot of questions. But there's nothing you two need to be concerned about. All right?"

Two small faces stared at their father across the kitchen table, their expressions wide eyed. Leigh marveled at her husband's clever and calculated phrasing. Nearly two decades as a successful politician had definitely taught the man how to spin. Somehow, he'd managed to describe her role in the fiasco without ever mentioning the word "body," nor had he been specific about exactly where it had been found—a point which they both feared could affect the children's enjoyment of their Aunt Bess's glorious woods. Thank goodness they knew nothing of their mother's historical proclivity in such matters... all *that* had happened before they were born.

The children remained silent. Allison's nose twitched.

Leigh's eyes met her husband's. *So far, so good. Thank you.* "So," she announced, "are you guys okay? Do you have any questions?"

"Yeah," Ethan said immediately, his gaze fixed on his mother with something like awe. "How many bodies have you found now? Like... six?"

Allison leaned over the table toward her. "Were his eyes open or shut?"

Leigh gulped. She threw a desperate glance at Warren, but he was struggling—curse him—to fight a grin. She turned to Ethan, "Why... What makes you think I've found other... I mean, *others?*"

Her son sat back with a snort. "Who doesn't know? You're like... legend. But we understand if you don't want to talk about it."

Allison nodded sagely. "If it grosses you out, Mom, it's okay.

Some people aren't comfortable with dead things."

Leigh found herself speechless. Warren, who was doing a really bad job of trying to look serious, stepped in again. "You guys are right; Mom doesn't like talking about it. But I'm glad you're taking it so well." He cleared his throat. "Now... back to whatever you were doing."

The children rose from the table.

"But," Warren continued, "don't talk to your cousins about this yet—your Aunt Cara and Uncle Gil need to be the ones to do that. Okay?"

The two looked at each other, then nodded. "We especially can't tell Lenna," Allison whispered to her brother as they turned and walked toward the back door. "You know how sensitive she is."

The door slammed shut behind them. Leigh rose, still stunned, and Warren wrapped his arms around her with a chuckle. "They'll be fine," he said good-naturedly. "They come from strong stock, you know."

Leigh looked up at her husband appreciatively. When they had first met, at eighteen, he had been tall, gawky, and a hopeless nerd obsessed with space movies. He was still tall, and he was still obsessed with space movies, but the gawky teen had been replaced by a confident, attractive man who still made her heart flutter after twelve years of marriage. Too bad it had taken twelve years of friendship first for her to realize what she'd been missing.

She was still determined to make up for that.

"Oh," Warren said heavily. Leigh heard the crunching of gravel that announced a car on the drive and looked up to follow his line of sight out the window.

"Oh, no," she added gravely.

"I really do have to get back downtown for that appointment," he said briskly, looking at his watch and reaching for his briefcase. "I rescheduled it once, but—"

"*Chicken,*" Leigh accused.

He grinned. "Not that I don't love your mother, Leigh. But if she's here for what I think she's here for—"

"She can't know yet!" Leigh protested. "Maura wouldn't tell her."

"No," he countered, kissing her quickly in passing as he made haste toward the garage door, "but your Aunt Bess would."

Leigh swore.

With deft timing, Warren managed to reach his car and start up the engine just as Frances Koslow's intent rapping sounded at the front door.

Leigh took a centering breath and opened it.

"Oh, poo," the woman on her porch exclaimed. "I just missed Warren, didn't I?"

Leigh surveyed her mother, who had clearly left home in a hurry. Never in Frances's sixty-some-odd years had she been known to leave her residence without a complete matched outfit (currently in fashion or not), a fully equipped bag (roughly the size of a newborn elephant), and a generous coating of lipstick (usually orange, occasionally pink, but never, *ever* red). And yet here she was— lips bare, polyester top and cotton slacks both alarming shades of olive. Thank God she at least had her handbag.

"He had to get back downtown," Leigh explained unnecessarily. In her mother's eyes, Warren could do no wrong under any circumstances.

It was Leigh that was the problem.

Frances shifted her gaze to her daughter and twisted her lips with disapproval. "He didn't have to make a special trip home, did he?"

Leigh considered her response. "Why would he?"

Frances' lips pursed further as she swept past her daughter and inside. "You know perfectly well why. Are the children around?"

"They're playing outside with their cousins," Leigh answered mechanically. "Did you know you forgot your lipstick?"

Frances gave a distressed little jump, then plopped down on Leigh's couch, dug out a gold hand mirror and orange tube, corrected the oversight, and stood up again.

Leigh felt better. "So, why did you come by?" she asked as politely as possible.

Frances scowled. "To make sure this fiasco goes no further, of course."

Leigh's brow furrowed. "Further than..."

Frances sighed. "If you must go around tripping over bodies, there's nothing I or anyone else can do to stop you. But really, dear... to involve your Aunt Bess? And poor, *poor* Gil?"

Leigh found herself, once again, speechless.

"Bess said she'd been trying to call you, but you weren't picking up," Frances accused.

Leigh cast a glance at her phone, which she had indeed been ignoring while she and Warren were talking to the children.

"Maura and her friend, the other detective, were very polite in their questioning, I'm sure," Frances continued. "But you know how Bess always plows into such situations head first — Lord only knows what she told them. She was raving on and on to me about how she caught the whole thing on tape, and how *you* knew but didn't tell her, and some nonsense about how some cat had made it all possible — always with those cats! — and then she suggested I come out and see how you and Cara were doing, because she was going to be busy running interference at the church all day."

Leigh's eyebrows rose. Her aunt might have said most of that, but no way had she sicced Frances' ministrations of support on Cara and herself. Bess might be dotty, but she was never cruel.

"Now," Frances began with a flourish, settling herself on the couch once more. "What we — " Her eyes narrowed. "These cushions could use a vacuuming, dear. And I daresay a little upholstery cleaner on these stains wouldn't hurt, either. Now, as I was saying, we'll need to plan what to do about this. Perhaps a family conference — "

"*No!*" Leigh interrupted, a bit more vehemently than intended.

Frances proffered the dreaded chin-down, eyebrows-up maneuver.

"I mean," Leigh backtracked, "it's too soon for that. Maura warned me not to go around telling anybody in the family what happened; she wanted to interview Bess and Gil first. That's why I couldn't say anything to Aunt Bess when I — "

"Well, the principals all know now," Frances interrupted. "Maura is interviewing Gil and his lawyer even as we speak."

"How did you — "

"Cara told her mother, of course. Your Aunt Lydie and I have already discussed this situation thoroughly. Clearly, what we need to do is — "

"Mom," Leigh interrupted again. "*We* don't need to do anything. I am not a suspect. Aunt Bess is not a suspect. It looks bad for Gil at the moment, but he does have an alibi — we just need to verify it."

"Aha!" Frances pointed a finger. "Yes, *we* do. Lydie and I already have a plan for that. We could use your cooperation. And as for your not being a suspect this time..." her eyes narrowed again. "What, dare I ask, is *your* alibi?"

Leigh bristled. Her mother wasn't actually accusing her of murder, merely of doing something stupid. Like being alone without proper documentation on the night a murder was being committed. "For your information," Leigh said proudly, "I was here with Warren and the kids. And Detective Maura Polanski. *And* her husband, Lieutenant Gerald Frank of the Allegheny County Police Department."

A smile played on Frances's lips. Then, much to Leigh's horror, her eyes began to water. "Oh sweetheart," Frances said heavily. "That's wonderful. I've been so worried, you know."

"Yes, mom," she returned with a sigh. "I know."

Frances recovered quickly. "So," she announced with a little bounce on the couch, "now we need to establish Gil's alibi."

"Cara said he was walking in North Park."

"Exactly!" Frances agreed. "Which is why we need runners and dog walkers."

Leigh's brow furrowed.

"Consistency, dear. Always look for consistency. People with dogs tend to walk the same time, same route each day. Same with serious runners. The walkers, the children, the bikers" — she waved a dismissive hand — "they're all over the place. We need to find the regulars. And we need to find them tonight."

Leigh blinked. In no family crisis had her mother ever been short of her trademark overreactive, occasionally hysterical plans of action — most of which involved the entire extended Morton family and the expenditure of vast amounts of unwelcome and generally futile effort.

But this idea actually made sense.

Wow.

"So we'll go to the park tonight and ask people if any of them remember seeing Gil last night?"

Frances smiled smugly. "Precisely. If we're lucky, Gil will remember someone he saw, and we'll have a specific target. It was right around dusk, so most of the people still out were probably regulars. We'll meet at the boathouse at 8:15. Lydie will have his route and any leads ready."

"Sounds good," Leigh agreed.

"And, dear?"
"Yes?"
"I can see dust on those dining room curtains from here."

Chapter 7

Diana Saxton clicked her long, perfectly French-tipped nails on the smooth glass top of Brandon Lyle's designer desk. Her nose ran. Her mascara was streaked to her chin. She wanted to go crawl into a hole and die. She also wanted to smash something.

She was determined that she would do neither.

She would remain calm, no matter how incredibly tempting it might be to pick up the framed portrait of Brandon and his smiling bride and hurl it through the twelfth floor window and out into the traffic of Grant Street.

No matter if Courtney Lyle's odious words still rang in her ears like swirling acid. The woman was a viper. A leech. A devil.

I'm so sorry to be the one to break this to you, sweetie cakes, the witch had sniveled into her phone. *But your sugar daddy's bit the dust. Gone. Cold. Dead. And you know what you are, you husband-stealing, gold-digging, silicone-implanted little wench? I'll tell you what you are. You're FIRED!!!*

Diana withdrew another tissue from the box she'd been carrying around the eerily empty office for the last two hours. She blew.

"He never loved you, you know that?" she muttered, staring daggers at the airbrushed woman in the photograph. "It was *me* he wanted. He would have divorced you in a heartbeat if his finances hadn't—"

Her words choked on a sob. *Close.* She'd been so damned close.

And now she had nothing.

Again.

She couldn't stand it. Couldn't bear for everything that had seemed so promising to go so suddenly, terribly wrong. But the blubbering and the sniveling had to stop, regardless. Her situation was precarious; she needed to focus.

She would not be in Brandon's will, she knew that. And even if she was, he'd have nothing left. The business had bled him out like a stuck pig.

Her stomach gave a lurch.

She grabbed another tissue.

Brandon had been right; it was Gil's fault. His good buddy Gil, who had pretended to help him, then dumped him in his hour of need. Mr. Hollywood-Handsome Gil March had walked away from Brandon—with a fat consulting fee in his pocket—and never once looked back. He was a fraud. A hack. A self-righteous, ungrateful, overstuffed prig.

God, how she hated him.

For more reasons than one. But this time, he would not walk away unscathed.

She'd made sure of that.

A ding sounded from the outer office; the door was opening. Diana wiped hastily at her cheeks, tucked the tissue box back under her arm, and walked through the open doorway and back into the reception area.

"Can I help you?" she asked, her voice rough as gravel.

The man and woman—at least, Diana thought it was a woman—surveyed her studiously. *Cops*, she decided immediately. Neither wore a uniform, of course, but the man had that quiet air of authority one usually associated with detectives, while the woman—good God, what a woman; she was huge!—looked like she could take down three drug dealers with one blow. They had come to tell her about Brandon. And to search his office for clues, no doubt.

With a discreet flash of their badges, the detectives solemnly introduced themselves.

"I already know about Brandon," Diana said simply, sniffling. "His wife called a couple hours ago." She moved to her own desk chair and dropped down with a plop. "I've been in a kind of daze, you know?"

The detectives nodded, then exchanged a glance and a gesture. The woman seemed to be in charge, but it was the man, a Detective Peterson, who did the talking. He began as expected with stiff condolences, then moved quickly to the heart of the matter.

"Could you tell me the last time you saw Brandon Lyle, Ms. Saxton?"

Diana sniffled, then reached for another tissue. She really should have planned these answers out already; the truth was hardly neat and tidy. On the other hand, when it came to her relationship with Brandon, why should she lie? To spare his poor, dear little wife the embarrassment?

She blew.

"I was with Brandon all weekend," she answered matter of factly, "at his apartment. The last time I saw him was yesterday morning. He went to work at the office but I didn't go with him. I had an... appointment in Harrisburg, and I didn't get back until late."

"What kind of appointment?" the detective asked. "And exactly when did you return to Pittsburgh?"

Diana sighed. "I had a summons to small claims court," she answered curtly, hoping to avoid further inquiry on that score. It was nobody's business, after all, whether she had or had not keyed the Ferrari of a certain liposuctioned, neurotoxin-injected high school classmate whose head had gotten far too big for her tiara. The point was, she could easily prove that she had spent most of the day a good four hours from Pittsburgh. "I didn't get back to town until around ten o'clock last night."

"And did you contact Brandon at any point?" the detective pressed.

"Yes," she answered. "I phoned him as soon as I got out of court—around five. He was upset, and I told him I was coming home and would meet him at his apartment."

The detective leaned in. "What was he upset about?"

Diana hesitated, but only slightly. "He had an important meeting scheduled last night, with the congregation of a church whose land he wanted to buy. He had hired a PR person to run the meeting, but she bailed on him at the last second. His management consultant, Gil March, was supposed to be there, but apparently Gil also refused to take an active role in the meeting. So Brandon got stuck running the thing himself." She paused. "Brandon felt like he'd been back-stabbed—especially since Gil was supposed to be a friend."

She looked up from her tissues long enough to see the detectives exchange a pointed glance. *Excellent.*

"Did you go to his apartment when you returned?" Detective Peterson probed.

Diana nodded. "I did, but he wasn't there. He wasn't answering his phone, either. I'd tried him several times since the meeting should have been over, but he never picked up. When he wasn't home, I got worried, and I drove to the church myself."

She allowed a suitable dramatic pause. Best not to appear too eager.

"And what did you find there?" the detective prompted.

"His car," she responded. "Empty. The church was all locked up, but he was nowhere in sight. And his car was the only one in the parking lot. I couldn't figure it out."

She sniffled again. This was the important part. "My first thought was that he had gone out with Gil March somewhere. I wondered if maybe they had gone out for a drink or something afterward. I... well, it seems silly now, since they weren't getting along very well. But I didn't know."

Both detectives were leaning forward now.

"So I called Gil on his cell, and he—"

Diana's voice caught, and she buried her face in another tissue. "To say that the man was no help would be an understatement. He practically screamed at me. Told me he didn't know where Brandon was, didn't care, and didn't want to hear from *me* ever again!"

The detectives were silent for a moment. "At what time did you make that call?" Peterson asked.

"I'm not sure," she answered honestly. "10:30, maybe? I can check it if you want."

"We'll do that in a minute, if you don't mind," the detective answered. "But first, can you tell us what you did next?"

Diana's eyes narrowed at the memory. "I went back to Brandon's apartment. I thought I would just wait for him there."

"But he never came home?"

Her head shook. "I never got in. I recognized his wife's car in the parking lot, and I left. I went back to my own apartment, sent Brandon about four texts, and then finally fell asleep. This morning I came in to an empty office. Courtney called here and told me that Brandon was dead. And then you arrived. End of story."

More or less.

"Are you certain that it was Courtney Lyle's car you saw in the parking lot?" the female detective asked. Her voice was civil, but commanding. Diana made a mental note not to get on the woman's bad side.

"Absolutely. She drives a bright yellow Porsche Boxster with the license plate 1BANANA."

The detectives exchanged a hard glance. "And you weren't expecting her to be there?" Peterson asked.

Diana snorted. "She has an apartment of her own in Chicago and breezes in whenever she feels like it. But I would say no — Brandon wasn't expecting her. If he was, he would have warned me not to come."

She looked up from her tissue and straightened, her voice level. "Courtney said he was shot. I don't suppose you know by whom."

The detectives let a beat pass. "That's what we're trying to figure out, ma'am," Peterson said glibly.

"Well," Diana remarked, "I certainly hope you do."

"You've worked for Mr. Lyle as an administrative assistant for the last six months, is that correct?" Peterson continued.

"That's right," she answered.

"And you seem to be admitting that you also had a romantic relationship with Mr. Lyle, is that correct?"

Diana restrained a smile. Smiles were not appropriate here. "We were intimate, yes. He and his wife led separate lives."

"And she knew about his relationship with you?"

"Oh, yes. We had... run into each other before."

Do NOT smile!

"Yet you said he would have warned you if he had known his wife was coming home last night, so she must not have been entirely approving of the relationship."

Diana hid her face in the tissue and sputtered. She hoped it sounded like a cough. "I wouldn't say that his wife approved, no," she said carefully. "But our relationship was no secret."

Suspect number one: CHECK.

"Did Ms. Lyle say anything else when she contacted you this morning?"

"Yes," Diana answered, visualizing nails pounding into a coffin. "She fired me."

She gestured to the banker's box that sat open on her desk, already packed half full with personal items.

Beautiful.

"Please think carefully, Ms. Saxton," the detective pressed. "Did Mr. Lyle's wife say or ask anything that would lead you to believe she suspected anyone in particular of harming him?"

Diana thought a moment. She decided it would be best to play it safe. "No," she answered. "I asked what happened to him, and all she said was, 'someone shot the bastard.'"

Take that, wifey-poo.

"I see. We also do need to ask, Ms. Saxton... do you personally know of anyone who may have wanted to harm Mr. Lyle?"

Diana drew in a breath. She had to be careful. Overeagerness would hardly do. She started to speak and let her voice catch appropriately. "Until this morning, I would have said no. But obviously, I would have been wrong." She met the detective's eyes. Peterson's, not the he-woman's. Hers were far too probing. "You have to understand, Brandon was a businessman. He was high spirited and ambitious, and I won't lie to you—he could be very temperamental. I'm sure he made his share of enemies in the business world. But I can't imagine a business grudge going this far. I just keep thinking that it had to be... well... more personal."

Like an old friendship betrayed, perhaps?

"Did Mr. Lyle ever mention being afraid of anyone?"

Diana's lips twisted. The detective was not taking the bait. "Brandon wasn't the type to be afraid of anyone," she found herself defending. "I'm sure he was caught totally off guard."

Watch it.

"I mean," she backpedaled, "he never gave me any indication that he felt threatened by any of his business associates. It was all just business, even if it did get heated at times. Except..."

She waited.

"Ms. Saxton?" the detective prompted.

"It's just that Brandon had become a lot more agitated recently, and I felt there was something he was hiding from me. I knew he was concerned over the financing for the Nicholson project, that much was obvious, but I wasn't privy to the details—he had an accountant for that, and Gil March, of course. But closing this particular deal with the church seemed so hugely important to him... I've never seen him get quite so... well... *emotionally* wound up."

She sat back with a sigh and let the implications drift.

The detective, sadly, missed the point once more. "Did Mr. Lyle ever give you any reason to suspect that he might have borrowed money from, shall we say, not completely legitimate sources?"

Diana's eyes widened. She hadn't thought of that. But of course she wouldn't; it was absurd. Brandon was far too much of a wuss to stoop to using a loan shark. Not when he could accomplish the same thing with a little blackmail between friends.

"No," she responded tentatively. "He never said anything like that to me."

Clearly, more bait was needed.

"The last thing he said," she continued slowly, "was that he was counting on Gil March to come through for him—one way or the other."

The detective's eyebrows rose.

Finally!

"And what do you think he meant by that?"

Diana squirmed in her seat. "I can't say for sure. I really don't know what was going on between the two of them. Not on a personal level, anyway. But I was pretty sure there was something, other than the business deal on the table. And I probably wouldn't have picked up on that, except..."

Silence hung in the air.

"Except," she continued without prompting, "that I happen to know both men very well, you see."

Suspect number two: CHECK.

"Gil March was my previous 'employer.'"

Chapter 8

"So," Gil said casually, his easy tone showing no hint of the anxiety Leigh knew to be brewing behind his shrewd hazel eyes. "What did you kids do today?"

His son Mathias paused in mid chew, a piece of macaroni escaping from his lips as he spouted excitedly. "We made twenty dollars!"

"We made $14.65," Leigh's daughter Allison corrected. "After expenses."

"How did you do that?" Warren asked, serving himself a generous second helping of casserole.

Leigh surveyed what was left of the meal a bit nervously. If Gil hadn't been picking at his plate like a gnat, the food would probably have run out already. But they would be okay. She should have realized she was due for a grocery run when she invited her cousin's brood over, but kitchen inventory was the last thing on her mind. Cara had been at her wit's end all afternoon, worrying about Gil on a day when she had unfortunately scheduled another of her Green Mommas shopping parties—an extravaganza of similarly-minded earth mothers who gathered to coo over the latest in compostable diapers while sipping carrot juice and nibbling on kale chips. Leigh had always avoided such events like the plague, which was easy to do when a babysitter was needed. This afternoon, however, she had almost gotten herself fired. Inviting her cousin's family to dinner seemed the least she could do.

Cara's cheeks flared with red. "Go ahead, Mathias," she said sharply. "Tell your father your brilliant idea."

Cara's daughter Melanie, who had been affectionately called Lenna ever since her older brother had trouble pronouncing his baby sister's name, sank miserably into her chair. Leigh could understand the sentiment. Cara was almost never this testy.

A sympathetic Ethan, sitting next to Lenna, elbowed his cousin playfully and smiled at her.

"Well," Mathias began tentatively, his tone no longer cocky. "We thought it might be fun to do a lemonade stand."

"Sounds like an enterprising idea," Warren said cheerfully, in an obvious effort to break the tension. Gil was covering his own anxiety well enough, but Cara looked ready to burst.

"We thought so," Mathias agreed, looking grateful for his uncle's support. "Aunt Leigh told us it was okay."

Gee thanks, kid.

Leigh met Cara's glare with a self-conscious smile. "That's true, I did. We had the necessary supplies, and it sounded harmless enough. I thought they were going to set it up out by the road."

Gil looked from his son to his wife, clearly baffled. "So what was the problem?"

"The *problem*," Cara fumed, "was that they set up the lemonade stand at the beginning of our own front walk!"

The men shot confused glances at one another.

Cara groaned. "Just as all the guests were arriving for my Green Mommas party!"

The children remained silent, staring hopefully at their fathers. Both men's faces strained as they tried hard not to smile.

"I guess that's what you'd call a captive audience," Gil said finally, losing his battle with the slightest of grins.

"That's what we thought!" Mathias agreed, his face beaming.

"It wouldn't make sense to set it up along the road, Mom," Allison piped up in her calm, quiet voice. "The cars drive by too fast, and there's nowhere to pull off. A business has to go where the customers are."

Now Leigh fought a smile.

"We didn't force anybody to buy anything," Mathias defended.

Cara sucked in a breath. "Yes, you did! The women knew who you were; it would have been rude for them not to buy anything!"

The children looked at each other blankly.

Lenna's rosebud mouth trembled as she spoke. "But, Mom... Matt said we were making the price a real bargain."

"I had free drinks inside!" Cara railed.

Lenna sank back down in her chair again.

"Cara," Gil said gently, "I'm sure the women didn't mind supporting a good cause."

"That's just it!" his wife continued, unappeased. "*The cause!*"

"I told you that would be a problem," Allison said accusingly, looking at Mathias.

"What?" the boy asked innocently.

"You know what!" Cara snapped. "Cheap instant lemonade mix, with artificial flavoring *and* coloring?"

Now it was Leigh's turn to sink in her chair.

"It was good!" Mathias defended.

"Those women came to our house specifically looking for healthy, organic, earth-friendly foods and household products," Cara continued, sounding like a television commercial. "*You sold them Styrofoam cups!!!*"

A wet explosion erupted as the mouthful of iced tea Warren had just imbibed spewed liberally across the table the same time as Gil, laughing equally loudly, accidentally elbowed a misplaced fork, sending it flying into the air and banking off the buffet.

Three adults and four children dissolved into gut-holding peals of laughter.

Cara stood up.

"I'm so sorry," Warren apologized, moving quickly to her side and placing a brotherly hand on her arm. "I know the whole situation was awkward for you, and it's been a wretched day all around. But maybe a little light-heartedness is what we all need right now, don't you think?"

The twittering dampened for a moment; all eyes fixed on Cara.

The glare she threw at Warren was fierce, but the seasoned politician merely smiled at her. After a long moment, she let out a breath. "I suppose so," she agreed, deflating.

A collective sigh of relief filled the room. Cara and Warren sat back down.

"Mom," Ethan interjected, "can we have that new ice cream you bought for dessert?"

Leigh didn't hesitate. So what if they had a junk food lunch and drank cheap lemonade all afternoon? You were only a kid once. "Sure," she answered. "But take it out on the patio, okay?"

She did not need to make the suggestion twice. Four chairs scooted back from the table simultaneously. Cara did not approve of her children eating double-donut pie-crust ice cream any more than she had approved of the hastily prepared concoction of ground beef, boxed macaroni and cheese, and canned tomatoes that Leigh called a casserole. But the women had a rule. "You serve what you like, and I'll serve what I like." And houseguests went with the flow.

"Budding little entrepreneurs, aren't they?" Warren said with pride after the children had gone.

Gil nodded, looking after the Pack fondly. "Chips off the old blocks."

The men fist-bumped. Cara's eyes rolled.

Gil leaned over and kissed his wife on the cheek. "It's all right, honey," he assured. "We'll get through this. I promise."

The mood turned instantly solemn.

"You're happy with your attorney, then?" Warren asked.

Gil nodded, and Leigh and Cara exchanged a glance. It was fortunate that Gil knew his own shark of a defense attorney. Leigh happened to know one of the best in the business — but that lawyer was also an ex-girlfriend of Warren's. Not that Leigh worried about such things... but *still*. Her entire experience with the criminal justice system was the kind of memory best left coated with a nice, thick layer of dust.

"Reg is highly regarded in the business," Gil praised. "At least by his clients. I gather the prosecutors aren't so enamored of him."

"That's probably a good sign," Warren noted. "What is he advising you to do? Anything we can help with?"

Gil let out a sigh. Accepting help had never been his forte. He was more the white knight type. "I can't do much about what the witnesses at the church heard and saw. It will be interpreted as motive — no matter how ludicrous. But that's all they could possibly have. There won't be any physical evidence, so I should be fine. It would help if I could verify my alibi," he acknowledged. "But I understand the Morton women are on it."

His wife smiled at him smugly. "In spades. We'll find someone who saw you at North Park last night, I'm sure of it. The rest of it is ridiculous anyway — no one who knows you could possibly think you had anything to do with that man's death."

A sour look flitted over Gil's still-smiling face. The breach lasted only a second, but Leigh read it like a neon sign, and so, naturally, did his wife.

"Gil?" Cara demanded. "What is it you're thinking of? *Who* would suspect you?"

Gil threw a pleading glance at Warren. Leigh's gaze moved to her husband, whom she expected to appear as clueless as she was.

He responded with nothing more than a slight, helpless shrug, but Leigh hadn't known the man since adolescence for nothing.

He knew something she didn't.

She hated it when that happened.

"Gil?" Cara repeated.

Gil breathed out with a groan, then rubbed his face in his hands. "It's nothing for anybody to worry about," he said finally, attempting a confident, comforting tone.

He failed. The man might look like a film star, but he was a lousy actor.

"There is one person I'm afraid might make trouble for me," he admitted. "Someone who seems to actually think I *did* do it."

"Who?!" Cara asked with a screech, her cheeks on fire again.

Gil cast another meaningful glance at Warren. Leigh fought an overwhelming urge to throttle the both of them.

"Diana Saxton," Gil answered quietly.

The name didn't register. "Who's Diana Saxton?" Leigh demanded.

No one paid any attention to her. Cara's face had gone from scarlet to white. Gil looked like he'd been flogged. Even Warren looked distinctly uncomfortable.

"Well?" Leigh insisted.

Somewhere, in the back of her mind, it occurred to her that the issue at hand might not really be any of her business. Cara and Gil were certainly entitled to their secrets. And if Warren happened to know also, what did that matter? Was her husband obliged to tell her absolutely everything, even if it had been told to him in confidence?

Damn straight, he was!

"Who is Diana Saxton?!" she asked for the third time.

"What did she say?" Cara asked Gil stiffly, ignoring her cousin.

Gil drew in a breath. "I don't know what she told the detectives. But she did call me today."

"I told you to block her number!" Cara fired back. Then almost immediately she swallowed, and her voice softened. "I'm sorry. I know it's not your fault. But why did you even pick up?"

"I had to know what she wanted," he defended. "Under the circumstances, it hardly seemed wise to antagonize her further. I was rude enough to her on the phone last night."

Cara harrumphed. "You could never be rude enough to that woman. What did she say?"

"Can't say I listened to all of it," Gil answered. "You could say she was ranting and raving. The gist was that she accused me of murder."

Warren leaned back in his chair with a frustrated sigh. Cara's body went rigid. Leigh still wondered who the hell Diana Saxton was.

"She won't have any evidence, so even if she does talk to the detectives, they'll know she's just blowing smoke," Gil insisted.

"No, they won't!" Cara argued vehemently. "Don't you see? If she wants to make you look guilty, all she's got to do is tell them you had an affair!"

Leigh's heart skipped a beat. She didn't believe it. They'd been through all this before. Gil was far too much of a prude to be a philanderer—besides, if anything like that had ever happened to Cara, Leigh would definitely know about it. That, and Gil wouldn't be sitting here tonight with all his parts intact.

"I'm afraid she's right," Warren said evenly, holding Gil's gaze. "You can't say nothing and let Diana define the relationship—it's way too risky. Did you tell your lawyer about the phone call?"

Gil shook his head. "It happened right after our meeting."

"Do that," Warren advised. "I have a feeling he'll tell you the same thing. By coming forward with the whole ugly story, you can level the playing field. And if you can verify that she's threatened you, that's a point in your favor."

Gil nodded solemnly. "You're right."

Leigh was seconds away from spontaneous combustion.

Cara rose from the table. "If you'll excuse me," she said stiffly, "I need to go break something. Leigh, can I help you with the dishes?"

Chapter 9

Leigh's dishes had thus far remained whole. Her sanity, not so much.

"Cara," she began finally, after restraining herself throughout the transport and rinsing processes. She was trying to be sensitive to Cara's mood, but no way could she make it through the loading. "You do realize I'm going to pop an artery if you don't tell me what's going on, right?"

Cara paused, dirty spoon in hand, and looked up at Leigh as if seeing her for the first time. "Oh," she said vaguely, straightening up. "That's right. I didn't tell you about Diana, did I?"

Leigh struggled to keep her voice even. "I think I would remember if you had."

"Sorry," Cara replied, dropping the spoon into the dishwasher's utensil tray and leaning heavily against Leigh's countertop. "I wanted to, at the time, but Gil was so uptight about it. He made me swear I wouldn't tell anybody, most especially you or my mother."

"But Warren knew!" Leigh said before she could stop herself. She hated it when she sounded like a teenager. She was forty-freaking-two years old; she could handle this stuff.

Cara's brow furrowed. "Warren did know, didn't he? Gil must have told him. I guess he thought Warren could sympathize."

"*Excuse me?*" Leigh spouted.

Cara's own brow furrowed. "For heaven's sake, Leigh — Warren's an attractive, successful man who's every bit as prominent in this town as Gil is. Of course he's been through it."

Leigh's arteries would never make it. She would bleed out right here on the floor, with the dishwasher only half loaded.

"*Through what?!*"

Cara's eyes flashed with impatience. "Through being hit on by a soulless, gold-digging homewrecker, that's what! What did you think?"

Leigh stared back at her cousin a moment, her blood pressure in free fall. "I... thought just that," she said lamely. "Of course."

Cara returned the briefest of glares, but moved on. "I don't know why Gil insisted on its being such a secret. It's not like he did anything wrong. But he was embarrassed by it—this incident way more than any of the others over the years. I guess because she went so much further. He said he didn't want to have to look at my relatives and know that they were trying to picture the whole thing."

Leigh's eyes widened.

Cara let out a short, rueful chuckle. "It was pretty ridiculous, really. I mean, the woman had no shame. If Gil had let me interview her when she first applied for the job, I would have had her number in thirty seconds, 'highly recommended' or no. But men can be so dense about these things."

She scooped up a few more utensils from the counter and dropped them in the tray. "Gil hired her about a year ago. Her credentials appeared impeccable. For the first few months, she was the picture of efficiency and professionalism. Then the claws came out. She started dropping hints, letting him know she was interested. At first, Gil ignored them. He was hoping"—Cara shook her head with an eye roll—"that she would give up and stop, without things getting any more awkward. But of course, she didn't. Her suggestions only got more blatant, until finally he had to address it straight out. He told her that he wasn't interested, and if she wanted to keep her position, she needed to act more professionally."

Cara sighed. "I wanted him to fire her then. And if she'd been any less fantastic at her job, I'm sure he would have. But apparently, the woman is brilliant at making herself indispensable. By the time any of this became a problem, she was up to her elbows in sensitive information, running processes she'd put in place that it would be difficult for anyone else to take over. Never mind how hard it is to find a decent administrative assistant in the first place."

"So it wasn't a spur-of-the-moment thing," Leigh reasoned. "She had a master plan?"

"She had him pegged as a target before she sent her resume," Cara confirmed. "And when he refused to cooperate, after she'd invested so much time and energy, she got desperate."

Cara picked up the knife Leigh had used to slice the watermelon and cradled it in her hands.

Leigh leaned in slowly and took it away from her.

"What happened?"

A growl rose from low in Cara's throat. "She made arrangements to go on a business trip with him. It wasn't the first—all his assistants travel with him from time to time. But she had a special agenda. She booked two rooms and they went their separate ways to unpack, but by the time he got out of the shower that first night, she had already moved herself into his room."

Cara's knuckles whitened as her hands clenched the countertop. "*Without* her clothes."

Leigh winced. "You really can't get any more blatant than that."

Cara sucked in a breath. "He threw her out and fired her, of course. And you might expect she wouldn't take it well. But there you'd be wrong. The woman is calculating and as cool as a cucumber. Once she gave up on Gil for good, she changed her whole tune. Apologized profusely. Claimed it was all a horrible mistake—she was just so deeply, hopelessly *in love* with him. But now, she respected his decision entirely, he was such a wonderful family man... yada yada yada."

Leigh frowned. "What a load of—"

"Clearly," Cara interrupted. "A load only a man would buy. What she wanted, of course, was her last paycheck and a spanking clean reference. What happened with Gil would never happen with any other boss, you see, because Gil was special, and because she'd learned how important it was to 'guard her heart.'"

"Oh, please."

"Tell me about it. But Gil believed her. At least a little bit... because he wanted to. And before you know it, the wench was working for the next most promising target on her list—a man that her job with Gil had already conveniently introduced her to."

Leigh's eyebrows lifted. "Brandon Lyle."

Cara put a finger to her nose. "You got it, cuz."

"But couldn't Brandon see—"

Cara threw her a look.

"Right," Leigh corrected. "The man thing. And Gil wouldn't say anything because, if he believed her story about having real feelings for him—"

"Then it would be like betraying a confidence," Cara finished. "He did wise up, eventually. Once Diana started working for

Brandon, Gil could see her playing the same games. But Brandon was a big boy who'd cheated before; as far as Gil was concerned, it was their business. He was just glad to be out of it."

Cara looked thoughtful for a moment. Her shoulders slumped. "Gil thought it was over and done with, Leigh. And I let myself think that, too. But I should have known better. When a woman lays it all out on the line like that... and I mean *everything*, and the man rejects her..." She bit a fingernail.

"I see what you mean," Leigh said gently. The image of Brandon's stiff face and glassy, unseeing eyes swept unbidden across her mind.

Shot in the back.

She straightened. "Did Diana have a falling out with Brandon, too? I mean, do you think she would be capable..."

"I have no idea what the woman is capable of," Cara responded grimly. "But at the very least, I intend to make sure Maura knows just how skillful a manipulator they're dealing with." Her voice caught. "Because if Diana Saxton resents my husband as much as I'm starting to think she might..."

The words hung unspoken in the air.

Gil could be in far worse trouble than he knew.

Diana drummed her fingernails on the steering wheel of her "preowned" Audi, contemplating which direction to turn. She should not have to drive a second-hand anything. She should be tooling around in an Aston Martin Roadster, telling people like that witch in Harrisburg exactly what they could do with their anchor-sized engagement rings and stiff, patronizing smiles. She hadn't chosen wisely in Brandon, that much was true. But she had done everything else right. She always did. It was other people who ruined everything.

The light remained red. Diana glanced to the left. Courtney Lyle was an idiot. Brandon's wife didn't need someone like Diana to bring her down; she was more than capable of doing it herself. It was clear from the detectives' expressions that they were unaware that Courtney had returned to the couple's Pittsburgh apartment last night—and yet they had obviously contacted her about his murder this morning. Had she lied to them on the phone, saying that she was still in Chicago? Or had she flown back to Chicago late last night?

All Diana knew was that Courtney had not been at the apartment this afternoon, which was fortuitous all the way around. One murder in the family was enough.

Diana's fingers drummed harder for a moment, then stopped abruptly as she reached a decision. Never mind the bubblehead. Courtney was her own worst enemy.

The light was still red. Diana let out an exasperated sigh and glanced at the empty seat next to her. Her prize was stowed underneath, waiting. It was a risky thing to do, but the temptation was just too great. Certain people had it coming to them. They were practically begging for it.

She glanced to the right. Would Gil March be at home now? Most likely he would, clutched in the loving arms of his older-than-dirt wife and his two sickeningly perfect children. Eating bean sprouts and sipping pomegranate juice. Going to sleep at night on top of giant piles of money...

Diana's eyes narrowed. Yes, it was worth it. Gil March would get his—and then some.

The light turned green.

But not *quite* yet, she mused, gunning the accelerator and shooting into the intersection with a squeal of rubber.

The Audi turned neither left nor right, but sailed straight ahead.

She would wait until the time was right.

Chapter 10

Leigh reached into the back of Cara's van and attempted to fasten leads on both Chewie and the March's Brittany spaniel, Maggie, without the two of them becoming hopelessly intertwined in the process. It wasn't easy. Maggie might be old and arthritic, but the dog was as much of a spaz as ever. Leigh finally managed to attach the spaniel's lead and put her down on the ground, only to struggle even harder to hook up the corgi while Maggie jerked her arm around like a marionette. By the time she got Chewie on the ground also he was panting as if he'd run a marathon, and he hadn't walked a step yet. The two dogs riled each other up under the calmest of circumstances; a mutual road trip was heaven.

"Why exactly did we need both dogs?" Leigh asked, handing Maggie's lead gratefully over to Cara and wiping corgi slobber off her other arm and onto her shorts.

"Mom wants us to split up," Cara answered, leading the foursome across the parking lot toward the light post under which the three Morton sisters—Bess, Lydie, and Frances—stood waiting. Leigh wasn't surprised to see Bess toting her Pekingese mix, but since neither her mother nor Cara's owned dogs, she was surprised to see Lydie and Frances each attached to a husky.

The women let the dogs sniff noses, then pulled them back out of leash-tangling range.

"All right, everyone," Frances announced in her best troop-leader tone, forestalling any attempt at pleasantries. "Now that we're all here, let's get the mission straight. Lydie?"

Leigh's Aunt Lydie, a lean, serious woman who resembled her identical twin Frances only to those who didn't know them, stepped around and handed everyone a small pad, a pen, and a large home-printed photograph. It was a picture of Gil, unfortunately cropped from a family photo of a summer vacation at Yosemite, in which he was dressed in shorts and hiking boots and sported a wide, carefree smile. If Leigh knew anything about her cousin-in-law, and she did, the appearance he had presented after leaving Brandon at the church last night would bear not the slightest resemblance. Lydie could have captured a better likeness by snapping a candid shot after pricking her son-in-law with a pin.

"It is critically important," Frances lectured, "that we not intimidate our potential witnesses in any way. That's why I've suggested that the men not accompany us — particularly Gil himself. And why each of us needs a — "

Frances' upper body bowled suddenly and violently backward. Lydie and Bess both made a dive for her, but after a brief cry of surprise, Frances threw back a foot and made a brilliant recovery, bringing her husky — which had apparently just noticed a wild turkey skulking near the edge of the woods — back to heel with a determined snap. "Sit, Denali!" she said firmly.

The dog obeyed with a sulk.

"As I was saying," Frances continued, unruffled, "people with dogs will gladly talk to us if we have a dog of our own. It will make the perfect conversation starter. Once you're accepted, find out if the person was walking in the same place last night, and if so, show them the picture of Gil and ask if they remember seeing him. But *don't* badger," she said accusingly, her eyes darting between Leigh and Bess. "It won't do us any good to find someone if they're not willing to testify."

Frances gave a nod to her twin, then took a half step back out of the way as if she was at a podium.

"Gil says he remembers getting here shortly before dusk," Lydie explained. "He parked in this lot and walked the whole loop around the lake. He's certain he passed several people with dogs before it got dark, but he can't recall any details, which I think we can all understand. He does remember seeing some younger people on roller blades, so you might keep a look out for that. The crowd thins significantly the closer it gets to sundown, so we need to work quickly right off the bat."

"Right," Frances agreed, taking the lead again. "We'll need to divide the loop into five sections. Not everyone walks the whole length of the lake, of course, and there are any number of parking lots or pavilions one could start from. So, as you can see here, I've taken this map and laid out a grid — "

"Oh, keep your panties on, Francie!" Bess huffed, tucking her notepad and photo beneath a flabby arm and pulling her feet out from underneath the rear end of Chester, who could take any cat in stride but was nervous around other dogs. "I think we've all got enough neurons to spread our carcasses evenly around a lake. I'll start by heading this way. And I'm telling you, you'd better hold on tight to those huskies. I'm sure they're otherwise well-behaved, but take it from me, if they get—"

"I am perfectly capable of handling a medium-sized dog, Bess," Frances retorted irritably. "And I'll have you know that Mr. Reynolds was grateful for our help in exercising them. He's always been a good neighbor, and ever since he had that knee surgery last month—"

"TMI!" Bess shouted over her shoulder, heading off. She threw a conspiratorial glance at Leigh as she passed. "Learned that from one of yours, kiddo," she said with a wink.

"What exactly did she just say to me?" Frances inquired of her daughter, eyes narrowed.

"Um... that means 'too much information,'" Leigh informed.

Frances sniffed. She muttered a few words after her older sister's departing form, clucked to her husky, and took off in the same direction.

Lydie cleared her throat. "Cara dear, why don't you and I head off the other way? Leigh, maybe you should stay in this area—catch people as they get out of their cars, maybe?"

"Sounds good," Leigh agreed.

The inquisition proved a bit more awkward than Leigh had hoped. Most people were happy to stop and chat—having a dog with giant ears and no tail helped with that—but as soon as she started asking questions, people's warning bells went off. Had she been trying to locate a lost dog, or even solicit a bone marrow donor, she might have had more luck. But no one seemed particularly eager to be a witness for a man who "may be accused of a crime he didn't commit," even if they did remember seeing him. Which so far, no one did.

After the first twenty minutes, Leigh found that a good portion of the people she met had already been approached by one Morton woman or other, and her spirits began to plummet. Quick texts to Cara, Lydie, and Bess showed that they'd turned up empty, too. Her mother she didn't know about, since Frances steadfastly refused to learn to text and only carried her Paleozoic era no-contract phone "for emergencies." Lydie and Bess had both tried to bring their sister up to speed, but Leigh—while professing her support for the idea—had secretly rooted for failure. If Frances ever figured out how to text, God only knew how many times a day she could remind her daughter to clean something.

It was nearly dark when a man about Leigh's age, walking alone, answered her welcoming smile with one of his own. Leigh introduced herself and asked the usual leading question, but before she could complete it, the man leaned in close and took a sneak peek at the picture she was carrying.

"This your husband?" he asked, smiling.

"No, he's my brother-in-law," Leigh fudged, stepping back. The man clearly had personal space issues. "We're trying to locate anyone who might have seen him walking here last night. Does he look familiar to you?"

The smile continued, and the hairs on the back of Leigh's neck pricked. The man never had answered her first question about whether he had been walking the same route last night.

"Yeah, I think I saw him," he said slowly, never taking his eyes off her.

Leigh heart sped up—but at the same time, she fought a cringe. The man wasn't what you'd call threatening... he was a good inch shorter than she was, overweight, out of shape, and the definition of a middle-aged nerd. But the intensity of his gaze and the slipperiness of his smile made her skin crawl.

"You did?" she asked civilly, reminding herself of the importance of her mission. "At what time? Do you remember?"

He shrugged. "About now, I guess."

He was still smiling.

Leigh swallowed. Why, of everyone she had questioned tonight, did *this* guy have to say yes? "Would you be willing to tell the police that if they asked you?"

His smile widened. "Sure."

"So..." she faltered. "You really are sure you saw this man, here, last night?"

"Absolutely." Smile.

Leigh pressed on. "Would you mind writing down your name and how we could contact you again?" she asked politely, holding out the pen and pad.

He took them both from her, his hand lingering against hers a little longer than necessary in the process. He scribbled something on the pad and handed it back. "You can come to my house if you want."

"I don't think that will be necessary," Leigh responded, stepping back another pace and trying hard not to scream. "But thank you. We'll... I mean, someone will be in touch."

"Awesome."

He didn't move.

Leigh glanced at her phone. "Oh my, I'm late," she gushed. "Sorry, I have to meet up with the rest of my group now. Thank you again!"

She turned tail and hoofed it. Chewie, who had not walked more than six feet in a straight line since jumping out of the van, launched into inchworm mode and galloped beside her obligingly as she jogged up the road in the direction Mr. Creepsville had come from. She didn't figure he would double back, and in any event, she didn't have the keys to Cara's van.

She felt a sudden urge to take a very long, hot shower.

"Leigh Eleanor!" her mother's voice barked unexpectedly from somewhere to her left. "Why on earth are you running?"

Leigh halted in her steps. Chewie, less quick on the draw, let his back legs pass his front ones, spun around inside his collar, and came to a stop on his rear end. Unfazed, he popped back up immediately and began sniffing at a signpost.

Frances was standing by a nearby clump of trees, allowing the handsome gray and white husky to do his business off the beaten track. She studied her daughter disapprovingly.

"I... um..." Leigh faltered. *Well, you see, there was this man wearing too-tight running shorts with black knee socks and loafers, and from the way he smiled at me, I'm pretty sure he was a serial killer...* "I just wondered how you were doing," she finished.

Frances frowned. "I thought you were supposed to be covering the parking lot."

"I did," Leigh defended. "I am. Have you had any luck?"

Frances clucked her tongue. "I'm afraid not. But wait"—she looked over Leigh's shoulder—"these people look likely. Gil said he saw roller skaters, didn't he? Here, you take Denali." Frances pressed the end of the lead against Leigh's closed hand and hurried back out to the road.

"Yoo hoo! What lovely roller skates!" she cooed.

Roller *blades*, Leigh thought to herself, making a perfunctory grab for the lead.

But the loop of nylon was no longer there. And neither was the husky.

Leigh spied the red ribbon of the lead snaking off through the grass as the husky made a beeline for the roller bladers. Dragging Chewie along with her, she launched into a desperate sprint — only too aware of the sound of several cars in the proximity. The dog was nearing the road. The lead was still traveling ahead of her... but she could reach it... just... if she made a dive for it... now!

The husky trotted off into the roadway unhindered.

Leigh did a face plant in the grass.

A wet corgi nose snuffled at her cheek. Leigh lifted her head and saw that the husky had gone no farther than the nearest roller blader, and that his lead had been picked up again — no doubt with minimal effort — by Frances.

She sighed and struggled back to her feet. Now she really, *really* wanted that shower.

"Well, that was a bust," Frances said testily, rejoining her. "Skaters just aren't creatures of habit like dog walkers." She looked up at the rapidly darkening sky and sighed dramatically. "Look, there's Bess coming our way. The walkers are all but gone; it's getting too dark. I guess we might as well head back. Let's hope the others had more luck. And by the way, dear — "

Leigh braced herself.

"You have goose poo in your hair."

Chapter 11

"So, did you find anyone to support Gil's alibi?" Maura asked, accepting the cup of coffee Leigh offered her and settling into a kitchen chair.

Leigh poured another cup and joined her. "Well, that depends on how you look at it. Cara did talk to a couple of women she was certain had seen Gil. They even remembered that he was wearing business casual, which stuck out a bit, as we'd hoped. But as soon as she mentioned the word 'testify,' they got skittish. Started saying they weren't so sure after all, that they couldn't possibly swear to it. Refused even to give Cara their names."

"That's not good," Maura said soberly.

Leigh shook her head. "Cara was distraught, as you can imagine. She tried so hard to be polite about it—but they just seemed terrified of having anything to do with the police."

"You have no way to contact them again?"

Leigh smirked. "I didn't say that. Cara being Cara, she let them walk off, then followed them covertly until they got back to their car. She hid behind a tree and scribbled down their license plate number."

Maura let out a smirk of her own. "Very enterprising. But we won't hassle them unless we have to; unwilling witnesses aren't much better than no witnesses at all. Anything else before you get to it?"

Leigh looked up from her cup. "Get to what?"

"Your attempted inquisition of me. Wanting to know everything Detective Peterson and I found out yesterday."

"So you're going to share?"

Maura reached out and grabbed a donut from the box Leigh had risen before dawn to acquire. "Hell, no. But I thought I'd take you up on the free breakfast, anyway."

Leigh groaned. "Knock yourself out."

A ball of black fur landed heavily in her lap, and she put out a hand reflexively to scoop it up. Her Persian, Mao Tse, was getting on in years. After the highly unpopular introduction of the barbarian dog two years ago, Mao had registered her protest with a self-imposed exile to the master bedroom—which Leigh had since kept both dog- and child-free in her honor. For Mao to discover an empty Leigh-lap in the middle of the kitchen on a quiet morning was a rare find the cat wasted no time capitalizing on.

"*Did* you find any other prospects?" Maura mumbled while she chewed.

"I found a guy who's ready to testify that he saw Gil, yes."

The detective's eyes widened. "Seriously?"

"He could be serious," Leigh said without enthusiasm, reaching for a chocolate-frosted. "But I'm guessing no, seeing as how he prefaced his contact info with *for a good time, call.*"

Maura spewed some donut crumbs. "Could still be legit, you know," she said when she'd recovered. "He might have actually seen Gil *and* want your body. Good thing you had Killer there with you." She pointed a thumb toward Chewie, who was laid out flat on the linoleum by the detective's feet, snoring. "This guy doesn't have your phone number, does he?"

Leigh frowned. "How dumb do I look?"

Maura grinned, but made no comment. "I'll take care of it, then. Guys like this make my day."

Leigh let that one go. Maura took a lot of grief for her size, but being a he-woman did have its perks, and being able to intimidate the crap out of perverts was one of them.

"Maura," she said thoughtfully, "is there anything else we can do for Gil? Cara's pretty frantic, under the circumstances."

"I know she is," Maura replied. "But Peterson's good, and I plan to be watching over his shoulder, whether the department likes it or not. He's got a full day's worth of search warrants to execute, so I'm sure something will turn up. The best thing you can do is keep trying to find a willing witness to Gil's alibi." She leaned over the table. "But that's *all* you can do. Any of you. Understood?"

Leigh offered her trademark salute.

"You know," Maura said with a frown, reaching for her third donut. "I never do believe you when you do that."

Leigh grinned. "Yeah. I know."

***

"We *won't!*" the Pack responded in unison, complete with eye rolling, as they piled out of the van and sprinted through the rain to the front door of the animal shelter. Leigh bit her lip. She hadn't meant to transmit her own anxiety, but clearly, she had given one too many admonitions about their staying out of the woods. She wished it hadn't been necessary, but she couldn't help but be suspicious of Ethan and Allison's sudden desire to pull an extra shift—and Matt and Lenna's sudden desire to accompany them. She would have said no if the shelter manager hadn't insisted she was short-staffed and could use the extra help this morning. Leigh knew that, unlike the majority of child volunteers, the Pack actually did help. And it was entirely possible that Matt and Lenna weren't looking for trouble so much as a way to get out of the house and escape their mother's unprecedented foulness of mood.

Leigh closed the van door, pulled out onto Nicholson Road, and headed for her Aunt Bess's house. The children's preoccupation for a few hours was timely, as she had a mission of her own to conduct this morning. A mission which had nothing to do with one Brandon Lyle—or at least, she hoped it wouldn't. The dog park was still a good idea, and she wasn't giving up on it. She couldn't very well abandon important plans every time she tripped over a body, could she?

She navigated the private road to her Aunt Bess's house warily as usual, mindful of the potholes that were quickly filling with the morning's rain. She had a fleeting fear of being trapped on the wrong side of the creek, but she suppressed it. It was July, for heaven's sake. And it hadn't been raining that long.

With her gaze kept firmly on the road, she didn't notice the visitor standing on Bess's porch until she was parked in the driveway. The man was gesticulating wildly. He was also holding a shotgun.

She fumbled in her bag for her cell phone, stuffed it into her pocket, and stepped out of the car. She would have called 911 if she didn't know who it was. Knowing who it was... well, it never hurt to have one's phone handy, did it?

"They wouldn't tell me a blasted thing!" the man was shouting. He was an older man, well past seventy, with deeply wrinkled, sun-damaged skin and dark eyes that brooded under bushy white eyebrows. Shabby clothes hung from his lean frame like a scarecrow, but his quick movements revealed a body as able as his spirit was willing. "Wouldn't you think we'd have a right to know," he railed, "seeing as how they're murdering people right here on our own doorsteps now?!"

"Now, Clem," Aunt Bess retorted, her voice calm, but firm. "You know perfectly well the police aren't going to answer our every question about an ongoing murder investigation. That's just silly. Some things, we have to find out for ourselves."

Leigh's eyebrows rose as she mounted the stairs and dodged under the porch roof out of the rain.

"Well, I was out there last night, wasn't I?" Clem fumed. "Got my flashlight and looked all over, soon as I heard. Should have known nobody was going to tell old Clem except the five o'clock news!" Chaw-stained spittle sprayed from the old man's lips as he talked, lacing the straggly white beard below.

Bess's eyes narrowed. "Now, don't you give me that line of horse pooey!" she said fiercely, dropping her previous facade of calm. "I knocked on your door three times yesterday, and the police tried, too. If you had a telephone and an answering machine like the rest of the modern world, you might not miss so much information!"

"Devil's work!" he spewed. "Bunch of techno-nonsense!"

"You figured out how to use that digital converter box fast enough!" Bess retorted.

The man's shoulders slumped slightly. "I gotta watch my shows, don't I?"

Bess sighed. "I left you a note to come and see me—it's your own darn fault you ignored it. Now, cut the self-righteous act and put away that fool gun before I crack it over that extra-thick skull of yours."

Clem uttered a low, growling noise, but to Leigh's relief, he leaned the shotgun obediently against Bess's porch rail.

"You remember my niece, Leigh?" Bess asked, her voice now all sweetness. Clem did not look up. He had yet to spare the newcomer a glance. "She's the one who found the body," Bess finished.

Clem looked up.

"What'd it look like?" he barked.

Leigh swallowed. "Um... he looked... dead."

Clem's eyes bugged. "Where was he? On my land?"

"Um... I—" Leigh looked to Bess for assistance. She wasn't supposed to be divulging crime scene information. For all she knew, the police were limiting what they told Clem for a reason. But Bess, curse her, looked every bit as expectant as he did. Bess had already given Leigh an earful for tipping off the detectives about the video before informing her dear, devoted aunt that there had been a murder in the first place.

"It was out near the pond," Leigh answered vaguely. Surely the five o'clock news had offered that much already.

"Really?" Clem said skeptically, his beard twitching.

"Don't sound so shocked!" Bess interjected. "If the body had been found on your property, the police would have contacted you first thing."

Clem grunted. "I don't know that. I don't trust the police!"

Leigh was not surprised.

"For all I know," he continued, "they whacked that young hustler themselves, and now they're trying to pin it all on us landowners! Well, I pay my taxes, and I'm telling you right now —"

"Clem," Bess said reasonably, with no trace of sarcasm, "Conspiracy theories notwithstanding, don't you think it's much more likely that a man like Brandon Lyle was murdered by a personal enemy? A business associate he'd double crossed? A jealous lover?"

Someone trying to protect their land? Leigh stifled the comment. Clem's shotgun was still within reach. Furthermore, such motive would apply equally to her own "eccentric" Aunt Bess, and one suspect in the family was enough.

Clem uttered a growl. "I don't frankly care who killed the bastard, as long as they stayed off my damn land while they were doing it! And the police had better stay off as well. Waking me up with their banging... lucky some heads didn't roll then, I'd say! Nobody trespasses on my land, understand?" He fixed his gaze on Leigh again. "*Nobody!*"

"Oh, leave her alone, you old coot!" Bess chastised, planting both hands on her generous hips. "She'll think you're serious."

"I am serious!" he bellowed.

"You're a pumped-up bag of wind!" Bess fired back. "You're just mad because you didn't hear the police coming. *And* because you didn't hear anything the night it happened, which we both know is because you're deaf as a post and too darn stubborn to get a hearing aid!"

Blue veins started to pop out on Clem's weathered temples, and Leigh's body tensed. Her Aunt Bess had always had a way with people — even crazy ones. But no one was perfect.

"Now, stop bullying my niece and get back on your own precious property and off of mine," Bess continued, her tone steely. "Before I start asking questions about how my extra gasoline cans keep going empty!"

Clem's gaze dropped like a rock. He scowled, swept up his shotgun, and stepped off the porch. Then he turned around and fixed Bess with another bug-eyed stare. "You'll tell me everything later, won't you?"

Bess returned a smug, conspiratorial smile. "Don't I always?"

Clem turned his back and stomped off.

Bess opened the door to her house and gestured Leigh inside, much to the delight of Chester, who burst from his captivity to spin around Leigh's ankles in greeting. "Would you like some tea, kiddo?" Bess offered, her voice merry.

Leigh shook her head. "Aunt Bess," she said nervously, "aren't you just a teeny bit worried about living next door to an armed lunatic?"

Bess's lips pursed. "Don't be ridiculous, Leigh. You've known Clem since you were a girl! He's perfectly harmless."

Leigh gritted her teeth. It was true that Clem had lived in the neighborhood even longer than Bess had, but the word "known" was an overstatement. In the last three decades, she might have glimpsed the man half a dozen times in the distance through the trees. His existence in her mind had always been on par with the wicked witch and the gingerbread house... smart children stayed out of his woods. Period.

"The man scared Hook's PR woman half to death!" Leigh retorted. "Sooner or later he's going to wind up in jail for brandishing a weapon like that."

Bess waved her hand in dismissal. "Clem's half deaf. He probably couldn't understand a word she said. But I agree he can't keep waving that fool gun at every person who bangs on his door. He couldn't hear with his telephone anymore, so he got rid of it.

Idiot won't listen to me when I tell him there are devices—" She broke off suddenly. "What's up, kiddo? You didn't drive all the way out here to lecture me about the company I keep. I have your mother for that. Are Cara and Gil all right?"

"I wouldn't say Cara is," Leigh answered honestly, remembering the bags she'd seen under her cousin's eyes when picking up the kids this morning. "She's still terribly worried about Gil. But that's not why I'm here. I'm here because I want the animal shelter to build a dog park, and I need your help."

Leigh explained the plan, which Bess took to immediately. "It's a splendid idea!" she agreed. "But you'll need to talk to Anna first. She has to approve any structures built on the property—that's in the lease."

"I know," Leigh agreed. "That's why I need you. I was hoping you could introduce us. I met her a long time ago, at the shelter's grand opening, but I doubt she would remember me, and if she's a tough sell, I figured your influence couldn't hurt."

Bess puffed herself up. "Well, it's nice to know you give your old aunt credit for *something*, at least."

Leigh sighed. Her Aunt Bess could forgive lots of things, like a neighbor pilfering gasoline, or a teenaged niece borrowing plaid polyester pants for a seventies party and "forgetting" to give them back. But there were two things Bess never forgot. The first was cruelty to an animal. The second was withholding juicy information she knew perfectly well she had no right to hear in the first place.

"I said I was sorry," Leigh repeated. "Maura swore me to secrecy until she could talk to you."

Bess arched one eyebrow. "Mm-hmm. Well, she's talked to me. Asked a boatload of questions and didn't tell me dip squat. I understand your not wanting to get into it last night with the others around, but now we're alone. So, shoot!" She plopped her ample rear end down on the couch, sending the requisite three cats flying off the cushions below.

Leigh pushed two more aside and joined her. "What is it you want to know?" she said without enthusiasm, wishing she could think and talk of something other than Brandon Lyle. She didn't know how morticians did it. No matter how many bodies she was unlucky enough to see, the last one creeped her out as much as the first. Brandon's sightless, staring eyes kept popping into her head...

his waxy face, frozen into an expression of utter shock...

"Yoo-hoo, kiddo," Aunt Bess's voice cooed. "You were telling me the leading police theory as to who killed Brandon Lyle."

Leigh shook her head. "I was?"

Bess nodded innocently.

Leigh sighed. "Maura won't tell me anything, either. But Cara and Gil are thinking maybe a loan shark. Brandon did seem pretty desperate for money."

Bess considered a moment, her lips twisted. "Nope," she announced finally. "Not buying it. They said on the news — not that *my own niece* would tell me — that he was shot in the back. A loan shark would want him to suffer, would want him to see it coming. No, I'm thinking it was more heat of the moment. A crime of passion."

Leigh squirmed. "I'd really prefer it wasn't. We don't need any more suspicion on Gil. Or on the church members who were at that meeting. What if one of them is nuts? Even more nuts than Clem?"

Bess dismissed the idea with a wave of her hand. "Not that kind of passion, silly. I'm talking the classic. The usual. *Love* triangle."

Leigh watched the sparks fly in her aunt's mischievous eyes. *This* was why Leigh got into trouble so often. It wasn't just bad luck. It was heredity.

"Brandon was cheating on his wife with his administrative assistant," she offered.

Bess's face lit up like Christmas. "Well, there you have it!" she said gleefully. "Now, we just have to figure out which woman killed him, and prove it."

"*No*, we most certainly do—"

"The first thing I need to know is exactly where you found the body," Bess began, getting to her feet. "Because everyone knows that the killer *always* returns to the scene of the crime. And with my handy new gadgets, we can have 24/7 surveillance, easy as pie!"

"Aunt Bess—" Leigh began hopelessly.

"Do you *want* to help Gil get out of this mess, or don't you?" Bess interrupted. "You know how worried Cara is. Looking for witnesses is good, but this is better, and it's not even illegal. At least, I don't think it is. The cameras will be on my property, after all. Anyway, grab some boots and an umbrella and follow me. Just point out the spot and I'll get the equipment moved before nightfall. Who knows... we might even catch Ferdinand and the other feral cats in the bargain!"

Leigh continued to sit, the wheels in her head spinning. Maura's disembodied head hung somewhere over her right shoulder, growling menacingly. But Cara's puffy-eyed visage was floating to her left, sobbing with worry.

Leigh's jaws clenched.

She got up and grabbed an umbrella.

Chapter 12

"I've always liked your aunt," the older woman standing before Leigh said fondly.

"Yes," Leigh agreed, "she's a real peach, isn't she?" Her words were not entirely sincere. She had been hoping that Bess would do more than make a brief introduction on Anna Krull's porch, assure Anna that Leigh's upcoming suggestion was brilliant, and then promptly disappear. Leigh knew perfectly well that Bess's suddenly remembered "appointment" was nothing but an excuse to go back and hustle her camera equipment to the pond. Bess would be watching every raccoon, squirrel, deer, and drunken teenager that approached the spot for weeks.

"Why don't you come on in and sit down?" Anna offered, leading Leigh the short distance to a worn couch in a small living room. "Would you like something to drink?"

"No, thank you," Leigh said as she sat, glancing around the room with widened eyes. Its interior was not what she had expected. She knew that, although the Krull family had once been prosperous farmers who owned all the land for miles around, Anna herself had been left with only a modest legacy, as her wastrel father and grandfather had sold off most of the land to pay their gambling debts. The outside of her house was always neatly kept and planted with seasonal flowers, but there was nothing fancy about it, and the car parked in her garage was half as old as Leigh. The house's furniture looked even older, which made it all the more surprising that the living room bubbled from end to end with state-of-the-art saltwater aquariums.

"Just a little hobby of mine," Anna explained, taking a seat beside her guest. "I adore fish. They're so quiet, you know. Seahorses are my favorite. I breed them."

Leigh studied the myriad bumpy-skinned creatures who clung to wispy sea plants with their tails, bobbing slightly in the artificial current. Her head filled immediately with nosy, more than likely inappropriate questions, but her hostess seemed ready for business.

"Now, then," Anna said briskly. "What can I do for you? Bess says you have a fundraising idea for the shelter. You took your Aunt's place on the board, didn't you?"

"Yes, I did," Leigh answered, happy to know that Anna was keeping up with things, even if she rarely visited the facility. The road-front property on which the shelter sat was worth a nice chunk of change, and not just to Brandon Lyle. The shelter was fortunate that Anna not only wanted to hang onto it herself, but was willing to lease it so reasonably. "We're all very appreciative of how generous you've been with your land. I can't tell you how much."

Anna waved away the sentiment, but offered a gracious smile. Her dentures had seen whiter days, but her blue eyes were lively, and she had the look of a woman who felt much younger than her seventy-some-odd years. Leigh wondered if she and Clem hung out much. "It works out well for me, too," Anna responded. "My taxes are covered, and I still have control over what's built out there. And what's not."

Leigh digested the subtle comment, and decided that her Aunt Bess was right. Anna Krull might not look intimidating, with her pixie-cut hair, alligator skin, and comfortable 100% cotton clothing—all of which together could not weigh more than ninety pounds soaking wet. But she and Bess clearly had mutual ancestors. Namely, a horse and a donkey. "What I'm suggesting won't sacrifice a single tree," Leigh assured. "The only thing we'd need to build would be a fence. I'm thinking of a dog park—a confined area where people can let their pets off leash."

Anna's smile disappeared. "How many people?"

Leigh tensed. She was well aware of how much Anna—like Bess, Clem, and anyone else who chose to live in the middle of the wilderness off a flood-prone road—valued their privacy. But as she delivered her rehearsed spiel on how the dog park could bring in extra revenue without bringing any extra traffic onto anyone's private land, she was gratified to see the smile gradually return to Anna's face.

"Well then, I think it's a fine idea," the woman praised. "I like the thought of all those cooped-up pooches having the chance to run a bit. Where would you put it?"

Leigh hesitated, unpleasant images once again threatening to unsettle her stomach. "I had been thinking that around the pond would be nice, since the dogs could go for a dip. But now, considering what's happened..."

Anna's brow furrowed. "Yes," she agreed. "We've always had trouble with trespassers out there, but now that..." she contemplated a moment. "No, that won't do, I'm afraid. That pond is already menace enough, attracting hippies and such, and your Aunt Bess is no help at all. She's close enough to hear when they're making a ruckus, but she absolutely refuses to shoo them off!"

Hippies? Leigh suppressed a grin. "Yes, well, that's Aunt Bess for you."

Anna's tone softened. "I suppose they've never really hurt anything," she conceded. "But I'd rather not make the public any more aware of that pond's existence than it already is. Besides, you couldn't fence it in anyway; it's not all on my property. My land, Bess's, and the church's all meet somewhere in the middle of water." She put up a hand and stroked her jaw thoughtfully. Then her eyes lit up. "Why don't you run the fence from the parking lot up to where the old house was? There's no pond that way, and it's a longer walk, but then you'd have a nice clearing for the dogs to play in. If you wanted to get the pump for the well working again, you could even have fresh water available."

Leigh envisioned picnic lunches and dogs leaping in the air to catch flying discs. She smiled broadly. "That sounds perfect!"

"Only thing is," Anna qualified, "I wouldn't want anyone trying to access the clearing from the private road. They'd have to walk from the animal shelter lot."

"I'm sure that wouldn't be a problem," Leigh replied. She had seen what was left of the gated drive that led off into the trees past Bess's house. The dead-end stretch was barely penetrable by goat cart, much less automobile.

"We've got enough traffic on this road already," Anna insisted. She was silent a moment, then she turned to Leigh, her voice suddenly earnest. "Your Aunt Bess is a strong woman, but lately, I've been a little concerned about her. Do you think... considering what's happened... that she's getting nervous about living out here all by herself?"

Leigh's eyebrows rose. No one who knew her Aunt Bess, even a little bit, would trouble themselves with that question. She got the distinct impression it wasn't really Aunt Bess that Anna was talking about. "If you mean, in regards to the murder behind the church," Leigh forced herself to say, "I don't think she worries about her personal safety, no. Do you?"

The older woman's face flushed slightly. "Oh, no. Of course not." She paused a moment, her eyes fixing on her front window. "Did your Aunt Bess tell you that he was here that night?"

Leigh leaned forward. "You mean, Brandon Lyle?"

Anna nodded. "He wanted my land, you know. I'd told him 'hell no' over the phone a dozen times, but he'd never come here in person before. The young woman did, Geralyn, but she was polite."

The older woman rose and stood over one of the aquariums; peered at a thermometer, adjusted a dial. Leigh restrained herself from comment. She knew the look of a person who wanted to talk when she saw it. And it was certainly the least she could do to listen.

"I knew there was a church meeting going on that evening, but I wasn't worried about it," Anna continued. "I didn't think they'd sell with Bess being such a big shot there, and even if they did—well, the development couldn't happen anyway, not without Clem or Bess. When I heard a car in the driveway, I couldn't imagine who it might be. I don't get many visitors, especially not at that hour."

The hand the older woman rested on the aquarium hood began to tremble slightly, even as her voice turned indignant.

"I was already in my nightclothes, for heaven's sake!" Anna exclaimed. "He came right up on the porch under the light, and I could see it was a man all dressed up in a fancy suit, but I didn't know who he was. The chain was on the door, so I did open it up a crack, and then as soon as he started talking, I recognized his voice. But..." she shook her head. "There was something about him that wasn't quite right."

Anna huffed out a breath and squared her thin shoulders. "I don't scare easy. Truly, I don't. But I have to say, that man gave me the willies."

Leigh stood up and moved closer. "What did he say to you?"

Anna shook her head. "I don't completely remember. Same things as always, about how he wanted to 'help' me. Said he could set me up in one of those luxury places for seniors—wouldn't listen when I told him I didn't want to leave here, that I already had everything I needed." She left the window and began to pace. "But I didn't argue with him about it then. I just told him to go away. He kept on, though, till he got downright weird—telling me I *had* to sell, because his entire future depended on it. Told me I was ruining his life!"

Leigh's teeth gnashed. Even posthumously, Brandon's rating on the egocentric ass scale kept climbing.

"By the end, he was practically sobbing," Anna continued. "Banging on the door, begging to be let in, demanding to see me face to face. That's when I'd had enough. I told him if he didn't get off my porch and off my land in the next ten seconds, the next thing he'd see would be the barrel of my granddaddy's Winchester!"

She paused in front of her small fireplace, over which an antique rifle was mounted. Leigh looked at the dusty weapon and the multitude of rusty screws and wires that held it in place, and couldn't help but raise an eyebrow.

Anna cracked a sheepish grin. "I suppose it was an empty threat," she conceded. "I couldn't get that thing down and loaded in ten seconds if a herd of wild elephants was after me. But he didn't know that."

She sank suddenly back down on her couch. "The thing is, I've never been afraid to live alone, never been afraid to defend myself, either. But this business... his spooking me like that, then dying that very night, and so close by! I'm ashamed to say, it's got me rattled."

Leigh sat down beside her. "It's got everybody rattled," she assured. "And if I was in your shoes, I'd be far more upset than you are, believe me."

A twinkle returned to the older woman's eyes.

"What happened after you threatened him?" Leigh asked, knowing perfectly well it was technically none of her business. "Did it work? Did he leave then?"

Anna nodded. "Finally. The second he drove away, I called your Aunt Bess. He wasn't headed her direction, but I was worried about her all the same. I was afraid he might head up to her place next."

"What about Clem? Didn't you call the police?"

Anna frowned. "Clem can take care of himself. And why on earth would I call the police? It was your aunt I was worried about."

Leigh decided not to press the point. Perhaps Anna and Clem really did hang out. They certainly shared the same lack of confidence in law enforcement.

Leigh stood. "Thank you so much for giving your approval to the dog park," she said genuinely. "I promise to keep in touch about how the plan is going. The board may vote it down, for all I know, but I'm glad to know you're not opposed to the concept."

"Bess knows I'm always happy to help her out with the animals," Anna replied, rising also.

Leigh's cell phone vibrated in her pocket. Ordinarily she wouldn't interrupt a conversation, but when she was away from the kids...

"Do you mind if I check this?" she asked, pulling out her phone.

Anna shrugged, and Leigh looked down. The call was from Gil's cell. That was odd. "I'm afraid I need to go now," she told her host, heading for the exit. "But thank you again."

"Come back any time. And tell that aunt of yours to watch herself!" Anna called out as she closed the door.

Leigh wondered as the door shut if Maura and Peterson had interviewed Anna yet. Surely, if they talked to Aunt Bess, they would know that Brandon had gone to Anna's house the night of the murder—apparently *after* the fight with Gil. Then again, her Aunt Bess hadn't passed on that particular intel to her niece, had she?

Leigh hopped into the van. Maura hated it when Leigh withheld information. But she really, *really* hated it when Leigh inserted herself into sensitive situations, asked questions that were none of her business, and through sheer dumb luck found things out before the police did.

Leigh was in trouble either way.

She drove back out to the intersection with Nicholson and pulled off on the side of the road. She would decide how to deal with Maura later. Right now, she needed to know what the heck Gil wanted.

He picked up his phone on the second ring.

"Leigh! Why didn't you answer?"

Her eyes rolled. Her cousin's husband was an honest, loyal, and devoted soul, but he was entirely too used to people jumping whenever he snapped his fingers. "I was driving," she white-lied. "Is anything wrong?"

"Not with me," he answered. "But I'm worried about Cara. Can you swing by my office today? Maybe around noon? I need to talk to you—in person."

Leigh sighed. Gil never "swung by" anybody else's office. He just expected others to come to him. "I don't see how," she explained. "I've got to be at Hook by one, and I can't leave now—I've got to wait and deliver the Pack home from the animal shelter first."

"The animal shelter!" Gil thundered. "You mean Cara's alone?"

Leigh's eyebrows arched. "Is that a problem?"

"Of course it's a problem!" he yelled.

Leigh pulled the phone away from her ear a little. She waited.

"I'm sorry, Leigh," he apologized. He always apologized. Gil March was an alpha male to the bone, but he was a chivalrous one. "I didn't mean to yell at you. I'm just so damn worried that she'll—" he broke off the thought. "Do you know where she is now?"

"She said she was going grocery shopping."

"Can you call her and ask if she can pick up the Pack? Tell her you've got an urgent meeting downtown. It's absolutely true. *Please*, Leigh. I can't get into all this over the phone."

Leigh contemplated for a moment. But it was only for show.

They both knew she would be there.

Chapter 13

Leigh stepped off the elevator with fine beads of sweat breaking on her brow and rainwater dripping from her shoes. She hated parking downtown. She always had, which was why she preferred Hook's offices on Pittsburgh's Northside. There was always a spot available around the stadiums, unless there was a game on, in which case she simply stayed home. She'd been working from home half the time since the twins were born anyway, and she remained perpetually grateful that her line of work made that possible. Cara might be the world's most nurturing earth mother, but if Leigh had been forced to quit work entirely when her kids were little, she no doubt would have gone completely insane. As it was, she had merely dropped back her hours as needed and then started writing increasingly bizarre ad copy. Interestingly, the latter had proved a boon to her career.

She walked down the plush corridor toward Gil's office, opened his solid oak door, and stepped in to find the reception desk untended. She was not surprised, knowing that Gil, like the principals at Hook, believed in giving employees a real lunch hour. But usually, when his assistant was out, Gil left his own door open. At the moment, it was firmly shut.

Leigh was not about to waste any more of her time, even if it was comparatively less valuable. She rapped on the door and opened it simultaneously. "Knock, knock. I'm here, Gil. What's—"

She paused in mid phrase with her mouth open.

Gil was standing to the side of his desk. Pressed against him, with her head nestled on his shoulder, was a buxom platinum blonde wearing an off-the-shoulder minidress and three-inch strappy heels. Gil's arms were around her, one hand resting on a bare, tanned shoulder blade.

He looked up at Leigh with the expression of one being seriously put-upon. "Hello," he said flatly.

The woman lifted her head and stared. She appeared to be around Gil's age, although her face was well preserved... or well injected. Jet-black mascara streaked her cheeks; her otherwise perfectly coifed hair was mussed on one side. Despite the raccoon effect, she was a strikingly attractive woman. At least until her eyes narrowed. "Who is *she?*" the stranger croaked, leaning her cheek back on Gil's shoulder again.

Gil put his hands on her arms and set her away from him. "Courtney," he said with exasperation, "this is my wife's cousin, Leigh. We have an appointment now. I'm sorry."

The woman's eyes flickered over Leigh as if she were no more significant than a mosquito. She turned her face back up to Gil, her red lips pouting. "You're throwing me out?"

"I'm afraid so," he answered, eluding her next attempt at a grasp and moving toward the door. "I'm very sorry about Brandon. I know it was a shock to you. But you're a strong woman; you'll get through this. Maybe you should go stay with your family for a while?" Leigh moved away from the door, and Gil held it open.

Courtney's expression melted to a frown. She shot Gil a look of pure resentment. "Maybe I'll just do that. It's nice to know that *somebody* cares!"

Gil uttered a growl low in his throat—one only Leigh could hear. "Of course I care, Courtney," he assured stiffly. "Just not the way you'd like me to. If there's anything *else* I can do for you, let me know. I am sorry for your loss. Truly."

Courtney let out a "humph," wiped her eyes on the side of her hand, and drew herself up straight. She walked to the door with a practiced flounce, displaying her various assets to their fullest. When she pulled up level with Gil at the door, she paused, tilted her strappy heels up to tiptoe, and kissed him full on the lips.

"See you later," she cooed.

Gil growled again, then slammed the door behind her. He walked past Leigh and returned to his desk. "Have a seat," he suggested gruffly.

Leigh remained where she stood.

Gil rubbed his face with his hands, then let out a breath. "Don't start with me, Leigh. Seriously. We're not having this conversation. I know what you saw, but—" he threw her a level, beseeching look. "You *know* better."

Leigh looked back into his magazine-worthy, smoky hazel eyes. He had acted with the utmost propriety ever since she had opened the door, true. How he had acted before then could be another story.

But it wasn't. Leigh had known Gil for almost twenty years, and despite his having ample opportunity to prove the adage that really gorgeous spouses are destined to cheat, he'd shown time and time again, in any number of ways, that he was truly, deeply in love with his wife.

"Yes, I do know better," Leigh said lightly, dropping into a chair. "But it would be a terribly fun conversation, don't you think?"

Gil's lips remained in a perfectly straight line. The man really did have no sense of humor.

Leigh sighed. "I take it that was Brandon Lyle's wife."

He nodded.

"I'm also assuming that you know her pretty well?"

He threw her a hard look. "I've known Courtney since college, same as Brandon. I've never cared for either one of them. Rich parents, spoiled, basically lazy. A well-matched set of reprobates. If you ask me, they deserved each other."

"How long had they been married?" Leigh asked.

"Not long," Gil responded. "Five years, maybe. But they've dated on and off forever. According to Courtney, they tied the knot as a lark when they got rip-roaring drunk in Vegas. According to Brandon, they tied the knot because he needed her money to shore up the loans he took out immediately before they got rip-roaring drunk in Vegas."

Leigh grimaced. "They didn't divorce, though."

"No," Gil replied. "Being rip-roaring drunk, they neglected to sign a pre-nup, which meant Courtney was stuck. At least legally. Last I heard, she was living with a twenty-seven-year-old African dancer in Chicago. You just saw for yourself how devoted she was to Brandon."

Leigh nodded. Her tone turned serious. "If all that's true, Courtney is bound to be a prime suspect. She seems to have as much motive as anyone. That's got to be good for your case."

Gil's face flickered with distress. "I'm sure she's being considered. But I'm also sure she didn't do it. I can hardly root for the police to hassle her just to get them off my back."

"How do you know she didn't do it?"

He shook his head dismissively. "I don't have any proof. I just know her. She's mischievous and shallow, but she's not evil. The tears you saw earlier were real enough; she's mourning Brandon in her own way, even if she didn't love him. But to pull out a gun and shoot someone? No, never. I'm telling you, she doesn't have it in her."

Leigh sat silently for a moment, mulling. How good a judge of female character was Gil? The fact that he had married Cara was a point in his favor. And once, well before that, he had even asked Leigh out. The man had to have some discernment.

"The reason I asked you here," he said suddenly, standing, "is Cara. I'm in enough trouble with the police already, as you know. I can handle that; I'm convinced we can all weather this just fine, with a little patience. But Cara can't seem to let it go. She wants to *do* something. And I don't mean just trying to substantiate my alibi. I'm afraid she's going to do something else, something... desperate."

Leigh sat up a little. She would like to assuage Gil's fears, assure him his wife would never do anything foolish in pursuit of what she considered to be her husband's best interests. But they both knew she'd be lying.

"I agree," she said flatly. "But as far as I know, she hasn't come up with any bright ideas yet. Do you know of something?"

Gil's teeth clenched, making a muscle pop in his square jaw line. "I'm afraid so. She's fixated on Diana Saxton. For some reason, she thinks the woman has it in for me, which is ridiculous. Diana went ballistic on the phone yesterday, true, and I was worried that she might babble the same nonsense to the detectives and make the whole situation worse for me. But she was understandably upset; she'd only just heard that Brandon was murdered! Now that she's had a chance to calm down and think things through, she'll realize how out of line she was to accuse me. She's high strung, but she's not irrational. The idea that she would coldly plot against me now is ludicrous. Our relationship was always polite and civil, at least up until I got short with her on the phone the other night when she was looking for Brandon—and that was my fault. As I've told Cara over and over again, despite the awkward circumstances, Diana and I parted ways very professionally."

Leigh slumped in her chair. So much for the understanding women thing. "What is it you think Cara's going to do?"

He began to pace. "I don't know. I don't know if she knows—yet.

But sooner or later, she'll think of something. And the worst thing she could do, the absolute worst, is to try and confront Diana herself."

An image of such a meeting popped into Leigh's head. She winced. "That wouldn't be pretty," she agreed.

"It would be disastrous," Gil stated. "Can you imagine how a prosecutor would look at something like that? But what worries me more is the danger to Cara herself. And I don't mean from Diana—she's harmless. But *someone* killed Brandon Lyle, and that someone is still out there. Who knows what Cara could put her foot into? I don't want her involved!"

Leigh looked up into Gil's earnest, troubled face, and knew that his fears were justified. Cara would walk over hot coals for him. "What do you want me to do?"

"That's simple," Gil said with relief, sitting back down. "All I want you to do is make sure she stays with the Pack. No matter how much she wants to help me, she would never put the children at risk. If she's responsible for them, she'll stay put. I know the two of you have a schedule, and you usually trade off, but I was thinking maybe you could tell her you had something urgent come up at work, and that you need her to pick up the slack. At least for the next couple weeks? You won't even have to lie to her. I'll give you the work. I can easily scrounge up two weeks' worth of stuff that the firm needs to have done, and I'll pay Hook's going rate. Please, Leigh?"

Leigh bit her lip. She was a lousy liar. She was lousy at fooling Cara even when she wasn't technically lying. But asking Cara to watch the kids more than her fair share was hardly an unusual request. And it was certainly for a worthy cause. With luck, the police would settle on a non-Gil suspect long before the two weeks were up.

"All right," she agreed.

Gil smiled at her. "Thank you."

"As long as you quit messing around with Courtney Lyle."

He frowned. "Is that supposed to be funny?"

Leigh couldn't resist a chuckle. There really was no point in answering that question.

"I'm surprised you're not more sensitive to the issue," Gil said, his tone reprimanding. "Considering everything Warren's been through."

Leigh stopped chuckling. "What do you mean?"

A loud knock sounded on the door. Gil rose quickly. "You know what I mean," he said as he moved across the room. "Women are always—" he broke off as he swung the door open.

Women are always what?

"Maura!" Gil said with surprise, ushering the policewoman inside. "Is this an official visit? I thought Peterson was in charge of Brandon's case."

"He is," Maura responded, surveying the room and taking in Leigh's presence with a visible look of chagrin. "I'm just doing him a favor. Hi, Leigh. Fancy meeting you here."

Gil waved the detective to another empty chair, then sat down again himself. "Should I call my lawyer?" he asked.

Maura shrugged. "That's up to you. I just need to ask you one question; you can decide after you hear it. And you too, Leigh, since you're here." She pulled a notebook and pen from her pocket. "Both of you had a working relationship with Brandon Lyle. What I'd like to know is, were either of you ever aware, at any time, that he was carrying a weapon?"

Leigh considered, fighting off another unwelcome image of Brandon's handsomely dressed body sprawled awkwardly on the ground. He had been wearing a suit then. He usually wore at least a sport coat, despite the weather. "I was never aware of a weapon," she answered. "But if he was concealing it, I wouldn't know."

Maura nodded and turned to Gil. He was frowning. "I knew that Brandon owned guns," he answered. "I heard him talk about them; he mentioned going to a shooting range. I never actually saw him with one, but like Leigh says, he could have been concealing it, and I wouldn't know."

Maura nodded, then fixed her gaze back on Leigh. "And you *would* have told me if you'd seen a gun on or around the body, right?"

"Of course," Leigh said defensively. "But I didn't. Not that I looked very hard. I told you that, too."

"Maura," Gil said soberly, sitting forward. "You should know that Courtney Lyle came to visit me here in the office about a half hour ago. She was upset about the apartment being searched. Or as she put it, 'torn apart.' And she told me about the handgun."

The detective breathed out heavily. "My, my. Word does travel fast, doesn't it?"

"What handgun?" Leigh inquired.

Maura tapped her pen on her notebook. "As Gil here is obviously already aware, Brandon Lyle owned several firearms, and one of them is missing. His wife claims it was in its place in the cabinet the last time she looked, though she's a little vague on when that might have been." She cast a glance at Gil. "Ms. Lyle is a little vague on a lot of things."

Gil met her eyes without difficulty. "She's a little vague, period," he stated.

"Did she say anything else to you that I should know about?" Maura asked.

Gil considered. "I don't think so. She came to talk to me about his memorial service. She's not having much of one, but she's concerned that no one will come. Brandon was an only child and both his parents are dead, so she may be right. She wanted me to call some of our mutual college friends, let them know. Mainly," he said heavily, "I believe she was trying to drum up my sympathy, and get me to take some of the logistical burden off her shoulders. Brandon's affairs were messy on several fronts; she's a bit overwhelmed."

"I wouldn't advise your doing any of that, under the circumstances," Maura offered.

"I won't be," Gil said succinctly.

Maura rose, then paused and looked at Leigh. "I don't suppose you want to tell me why you're here?"

Leigh shrugged. "Gil and I were putting our heads together, trying to figure out how to keep Cara from doing something stupid."

Maura let out a long, exasperated sigh.

"What?" Leigh said, offended. "How could keeping someone else *out* of trouble possibly get me into it?"

"I don't know, Koslow," Maura said gloomily, turning to leave. "But I'm sure you'll find a way."

Chapter 14

Leigh stepped off the elevator into the lobby of Gil's office building. She hoped it had stopped raining. Her shoes were still clammy from her last hike in from the parking garage. Before she could reach the doors she was approached by a familiar—albeit unexpected—figure.

"Excuse me, Leigh? That is your name, isn't it?"

Leigh looked into the smiling, yet obviously anxious face of Courtney Lyle. The woman's raccoon eyes had been repaired. A fashionable suit jacket now covered her bare shoulders.

Leigh resisted the urge to give a wary look around. All evidence pointed to Brandon's widow having laid in wait for her, which was disconcerting. She must have waited quite a while. It had taken Gil at least twenty minutes to describe the copywriting he conveniently wanted a rush-job on, and that was after Maura had left. But the lobby was safe enough. And the woman's demeanor was hardly threatening.

Just a little weird.

"Yes," Leigh answered. "That's me."

"I'm sorry to interrupt you," Courtney said insincerely, still smiling, "but I wondered if you had a minute? There's something I need to ask you."

Leigh sighed. The fact that Maura always blamed her for these situations was so unjust. Had she *asked* to attract the attention of the widow of the man she'd found murdered who coincidentally had just tried to seduce her cousin-in-law?

"Um..." Leigh looked over her shoulder into the reception area. A uniformed security attendant sat behind a desk, looking down at what might be a security camera, but more likely was the internet. "Sure," she answered. "Let's sit right here." She pointed to two chairs near the door, and dropped into one. The security guard glanced over briefly, then resumed staring downward. Courtney looked around uncertainly at first, but then—perhaps after assessing that the ambient noise level made them unlikely to be overhead—she sat down also.

"You must be the one who found... Brandon," Courtney began. Her voice wavered as she talked, but her eyes were dry, the set of her mouth determined. "I didn't realize. I knew it was someone he had worked with, and a relative of Gil's, but when he mentioned your name it didn't sink in at first. It was you, wasn't it?"

Leigh tried not to bite her lip. She had the distinct feeling she was being not only questioned, but analyzed. Or maybe... suspected?

It made sense, she supposed, from Courtney Lyle's perspective. If Courtney hadn't killed Brandon herself, she must be wondering who had. All she knew about Leigh was that she had "found" the body, and that she had "worked with" Brandon before.

Leigh had to admit, she would suspect herself, too.

"I was the first to find his body, yes," she answered, doing her best to sound direct, but not defensive. "But only because I'm on the board of the animal shelter that leases that property. I was walking the grounds with my dog. I wasn't at the church meeting the night before—I didn't have anything to do with any of that. I wasn't even doing his PR; that was handled by someone else at my firm. And I have no idea who might have killed him, except to say that I'm sure it wasn't Gil. Is that what you wanted to ask?"

Courtney's brown eyes looked at her probingly. After a very long, decidedly uncomfortable moment, Courtney raised a hand, fluffed her blond bangs, and sighed. "He wasn't doing you," she announced.

Leigh's eyebrows rose. She didn't know if—under the circumstances—she had been complimented or insulted. Either way, the conversation was over.

She got up and headed back out the door.

"Wait!" Courtney cried, following her through the lobby and out onto the plaza.

Naturally, it was still raining.

"What do you want?" Leigh said testily, opening her umbrella. Courtney reached into her own handbag and did the same.

"Don't take it personally!" the woman insisted, her tone pleading as she followed Leigh into the crosswalk. "I know Brandon would sleep with anyone. I just want to know who killed him. I thought maybe you could help."

Anyone? Gee thanks, you surgically enhanced —

Leigh stopped with sudden lurch; a car turning left had nearly grazed her thigh. She swore. She hated downtown traffic. Pedestrians were always taking their lives in their hands, even when it wasn't pouring rain and they didn't have crazy women in weather-inappropriate heels dogging their every footstep.

"Look," Leigh said firmly, still moving. "I'm sorry you lost your husband, but there's nothing I can do to help you. I already told you everything I know." It was a white lie, of course. But she felt no compunction.

Courtney continued to follow her.

"I *need* to know," the woman squealed from somewhere over Leigh's left shoulder. "I need to know if it's realistic that a business associate might have done it. You've worked with him... if you suspect anyone in particular, would you tell me? I thought that Gil would help me, but he won't!"

The last words were a girlish whine, but they were punctuated with a stinging animosity. Leigh stopped.

"What do you have against Gil?" she asked.

Courtney reeled back in surprise. "Nothing," she answered.

Leigh started walking again.

Courtney caught up with her, her voice becoming suddenly earnest. "Look, we both know that Gil's no murderer. He's no philanderer, either. I was only messing with him just now for the fun of it. The guy's always had such a rod up his butt! It's hard to resist, you know?"

The corners of Leigh's mouth twitched.

"But he won't help me with anything, and there's so much to do, and I *have* to know who's the likeliest person to have killed Brandon, or else I can't—"

Courtney cut herself off, and Leigh stopped moving and looked at her. Although virtually everything about the appearance and manner of Brandon's widow screamed "ditz," Leigh found herself suddenly skeptical. Between those eyeliner-tattooed eyelids she could swear she caught a flash of long-suppressed intelligence. "Or else you can't what?" Leigh asked.

Courtney stepped back. She lowered her umbrella for a moment, hiding her face. When she lifted it again, her expression was composed. "I can't sleep at night," she finished. Her eyes fixed on some point in the distance, and her next words were a mumble. "I'll get another room."

Leigh considered. Courtney was hardly an easy woman to read, but the fear in her last words seemed genuine. The question was, fear of what? "If you're concerned for your own safety," she suggested, "you should tell the detectives."

Courtney's eyes snapped back to attention. "I'm perfectly fine," she insisted. "But if you hear anything about the case —"

"You would hear before me," Leigh white-lied again. "You're his widow, after all." *I just have a knack of being in the wrong place at the wrong time.*

She looked down and noticed that she was standing in a puddle. *Like now.*

"I'm also a suspect," Courtney said bitterly. "Which means they won't tell me anything. All I know is that Brandon was shot, most likely with his own gun. Which means nothing, other than that he was stupid enough to let somebody get it off him. He never could shoot the damn things anyway. Some *protection!*"

Courtney began to fumble with something in her bag, and Leigh tensed. *Stop that,* she chastised, reminding herself that she was standing on a crowded city street in the middle of the business district.

"Here," Courtney ordered, pulling out a limp business card and pushing it under Leigh's umbrella. "That's my cell at the bottom. I don't need a judge and jury... I just need to know if the police are convinced it was somebody here. Can you do that much for me? Please?"

Leigh blinked. She couldn't think of a reason why Courtney Lyle would assume Leigh owed her anything. But perhaps a woman like her didn't need a reason. Growing up rich and pampered, looking as attractive as she did, she might easily take other people's obsequiousness as a given.

Leigh pocketed the card without comment. She supposed Courtney had given her something. She'd given her a prime piece of intel for her next conversation with Maura. Of course, then she'd have to *tell* Maura they'd had this conversation in the first place.

Rats.

Leigh sighed. "I really can't help you, Courtney," she repeated. "You should just stay in touch with the police."

Courtney frowned. "Thanks," she said sulkily. Without another word she tilted her umbrella, pivoted on her heels, and disappeared.

Leigh did not get wetter watching her go. She put her head back down and concentrated on avoiding the rest of the puddles between her and the parking garage.

"Somebody here," she muttered to herself as she walked. "Somebody *here*."

Whatever had the widow Lyle meant by that?

A full afternoon's work at Hook, one hasty chicken dinner with the kids, and half a turn around the North Park lake trail... and it was still raining.

Furthermore, it smelled bad. Cara's van, like Leigh's own, did not smell pleasant under the best of circumstances. But when it was crammed full of five wet women and four wet dogs, one of which was a borrowed bloodhound that drooled so much Frances kept pushing a pie pan under its nose, the odor was nearly unbearable.

And it was raining too hard to open the windows.

"I think they're looking for another body," Bess insisted, her hackles raised by yet another disagreement with her equally headstrong younger sister.

"That's patently ridiculous," Frances fired back. "No one else is even missing!"

"Well, you don't drag a pond for nothing, that's all I know," Bess retorted, fanning her face with a cardboard store flier she had plucked off Cara's dashboard. "It costs money to bring out the tractor and all that equipment—the people don't work for free, either."

"When did the police say it would happen, Bess?" Lydie called from the backseat, struggling to stay in the conversation while a blurred conglomeration of wet spaniel and corgi bounded in a continuous loop around her lap, the seat next to her, and the floor around her feet.

"They wouldn't pin it down for me," Bess answered. "They just asked my permission, seeing as how the pond is partly on my property. They also asked Anna and the church board chairman, and of course we all said yes. Anna was a little concerned about the fish, but I told her if anything they'll filter out about a hundred years' worth of beer bottles and trash. Anyway, they said sometime tomorrow; that's all I know." She let out a sudden groan. "Ugh! Chester, will you please stop that! It's too hot to cuddle." She placed the soggy Pekingese mix on the floor by her feet. "Just sit right there. The bloodhound won't hurt you, for heaven's sake!"

Chester hopped back up onto Bess's lap immediately, burrowed his wet fur under the crook of her arm, and whined.

"Perhaps a little air conditioning, Cara?" Leigh panted from the middle seat.

Cara's brow furrowed. "Just open the windows a crack," she suggested. "No need to pollute the planet."

Cara turned the key, and the women all lowered their windows as much as possible without soaking the upholstery. Leigh made a mental note to bring her own van next time.

The bloodhound sneezed.

Leigh changed her mind.

It had been a trying evening all around, after they had arrived with such high hopes. Gil had remembered seeing a young woman with two babies in a stroller, and the rain seemed to let up just as they set out to find her. But the lull was only temporary, and the park had proved nearly deserted anyway. Now it was pouring again and growing darker. No woman in her right mind would have her babies out tonight.

Leigh had rarely seen Cara in a fouler mood.

"I hope they do it soon," Bess continued, looking at Leigh. "I had just moved all that equipment out to the pond when they called, and then I had to move it back again! Not that I was doing anything illegal, mind you—"

Frances snorted. "Certainly *that* would never happen."

Bess ignored her. "But I prefer to keep my little spy camera a secret, for now." She winked at Leigh. "We wouldn't want the feral cats to catch on, would we?"

Frances drew in a breath as if to say something else, but Lydie mercifully interrupted. "But what *could* the police be looking for in the pond?"

"The gun," Cara said stonily, her eyes gazing out the front windshield into the rain. "They're looking for Brandon's gun."

The women in the back of the van exchanged glances.

"What makes you think that, kiddo?" Bess asked gently.

Cara exhaled. "When the police searched Brandon's apartment, they found his handgun missing. His wife pointed it out, actually — said it was there when she left town. Now it's gone. And it wasn't found with the body, obviously. They asked Gil if Brandon ever carried it concealed, and of course he didn't know — it's not like he waltzed with the man. But Brandon must have been wearing it when he went to the church that night." She paused a moment, her voice still a disturbing monotone. "Which raises a lot of interesting questions. Why would the man pack a handgun to a church meeting? Not that the Church of the Horizon hasn't had its problems... but still. It seems far more likely to me that Brandon was planning on meeting someone else that night. *After* the church meeting."

The women digested her words thoughtfully.

"It makes sense," Bess agreed. "Look at the facts. After his fracas with Gil, Brandon drove away from the church. We don't know where he went then, but he couldn't have gone very far, because it wasn't long before he doubled back and confronted Anna on her front porch. He was acting so bizarre, so "desperate" that he gave the poor woman the heebie jeebies — and believe me, Anna's no shrinking violet. Then, after everyone else had left the church, he drove back and parked in the empty lot again. Why? He *must* have been going to meet somebody!"

"The somebody he had packed the handgun in anticipation of meeting," Leigh finished. "Somebody he knew to be afraid of."

"Of course," Frances interjected. "The only question is who."

A low growl uttered from Cara's throat, and all four women turned to look at her. "Diana Saxton," she said bitterly.

Leigh and Bess exchanged a glance. Lydie and Frances looked down at their laps in silence. It was clear they had all heard the story.

"It's possible, honey," Cara's mother said gently. "But I don't think it's very likely. She wouldn't seem to have much to gain and, well, it's hard to imagine a man like Brandon being afraid of her."

Cara uttered another growl, this one distinctly animal-like.

Chester burrowed himself further under Bess's arm and whimpered.

Leigh could understand the dog's sentiments. Her cousin was a good-natured and fundamentally reasonable person... but in this case, Gil was right. Cara was fixated on Diana's being to blame, both for Brandon's death and for Gil's current difficulties, and her protective instincts were making her anything but reasonable. She was a lioness defending her mate and cubs. And her claws were most definitely out.

"Aunt Bess," Cara said suddenly, swiveling in the driver's seat. "Do you have more than one of those motion-activated cameras?"

Bess drew back in surprise. "I have two, actually. Why?"

"Because I'd like to borrow one. If that woman comes onto our property, I want to have proof she was there."

"But honey," Lydie tried again, "Why on earth would she—"

"To make Gil look guilty, of course!" Cara interrupted, her cheeks flaring. "You don't really think they're going to find that gun in the pond, do you? I've been stupid not to think of it already—it might be too late." She turned back to her aunt. "Could I come by now and get the camera? You can show me how to set it up."

Bess's eyes turned, ever so subtly, in Leigh's direction. Leigh thought quickly, then offered a subtle nod. Camera surveillance of Snow Creek Farm, while almost certainly purposeless in terms of Gil's defense, would make the ideal preoccupation for Cara. What could be safer for her than sitting in her own living room staring at a TV screen that showed nothing but the end of her driveway?

"Sure thing, kiddo," Bess said cheerfully. "We might as well call it quits, here. This rain's not letting up before nightfall."

"Same time tomorrow, ladies?" Frances demanded.

All agreed.

Leigh breathed in a welcome gasp of fresh air as the van doors opened and three women and three dogs scrambled out. Only two dogs were supposed to get out, however, and by the time the hyper spaniel had been corralled back into the van, both Lydie and Cara were thoroughly soaked. Leigh gave Chewie a grateful pat on the head. He would have been out with Maggie in a flash under ordinary circumstances. Fortunately for her, he hated the rain.

Leigh's house was more or less on the way to Bess's from the park, so Cara dropped her and Chewie off before driving out to fetch the camera. Cara spoke little en route, her mind obviously elsewhere, and Leigh had to admit relief when she at last walked through her own front door and—for the last time, at least tonight—

out of the rain.

Warren stood in the living room, waiting for her. "How did it go?" he asked, not sounding particularly hopeful.

"Lousy," Leigh confirmed, shrugging off her things. "Kids in bed?"

Warren nodded, and Leigh walked into his embrace, feeling blissfully comfortable until she remembered the nagging question that had been bugging her for the last twenty-four hours.

She drew back and looked at him.

Warren, who was well acquainted with his wife's "studying" look, lifted an eyebrow. "What is it?" he asked.

Leigh continued the examination. "Tell me the truth. Do women hit on you? I mean, at work?"

He blinked. "Excuse me?"

Leigh let out a sigh. "You heard me. You're only buying time so you can figure out how to answer. Fabulous. I'll take that as a yes."

Warren smiled a little. "If I'm not needed in this conversation, can I just go?"

"Hell, no," Leigh chastised, collapsing on the couch and pulling him down beside her. "Why wouldn't you tell me? Now I feel like an idiot. Cara knows about all the women who hit on Gil."

"No, she doesn't."

Leigh sat up again. "Are you kidding me?"

Warren wrapped a long arm around her. "Look, it's not the most pleasant conversation for a man to have. Do you say something and make your wife upset, or do you not say anything and risk her getting even more upset later? It's lose-lose."

Leigh's teeth gritted. "I wouldn't get upset."

"Liar."

"Okay, I would get upset," she amended. "But I would still want to know."

"Why? How would that help anything?"

"I don't know!" Leigh wailed.

"You're already upset," Warren pointed out, "and I didn't tell you a thing."

"Yes, you did!"

"I assure you I didn't," he argued, his brown eyes smiling. "I was quite careful not to, actually. Would you like to see the transcript?"

Leigh groaned and sank back into his arms. "You should have

been a lawyer."

He shook his head. "I hate paper cuts."

Leigh laughed. Despite the disadvantage of being an honest man, her husband had made a successful career for himself as a local politician. But after a long and lauded run as chair of the County Council, he had decided to retire to a life of relative anonymity as a private financial consultant rather than continue on the Presidential track. He claimed that at long last, politics had jaded him, and that he wanted to make a difference on the other end — by working with nonprofits. But Leigh knew the real reason was even more elemental. Despite his ambition, her husband was a family man, enjoying home and hearth a whole lot more than planes, trains, television mics, and assembly halls.

She leaned over and kissed him. "You're just lucky I trust you," she declared.

"Thank you," he answered. "I'm so glad we haven't had this conversation. Now maybe we can talk about how, other than dog walking at the park, you've managed to stay completely out of Brandon Lyle's murder investigation today?"

She hesitated.

Warren's eyes narrowed knowingly. "Lose-lose?"

Leigh grinned and cuddled closer. "I just love it when we don't have these conversations."

Chapter 15

Leigh was awakened the next morning by a rapping on her bedroom window. She didn't need to lean over and pull up the shade to know who it was, but she did anyway. The blur that was her cousin gestured anxiously toward Leigh's back door, then disappeared.

Leigh sat up and tried to focus her eyes. Warren had left for an early meeting already, and the house was quiet, which meant that Ethan and Allison must still be asleep. She grabbed a robe from the closet and stumbled out to open the back door.

"I'm sorry to wake you," Cara apologized promptly, hastening inside and making a beeline for one of Leigh's kitchen chairs. "There's no emergency. At least I don't think there is. But I don't know. Oh, Leigh! What am I going to *do?*"

Mao Tse, who had been lounging on one of the other kitchen chairs, flicked her bushy tail with agitation. She had always tolerated Cara better than other non-Leigh humans, which was to say, she didn't usually hiss at her on sight. But the tension Cara now radiated was palpable, and Mao had no patience for drama. The cat stretched, wrinkled what little nose she had to wrinkle, and padded sulkily out of the room.

"Coffee?" Leigh offered, still blinking away the cobwebs.

Cara laughed ruefully. "Caffeine is the last thing I need. But you go ahead."

Leigh studied her cousin as she poured herself an already steaming cup from the pot her thoughtful husband had left warming for her. Cara was indeed jittery; she fidgeted with both hands and feet, and her face showed new and unusual worry lines.

"This isn't like you, you know," Leigh said lightly, sitting down. "Your mother is the normal one. It's me who got the anal-retentive hysteria genes."

The ghost of a smile flitted across Cara's face. "They're identical twins. They have the same genes."

Leigh waved a dismissive hand. "Don't distract me with

technicalities. You walked all the way over here and woke me up from a perfectly nice dream that I'm pretty sure involved chocolate. So, spill it. What's happened?"

Cara glanced at her phone. "There was a bomb threat at the gym this morning. I heard about it on the news just now."

Leigh's eyebrows arched. "Which gym?"

"Gil's gym. The one he left to go to about half an hour ago."

Leigh took a sip of coffee and waited for more. "Well," she said finally. "There wasn't a real bomb, was there?"

"They're still looking," Cara answered. "The gym never opened, of course."

Leigh took another sip. Her cousin's behavior was growing more bizarre by the minute. "Cara!" she exclaimed finally. "Clearly, Gil never stepped foot in the gym. It was almost certainly just some prank to begin with. Why are you so upset?"

Cara stood up. She began to pace. "I can't reach him. He's not answering my texts or my calls."

Leigh willed herself patience. "He's *driving*," she reasoned. "He probably just went on into the office. You want him to text in the middle of the Parkway North?"

Cara's blue-green eyes misted over. She sank back down into her chair. "I don't think it's a coincidence, Leigh," she said softly. "I can't explain why, exactly, but I just know. It's going to happen exactly like I was afraid it would, and I don't know how to stop it."

"Stop what?" Leigh urged.

The sound of wheels crunching on the gravel drive outside echoed into the quiet kitchen, and Cara leapt to her feet again and moved to the window. "It's Gil!" she exclaimed with relief. Then she turned to Leigh and grabbed her arm. "Come with me. I want you to tell him I'm not being overly dramatic, that he *has* to take the risk seriously. He won't listen to me—he thinks my judgment is too clouded by my own feelings about her. But you know it's not!"

Leigh's head spun a little, but as the words gradually fell into place, she began to understand. Cara wanted her to help convince Gil that Diana Saxton's supposed vendetta against him was more than a figment of his wife's superb and well-documented imagination.

But was it?

Leigh hesitated.

"He'll listen to you, Leigh," Cara insisted. "I know he will."

Leigh lifted an eyebrow. On what planet she had any influence whatsoever over the all-knowing Gil March, she had no idea. But as she had spent her entire childhood and most of her adult life playing protector to her headstrong and impulsive "little sister," she could hardly refuse the impulse now.

"Just let me get dressed," she responded. "I'll wake the kids up and get their breakfast, they should—"

She broke off as she spotted her daughter, slim as a broomstick, leaning silently against the doorway to the hall. Leigh's heart skipped a beat. How much Allison had overheard this time was anyone's guess. The child had earned a black belt in reconnaissance by the age of three.

Leigh opened her mouth to protest, but changed her mind. Chastising Allison for eavesdropping was ineffective; the girl had inherited way too much talent for playing lawyerball from her father. If reproached, Allison would simply point out—quite calmly and rationally—that (1) she had been in plain view the whole time, and (2) no one had told her it was a private conversation.

Leigh sighed.

"I can get our breakfast, Mom," Allison said helpfully, stepping towards the kitchen. "Ethan's up, too. He's just lying in bed trying to get to level seven on Ninja Snowblast. Hi, Aunt Cara."

"Hi, sweetie," Cara returned with a motherly smile, all traces of anxiety well hidden. "Say, if I send Matt and Lenna over here, can you guys entertain yourselves for a while? Your mom and I need some time alone with your Uncle Gil."

"No problem," Allison said expressionlessly, opening a kitchen cabinet and removing a box of cereal. "I'll watch everybody."

Leigh and Cara exchanged veiled grins. Allison was a head shorter than any of the other children, but her moral authority had always gone unquestioned.

"Thank you," the women answered together.

Ten minutes later, Leigh rapped on the door of Cara's farmhouse and was let in by a strained-looking Gil, who glanced over her shoulder as if expecting someone else.

"Detective Peterson is on the way over," Cara announced grimly as Leigh stepped inside. "That's why Gil came home, instead of going into town. His lawyer is meeting us here, too."

"I see," Leigh responded, trying her best to sound upbeat. "Did he say why?"

"No," Gil answered, closing the door behind her. "Only that he had more questions for me."

An awkward silence followed. After a moment, Cara led them all back into the living room.

"So," Leigh began, breaking the uneasy silence and dropping down into a chair. "I hear there was some excitement at the gym this morning?"

Gil shrugged. "All I know is that it was closed. The lot was swarming with police cars."

More silence.

Leigh's arrival had clearly interrupted something. Cara and Gil were rarely present in the same room without displaying some honeymooner-like affection, yet now they stood well apart, with a distinct chill in the air. "Well, you could always use the workout center in your office building," Leigh babbled. "That's a nice one. I used to walk by it daily when I had copywriter job #2. Not that I ever made use of it myself, of course."

Gil nodded and sat down. "I thought about that this morning, actually, but I didn't have my gym bag. Besides, the detective called just as I was pulling out of — "

"What do you mean?!" Cara shrieked, whirling to face her husband.

Gil started as if he'd been struck. Leigh felt herself do the same.

"What do I..." he repeated in confusion. "What are you talking about?"

"*Your gym bag!*"

Gil looked helplessly at Leigh. She looked helplessly back.

Cara collapsed onto the couch beside him. "You said you didn't have your gym bag. Why not? Where is it?"

"It's in the gym," he answered calmly. "I guess. I don't know for sure. I thought I brought it out with me yesterday and put it in the car like always, but it wasn't there last night, so I must have left it in my locker."

Cara's face went pale as chalk. "You thought it was in the car, but then it wasn't?"

Gil raised a tentative hand and placed it on his wife's shoulder. "It doesn't matter, sweetheart. There was nothing important in it."

"Cara," Leigh pressed, "What are you getting at? We're baffled here."

Cara sat slumped for a moment, looking defeated. "It may be nothing," she said finally, her voice a choked whisper. "I'm sorry I yelled at you. I didn't mean to. It's just that—" she raised her chin and looked at Leigh. "Well, tell him, Leigh."

Gil looked over at Leigh expectantly.

She shrank in her chair.

This is awkward.

"Um..." she began, trying to remember exactly what she had promised to do. "It's just that Cara thought you should hear a second opinion about... well, about how women think."

Cara nodded at her encouragingly. Gil's expression turned stormy.

Leigh swallowed. "Look, I don't want to get into this any more than you do, but the fact is, Gil—"

The man looked like his face would explode.

Leigh plowed on. "Women don't take rejection well. The more aggressive the woman, the harder she takes it. The more intelligent the woman, the more personally she takes it. The more attractive the woman, the worse she's insulted by it. All of which makes someone like Diana Saxton a triple threat."

She took a breath. Gil hadn't exploded yet, and Cara looked pleased. "I don't know the woman, and I don't know how much trouble she's willing to go to to make you suffer, but trust me," she leaned forward for emphasis. "You did *not* part on good terms, no matter what she told you. She's clearly a liar and an actress, because there's no doubt she still resents the hell out of you. Thinking anything less, giving her the benefit of the doubt in any way, is opening up yourself, *and* your family, to one whopping sucker punch."

Leigh dropped back against the couch cushions, her duty discharged. Cara looked hopefully at Gil. Gil continued to glower, but when he spoke, his voice was mellow. "I hear what you're saying, Leigh."

The front doorbell rang.

The pall of tension already blanketing the room grew heavier. Gil rose and walked to the door. A few moments later he returned with two men whom he introduced as Reginald Bloom, his lawyer, and

Detective Andrew Peterson. Leigh shook both men's hands, thinking that if they hadn't been introduced, she would have reversed them. Gil's "Reg" was sixty if he was a day—a grizzled, pot bellied man with frizzy mad-scientist hair and a mischievous glint in his eye. Maura's detective friend was barely thirty, a slight, serious fellow with narrow spectacles and an intellectual air.

Neither man wasted time.

"As you know, we made an exhaustive search of Brandon Lyle's home and office yesterday," Peterson began as soon as they were seated. The detective was unexpectedly soft-voiced, and Leigh was embarrassed to catch herself leaning forward to hear. She was lucky no one had thought to kick her out yet.

"I don't recall your mentioning that Mr. Lyle had asked you for a loan?" the detective inquired of Gil.

"You didn't ask," the lawyer interjected quickly. "But my client is happy to answer now that you have." He gave Gil a nod.

Gil sat forward. "Brandon did ask for a personal loan, maybe three weeks ago. We had broken off our official business arrangement nearly a year ago, as I told you. I declined the loan because I considered the man a very poor risk, but I did offer him some informal, unpaid business advice at that time, as I explained already."

"Yes, you did," the detective agreed. A painfully long period of time elapsed. Leigh could hear Cara's grandfather clock ticking in the upstairs hallway. "In examining Mr. Lyle's papers, we've found indications that he considered you among his potential 'fallback' assets should his current real estate venture collapse. Specifically, he listed your name next to an anticipated sum in the neighborhood of seven figures."

Cara's face paled further. Gil's flushed red as a fire engine.

"Seven figures!" he exclaimed, rising from his chair. "That's insane! He only asked me for six figures, and I wouldn't give him that!"

"The victim's delusions regarding his own appeal as a credit risk are hardly my client's concern," the lawyer purred smoothly, stroking his mustache with a bejeweled finger. "Is there anything else?"

The detective remained unruffled. "Yes. The whole question of Mr. March's history with Mr. Lyle's firm, as well as their personal relationship, appeared to be of considerable interest to Mr. Lyle immediately before his murder."

"How do you figure?" the lawyer asked.

"We found a file—several files, actually—of printed materials, correspondence, even some university-related documents going back several decades, placed quite prominently among Mr. Lyle's things, as if he had reviewed them recently. This, in conjunction with the stated threat Mr. Lyle made in the hearing of multiple witnesses on the night of the murder—"

"We explained that already, I believe," the lawyer interrupted.

The detective paused. "You offered an explanation, yes. I was wondering if you could offer some additional explanation for why Mr. Lyle might have been under the impression that a large sum of money might be coming to him from Mr. March."

Gil sputtered and started to speak, but the lawyer stopped him with a hand. "My client can hardly be expected to account for whatever vagaries were going on in Mr. Lyle's mind in the midst of impending financial ruin," he said placidly. "Mr. Lyle asked for a loan and was refused. He made a threat which we have previously established to be empty, as my client has no culpability with which Mr. Lyle could hope to extort seven cents, much less seven figures. Is there anything else?"

The detective studied Gil for another long moment. Then he returned his notebook to his pocket. "No, that will be all for now. Thank you." He rose to leave, and Gil showed him back out without another word.

"Interesting," the lawyer said when Gil returned. "What could Lyle hope to accomplish by looking through files with your name on them?"

"I haven't the faintest idea," Gil said with frustration. "Even if he was stupid enough to believe he could blackmail *me* over that wretched Philadelphia business, he wasn't going to find anything incriminating in a business file." His brow furrowed. "It doesn't even sound like Brandon. I can't see him keeping hard copies of our 'correspondence' in the first place—he kept terrible records. That was part of his problem. If such files exist, it would only be because—" his voice broke off abruptly.

Cara stood up. "Because Diana Saxton printed them out!" she finished fiercely. "Which she would, if she was trying to frame you!

Who knows how much Brandon told her? About the loan request, about the blackmail? She could have known the whole story! And she could have easily pulled your files to the front and laid them out for the detectives to find. She could have created them all herself in the first place!"

Reg looked from Cara to Gil. "That possible?" he asked.

The couple exchanged a hard stare. Gil exhaled. "Yes," he conceded. "It's possible. She's certainly tech savvy enough. I wouldn't have thought Diana would exert that much effort in my honor, but if the woman wanted to screw me over..."

The lawyer made a clucking sound with his tongue. "Well then, old chap, we're damned fortunate we brought to light the spurned secretary issue yesterday. They can't very well ignore the possibility of sabotage, far-fetched as it may seem." He rose suddenly and gave Gil a hearty clap on the back. "Don't lose sleep over it. The motive they're chasing is sketchy, at best. The fact that you refused a loan request previously is helpful—it shows you weren't afraid of him. In any event, there's not a scrap of physical evidence to tie you to the murder scene."

The doorbell rang. Everyone looked at each other blankly for a second, then Gil walked toward the door. He returned a few seconds later with the detective in tow. "Terribly sorry to bother you again," the slight man said softly, making no move to sit. "But I just received a rather intriguing call. Perhaps you heard that the Ironworks Health Club on Perry Highway was closed early this morning due to an anonymous bomb threat?"

Leigh shot a glance at Cara. Her cousin stood ash-faced; her hands began to tremble.

"Yes," Gil answered. "That's where I go. I was pulling out of the parking lot when you called this morning. What of it?"

The detective cleared his throat. "It seems that in the course of searching the building, the bomb squad came across a bag with your ID tag on it, which was left underneath a bench in the weight room."

Cara's quick intake of breath was slight, but Leigh heard it. She only hoped the detective had not.

"The bag contained an item that drew their immediate attention," Peterson continued. "A handgun registered to Mr. Brandon Lyle."

Chapter 16

Maura grimaced as she picked up a stick from the ground and attempted to scrape several inches of mud off the bottom of her left shoe. The women were meeting once again at the picnic table behind the church, where the detective had summoned Leigh after finishing the unenviable duty of overseeing a pond-dragging on the heels of a rainstorm.

"So, I hear the bomb squad stole my prize," the detective said dryly. "And they weren't even looking."

Leigh sighed. She felt terribly guilty leaving the Pack with Cara. She could have watched them easily; the project Gil had scrounged up was five afternoons' worth, tops, and she could work with the kids at home if they were occupied. But under the circumstances, it was Cara who needed watching by the Pack.

"What's going to happen now, Maura?" she asked, restraining Chewie by his lead as he lunged toward a nearby squirrel. "Is there enough for an arrest?"

The detective blew out a breath. "Don't get ahead of yourself, Koslow. The ballistics aren't back yet. If Brandon's handgun was the murder weapon, well... all I can tell you is that Peterson is nobody's fool. If he were," she added with a scowl, slinging a long rope of mud off the stick and into the bushes, "he would have volunteered for this crap job himself instead of conning me into it."

She finished scraping one shoe and moved to the other. Leigh could barely tell a difference.

"If Cara is so sure that Diana is responsible," Maura began thoughtfully, "how does she figure the woman got hold of Gil's gym bag?"

"His car has keyless entry," Leigh answered. "Diana must have memorized the code when she was working for him. She certainly knew all his habits. She even joined the same gym so she could 'run into him' in a sports bra and spandex."

Maura whistled under her breath. "Sounds like one scary chick." She took off her right shoe altogether, then heaved it against the table leg with enough force to crush a melon.

Leigh restrained a grin. "Yeah. Some women are like that."

The detective replaced the now notably cleaner shoe on her foot. "Peterson will keep an eye on Diana Saxton," she assured. "And the flaky widow besides. Which reminds me, what's this vaunted intel of yours? Spill it. I'm overdue at the station already."

Leigh described her encounter with Courtney Lyle, highlighting the enigmatic "somebody here" comment. With Diana almost certainly having planted Brandon's gun, Courtney's foibles didn't seem as important anymore. Still, adding any names to the list of non-Gil suspects could only help his case.

Maura's eyebrows rose. "Interesting," she remarked. "You say Courtney seemed afraid of something? Or someone?"

Leigh nodded. "Gil said she was living with another man in Chicago. I was thinking... a little jealous rivalry, perhaps?"

Maura smiled. "You know what, Koslow? Sometimes your instincts aren't all bad."

Leigh smiled back. "Can I have that in writing, please?"

Maura's grin widened. "Hell, no."

Leigh did not find Maura's mud problems nearly so amusing an hour later, when she found herself trudging along in soggy muck on the opposite side of the pond with her Aunt Bess, Chewie, and an awkward armful of camera equipment.

"Couldn't we wait until the sun dries things out a bit?" she suggested, dropping her aunt's tripod for the second time as the corgi lurched backward, jerking her elbow with him. She looked around the now empty woods, unclipped the dog from his lead, and picked up the tripod again. "Stay close, Chewie," she ordered.

"Oh, don't be such a priss," Bess chastised good-naturedly. "I want to get everything set up and concealed before any more curiosity seekers make it out here. It was quite a show this morning."

Leigh's eyebrows arched. "You mean there were spectators? For a pond dragging?"

Bess frowned. "Well, not *so* many. But then, not everyone is as devoted to the cause of law enforcement as I am. It was a long and messy process, but ever so interesting."

"You stood out here and watched the whole time?" Leigh inquired.

"Of course not, silly. I brought a lawn chair."

Leigh let that one pass. "What did they find?"

"Oh, all sorts of things," Bess answered cheerfully. "Hordes of glass bottles, as I expected. I pulled a few that might be worth something... if so, I'll give them to Clem. He has a collection, you know. Flashlights, some aluminum cans, some canvas that looked like it might have been a tent, deflated innertubes, a camp lantern, some mangled pieces of metal farm equipment, a drink cooler, three tires, and my personal favorite... a bed pan. It was all very enlightening. I felt like an archeologist!"

Leigh tried to imagine Clem's house containing a curio cabinet of carefully tended antique bottles, but all she could picture was a dusty shelf heaped with broken glass and empty chaw tins. Perhaps she was being presumptuous. Had she not expected Anna's house to contain a canary cage, cutesy china figurines, framed pictures of grandchildren, and perhaps a velvet Elvis? For all she knew, Clem's living room was filled with sophisticated computer equipment and he and Anna had been carrying on a wild affair since the Cold War.

"That reminds me," Leigh asked. "Are Anna and Clem buds? I mean, they're about the same age, and they've both lived out here forever, right?"

"I don't know if 'buds' is the right word," Bess answered, her voice chipper despite the effort of walking in mud that sucked down their boots with every step. "Their fathers were friends; Anna's father sold Clem's father his plot way back when theirs were the only two houses around. Clem and Anna not only grew up together, they were all each other had in the way of playmates. So you could say they're like brother and sister."

"Oh," Leigh said with disappointment. "I guess there goes my 'wild affair' theory."

Bess chuckled. "Well, they do bicker like an old married couple, but that's as far as it goes, I'm afraid. Lord knows they'd both be happier if they were getting a little action somewhere."

Leigh allowed herself a grin. Her forthright aunt had been married three times: once to her high school sweetheart, who had died in Korea; once to a lovely, educated man who had died too young; and once on the rebound to a bohemian drifter who was too young, period. Bess had divorced the third one promptly and vowed never to marry again—but she was still the biggest flirt in three counties.

"Have either of them ever been married?" Leigh asked.

"Anna was once," Bess replied. "Total disaster. Worthless scum cleaned out their joint account and skipped the country. Sent her a postcard a couple weeks later—from Rio de Janiero, no less—saying he'd met someone else and didn't want to be married anymore. To top it off, the card was one of those—"

Bess stopped short as her right foot dropped into an unexpectedly deep hole. She tottered dangerously, camera in tow. Leigh slogged over to lend a hand, but with some impressive one-armed windmilling, Bess miraculously managed to right herself.

"Good save," Leigh praised with relief. The last thing her drama-loving aunt needed was another broken ankle, seeing as how the last one had nearly gotten her sucker of a niece killed.

"As I was saying," Bess continued, unaffected, "as if dumping Anna weren't enough, the bastard picked one of those cheesy, practically pornographic postcards of a busty sunbather in a string bikini that said: *Wish you were here.*"

Leigh winced. "Ouch. And she never married again?"

Bess shook her head. "She couldn't find the SOB to divorce him, so her legal affairs were a mess for a long time. But even after she was free, she wanted nothing more to do with men." Bess paused for a moment to readjust her load, letting out a dramatic sigh as she did so. "Sad, isn't it? And Clem's no better. That old geezer hasn't gotten any since Eisenhower was President. The man's healthy as a horse, but I can't tell you the last time I saw a woman anywhere near that cabin of his!"

Leigh's eyebrows rose. "This surprises you?"

Bess smirked. "Well, if he'd mixed it up a little more often over the years, he might not be such an old geezer now, would he?"

Leigh considered a moment. "Good point."

At long last, Bess reached her desired position near the edge of the pond and set the camera down on a fallen tree limb. "We'll set up the tripod here," she announced, pointing to a cluster of brush, "and then cover it with branches and such. If we're careful about it, it will be almost impossible to see the camera from the far bank of the pond—and that's where our guilty party will be headed."

Leigh swallowed. She had no desire to look at the spot in question, but Chewie, of course, was already making a beeline for the place where the body had lain. "Chewie," she chastised. "Get away from there! Go dig someplace else."

The dog's ears perked. He glanced quizzically at her for a moment, then bounded off to sniff around the water's edge. Not only were his previously white paws now brown up to his oxters, but his whole underbelly (none of which was particularly far removed from the ground) was dripping with mud. Leigh sighed, hoping Bess would have a hose handy when they returned to the house. She spared a glance around the rest of the pond and was dismayed to see the havoc that the dragging equipment had caused. The water was still as opaque as a cup of hot chocolate, and the bank on which the tractor had driven was gouged with deep, crisscrossing tire ruts.

"Don't worry," Bess said dismissively, following her gaze. "It'll heal. Besides, maybe the mess will keep people from walking across to this side of the pond and out of our viewing range." She fiddled with the tripod, placed the camera securely upon it, and then began to gather up nearby branches. "Feel free to help anytime," she suggested dryly.

Leigh started. She had been absorbed by more unpleasant memories. "Sorry," she apologized. She looked around. "Do you want me to find more of the—"

The crack of a gunshot split the air. Leigh jumped out of her boots... literally. Her too-big borrowed galoshes were stuck fast in the mud, and when she came back down to earth, heart pounding, it was with one sock-clad foot resting on a collapsed boot and the other sunk in muck up to her ankle.

She and her aunt swore simultaneously.

"Knock it off, Clem!" Bess yelled loudly, cupping a hand to her mouth. "We're at the pond!"

A moment's silence followed. Then a disembodied, whining voice carried back to them through the trees. "Sorry!"

"Don't worry, kiddo," Bess assured. "That shot was a lot farther away than it sounded. Clem's just doing some target practice. He usually makes sure I'm out of the way first, but I guess he thought I was in the house, since your car was out front."

Leigh pushed her feet back into her boots and tried to keep her teeth from chattering. The sudden shot had scared the crap out of her, as it obviously had Chewie, who had appeared from nowhere to attach himself to her shins like a barnacle. "Do—" she stammered. "Does he shoot like that often?"

"Not too much anymore," Bess said lightly. "For all his love of hoarding guns, he never was a very good shot. But he's always been careful with his target practice—he stays on his own land and makes sure no one else is around. He's never been shooting when you were at my house before, has he?"

Leigh shook her head. *That*, she would definitely have remembered.

Bess's expression turned thoughtful. "He had an accident once, when he was a boy. He and Anna used to practice hitting cans behind her house, and one day they set up the targets poorly, and Clem aimed too high. A stray bullet went out to the road and hit the car his mother was driving. She wasn't hurt, but it had a big effect on Clem. Even when he shoots in his own yard now, he climbs up to his deer stand and aims down toward the ground."

Leigh blinked. She would hardly have pegged Clem as a gun safety devotee. "Why shoot at all then?"

Bess shrugged. "It's a macho thing."

Leigh reached down to pet Chewie, who was still attached to her leg, and was dismayed to note that what part of his coat wasn't muddy was now laced with burrs. "It's okay, boy," she comforted, feeling less than comforted herself. "You go back and do some more excavating. We'll be done here soon." The dog seemed pacified enough to detach, but his eyes were wary and his ears remained perked as he trotted off toward the pond again.

Leigh's hands were still shaky, and her thoughts darkened. "Aunt Bess," she said soberly, "are you absolutely positive that Clem couldn't have shot Brandon Lyle?"

Bess's lips pursed. She faced Leigh squarely. "Of course I am! Clem's got no stomach for violence; he doesn't even hunt. He's such a nervous Nelly I've wondered if there weren't more to the story about his mother, or if some other accident didn't spook him somewhere along the line. But however he got this way, he's perfectly harmless!"

"All right, all right," Leigh conceded, moderating her tone. One could only go so far in impugning a friend of Aunt Bess's before having to duck. "But you have to admit, he *is* a bit wacko."

Bess dismissed the concern with a wave. "Clem may be a little wacko, but there's no harm in that. Hells bells, some of my best friends are complete crackpots!" She surveyed her camouflage job. "Perfect! We're all set to spy on smoking teenagers, mating cats, and panicky murderers. You want some tea?"

Leigh let that one pass, also. "Maybe after I hose off the dog. Aunt Bess, even if Clem isn't dangerous, *somebody* shot a man not twenty yards from here, practically in your own backyard. Doesn't that worry you?"

Bess looked at her with surprise. "Why should it? I told you before—and the gun being planted on Gil proves it—this was a crime of passion. *I* certainly didn't sleep with Brandon Lyle. At least, I don't think I did. Then again, the mind does wander when you're older. There was that one time last month, after Noreen made me that third fuzzy navel—"

"Aunt Bess!"

"Yes, Francie?" Bess drawled, one eyebrow raised high.

Leigh frowned. "Never mind. Are we done here, now? My foot is soaked, and I believe I was offered tea."

Bess cracked a grin. "You certainly were." She gestured for Leigh to follow her toward the house, then put a hand to her mouth and produced an ear-splitting whistle. "Chewie!" she called, "You've got a date with a hose, my dear!"

The brush rustled, and in a few seconds the corgi reappeared, toting an equally filthy prize in his mouth that looked like a much bigger dog's long-lost rawhide chew bone. The mud-covered mess collected more mud as Chewie half-carried, half-dragged it along the ground—which of course was only inches from his mouth to begin with. "Chewie!" Leigh warned. "You do realize that thing is *not* going home with us?"

The dog, who looked extremely proud of himself, ignored her and scuttled ahead.

Bess snickered. "Well, Chester will enjoy it, anyway. If he ever comes out from hiding. I've never seen him act so skittish with Chewie! I do hope your mother refrains from borrowing any more dogs this evening. He's still traumatized from being forced to fraternize with the huskies and the bloodhound. So, other than trying to shore up Gil's alibi, what's next on the Morton power agenda? I haven't had any orders from Sergeant Frances for" — she looked at her watch — "a good three hours now."

Leigh let out a sigh. She had received a cryptic voice mail from her father a little while ago, asking Leigh if she had anything for her mother that needed sewing, mending, patching, or cleaning. Randall hadn't said why, but Leigh suspected her mother was once again attempting to burn off nervous energy by "helping out" at the clinic. The last time she was stressed over a family emergency, Frances had rearranged every bottle in the pharmacy by height, assigned numbers to the nylon leashes, and disconnected all the appliances to sanitize their power cables.

"I think she's at the clinic," Leigh responded.

"Oh, dear," Bess said sympathetically. "I suppose you had best get out there and rescue your father, then."

"I suppose so," Leigh agreed.

Chewie popped out of the brush in front of them, and both women let out a gasp. In addition to the mud and the burrs, within the space of the last few seconds he had somehow managed to cover his entire front end with tiny brown and white feathers.

"Oh, my," Bess remarked, her voice holding noticeably more mirth than chagrin. "I do believe he's found some of Ferdinand's leavings. That cat does wreak havoc with the sparrow population."

The corgi looked up at Leigh with a canine smile that was all innocence. One fluffy feather detached from the mud between his ears and drifted down to catch again on his jowl.

Leigh groaned.

"At least he dropped the bone," Bess commented.

"It's going to take more than a hose to handle this," Leigh said miserably. Then, as the thought occurred, she smiled.

"It's going to take... a Frances."

Chapter 17

Diana Saxton let out a sigh. She wasn't ordinarily the sighing kind, but assessing her bank records brought out the worst in her. She clicked the program closed and leaned back in her zebra-striped desk chair. So she had expensive tastes. What of it? Her big payout had always seemed close enough, and she knew how to manage a budget.

The loss of a steady paycheck, however, was galling. She had been fired twice in the last sixth months, through no fault of her own. She couldn't possibly have predicted that Gil March's rugged good looks masked the ardor of a frozen halibut, and she had every reason to believe things would work out with Brandon... until they didn't. So here she was again. Unemployed. And in serious need of some new satin sheets.

The doorbell rang.

Diana looked up warily. She wasn't expecting anyone. No one ever came to visit her at her apartment. Even Brandon had found it too sterile for his tastes, which was fine by her, since he was a slob. The tastefully decorated, meticulously kept studio was her private abode.

The doorbell rang again.

"Diana!" a shrill voiced called. "I know you're in there. Let me in, now! We need to talk."

Diana's irritation gave way to a slow, sly smile.

She was about to get lucky.

She rose, crossed the small room, and swung open the door without haste. "Yes?"

Courtney Lyle's upraised hand froze in mid knock. "You *are* home."

"Clearly."

Courtney opened her mouth to say something, then seemed to think better of it. She was looking less than her best today. Diana had rarely seen Brandon's wife dressed in anything but a skirt and heels, and her platinum hair was always perfectly coifed. This version of Courtney, wearing khaki pants and a polo shirt with her hair in a ponytail, was not exactly slumming it. But she probably thought that she was.

Courtney continued to stare at Diana, who was dressed exactly as she always dressed during the day: consummately professional, surreptitiously sexy. Never mind if all she had to do was distribute resumes via email. It paid to be prepared.

Brandon's wife was struggling. All manner of emotions flitted across her face in the space of a few short seconds: jealousy, hatred, disdain, resignation, and— interestingly enough—apprehension.

"Can I help you?" Diana purred. She could help her guest quite easily. She knew exactly what the other woman wanted. But what would be the fun in that?

"Can, um—" Courtney stammered, "Can I come in?"

Diana wordlessly stepped back and out of the way. Courtney entered. Both women continued to stand.

"Just so you know," Courtney said stiffly. "I left Detective Peterson a voice mail earlier. I told him I was coming to see you here."

Diana's eyebrows rose. Either Brandon's wife suspected her of the crime, or she wanted to make the authorities think she did. Either way, her appearance here, now, marked desperation.

Diana made no response.

"Could we sit down?" Courtney suggested. Her face strained with the effort of faking politeness.

"Certainly," Diana proffered, gesturing to her cream-colored suede and chrome couch.

Courtney sat. She pulled her purse into her lap and fidgeted with the clasp.

Diana lowered herself into a matching chair. She waited.

"Look," Courtney said finally, leaning forward. "We don't like each other. That's obvious. But I need your help."

Diana waited some more.

Courtney breathed out with a groan, stood, and began to pace. "The business is a disaster. Everyone's calling and wanting to know where things stand—and the accountant can't begin to figure it out by himself. I hired some supposed business guru to come in and get things straight, but he quit after half a day. He says nobody can figure out what the hell's going on except you—that you organized everything with some funky filing system, and that all kinds of important documents are written in shorthand. Not regular shorthand, either, but some weird version of it that he's never seen before. He said if I couldn't get your help, I might as well hire somebody to burn the office down, because the creditors were bound to sue, with all of Brandon's investors right behind them!"

Courtney stopped by Diana's chair and glowered down at her. "I don't *want* Brandon's stupid development business. I couldn't care less if it's sold off, dissolved, or baked into apple pie. But apparently," her voice changed to a whine, "just because I was idiot enough to marry Brandon, it's suddenly *my* responsibility!"

"Hmm," Diana responded, crossing her legs with flair. "That is a problem." She felt a sudden twinge of regret. Lyle Development was clearly worthless; living or dead, Brandon would have been bankrupt within the year. If it *were* worth something, she could easily manipulate Courtney into signing it over lock, stock, and barrel. But Diana didn't want Brandon's company now. No one would. Why couldn't Gil March have gotten whacked while she worked for him?

"I'm prepared to pay you for your time," Courtney continued. "And not from the business—I have money of my own."

Diana resisted the urge to bristle. Like she didn't know *that?* If it weren't for Courtney's precious inheritance, Brandon would have agreed to the damn divorce the first time his wife asked for it. And if Diana had *known* Brandon had no intention of agreeing to any damn divorce, ever, the current vile situation could have been avoided altogether. The nerve of the woman to come here and whine! Courtney had been a fool to marry Brandon without a prenup, and an even bigger fool to give him grounds for restitution by deserting him. If she couldn't get out of the marriage, it was her own stupid fault. "What is it you want exactly?" Diana asked without expression.

Courtney sat back down. "I want you to come back to the office. Work with the accountant; and with this other consultant I'm bringing on. All you need to do is answer their questions and translate the shorthand. They'll get a grip on where things stand and figure out how the hell I can unload this mess. Okay?"

Diana considered.

She crossed her legs the opposite way.

She considered some more.

Watching the sweat rise on Courtney's brow was immensely gratifying.

"I'll expect payment in advance," Diana said finally. "For two weeks' worth of work. I may finish before that. If it takes longer, we renegotiate."

"How much?"

Diana named a figure ten times her normal rate.

Courtney gave a little bounce. "Done!"

Diana's lips twisted. She should have asked for more.

Courtney reached into her purse, pulled out a checkbook, and started scribbling. After a moment she ripped out the check, handed it to Diana with a flourish, stood up, and headed for the door. Diana accepted the check, examined it, then rose to usher her out. But with one hand on the doorknob, Brandon's wife suddenly stopped and turned around.

"Before I go..." she said tentatively.

"Yes?" Diana snapped, still irked at underselling herself.

Courtney hesitated. "I need to ask you something. The day Brandon died, did you by any chance see a man hanging around him that you didn't know? I mean, a man who didn't look like one of Brandon's usual business acquaintances?"

Diana was intrigued. "A man who looked like what, for example?" she inquired.

Courtney bit her lip. "A man dressed well, probably, but not for business in Pittsburgh. More... cosmopolitan. A tall, powerfully built man with gray hair and dark eyes."

Diana considered. "Good looking?"

Courtney frowned. "Extremely."

"My, my," Diana purred. "If only I had been in town."

The other woman's brow furrowed. "What do you mean? You weren't here?"

"On the contrary," Diana explained casually, moving to her desk and placing the check carefully under a glass paperweight. "I spent the entire day in Harrisburg, being legally harassed by an old nemesis. I didn't get back to Pittsburgh until after ten. A fact easily provable by the records of the Turnpike commission, by the way. Which should reassure you that I'm no murderess. Unless you think I hired someone else to drive my car while I flew in on a private charter for the express purpose of eliminating my primary source of income."

"I didn't—" Courtney cut off the protest.

"But you know who might have, don't you?" Diana accused, her voice even.

Courtney's cheeks reddened. "I didn't say that!"

"Of course you did," Diana argued. "Who is he? And why did you lie to the police about being at Brandon's apartment the night he died?"

The color in Courtney's face drained instantly. Her voice dropped to a whisper. "How do you know that?"

"I was there, of course. I went by the apartment looking for Brandon, but I didn't go in because I saw your car. I thought maybe he was with you. Evidently, somebody else was."

"No!" Courtney screeched, crossing the distance between them. "It wasn't like that! I never saw —" she bit back the words. Her eyes glared at the other woman maliciously. "It's none of your damn business why I was there. I had nothing to do with Brandon's death."

"But you're afraid your hottie did, eh?"

Courtney whirled away from her. "This conversation is over. Go cash your check and—" she stopped abruptly. She turned back to Diana with a look of alarm. "Did you tell the police you saw my car?"

Diana smiled. "Of course not. Why would I?"

Courtney released a long, slow breath.

"As I mentioned before," Diana continued. "I have an interest in protecting my sources of income."

Courtney's breath drew in again, sharply. She gave a long, hard stare. "Brandon was out of his league with you, wasn't he?"

Diana grinned. "He thought I was brilliant."

Courtney stared another moment, then gave an undignified snort. "Brandon thought a lot of things," she muttered, heading for the door. "He thought he was a good lover, too."

Silence hung in the air for a second. Then Diana exploded with laughter.

Courtney stopped with her hand on the doorknob and looked sideways back at her.

The women exchanged a smile.

***

"No, Mrs. Koslow, Please Mrs. Koslow. Those cats like the little pans, Mrs. Koslow!"

Leigh heard the note of panic in Jared's voice the second she opened the clinic's basement door. Clearly, her father was not the only one requiring rescue.

"Now, Jared, don't be foolish," Frances' voice soothed. "The cats don't know the difference. It makes much more sense for the size of the pan to match the size of the cage."

Leigh turned the corner into the downstairs kennel room to see her mother's ample behind sticking out of an aluminum cage on the bottom row. Her father's longtime kennel cleaner and most trusted employee, Jared Loomis, stood in the center of the room, wringing a cleaning rag anxiously in his large, broad hands.

"But Mrs. Koslow—" His face brightened as he noticed the newcomer. "Hello, Leigh Koslow! I'm so glad to see you, Leigh Koslow!"

I bet you are.

"Hello, Jared," she said with a smile. "How's everything going today?"

The blond giant of a man, who was born with Down Syndrome but at times could show the wisdom of Solomon, contemplated the question a good five seconds. "It was going all right earlier, Leigh Koslow," he remarked.

Leigh tried hard not to laugh. Jared, bless his soul, was nothing if not brutally honest.

Frances's rear end backed out of the cage. She grabbed the bars for support and rose. "Now, that looks much better!" she said proudly, wiping her hands on a towel she had wrapped around her waist like an apron. "Big pans in big cages and little pans in little cages. Now everybody's happy!"

"Angus is not happy, Mrs. Koslow," Jared said miserably, pointing to a brown Maine Coon on the top row. "Angus likes to sleep in a big pan. The little ones he just flips over, Mrs. Koslow."

On cue, the cat shoved one meaty paw under the tiny metal pan and batted it up and sideways against the wall of the cage with a clatter. Spilled litter sprayed liberally out the front and skittered across Jared's shining floor.

Frances' lips pursed. She turned to her daughter. "And what are you doing here? I thought you were going to keep your Aunt Bess out of trouble this afternoon."

Leigh sighed. She could only keep so many relatives out of trouble simultaneously. "I just dropped by to pick something up," she said vaguely.

"Hello, Chewbacca!" Jared called, passing Leigh and moving to the alcove behind her. Leigh could see nothing except the other end of her lead trailing around the corner. Chewie hated coming to the clinic.

"Don't be afraid, Chewbacca," Jared soothed, getting to his knees and attempting to coax the trembling corgi out into the open. "Nothing to be afraid of, Chewbacca."

Leigh grinned at Jared's use of the dog's "formal" name. Warren had originally named the puppy after a Star Wars character, of course, but they had all long since forgotten that. Except Jared. Jared never forgot anything.

"Oh," Frances exclaimed suddenly. "You mean Allison, of course. You should have called me. I could have taken her home."

Leigh's eyebrows rose. "Allison?"

Frances' attention diverted to Chewie, who had just crept out into full view. Leigh had hosed and dried off his underside just enough to preserve the floor of the van—but her efforts had barely made a dent in his impressive overall appearance.

"Merciful heavens!" Frances exclaimed, "Leigh Eleanor Koslow, what have you done to that dog?!"

Leigh steeled herself. It would never do for her to *ask* her mother to clean something for her. Such a request would be too far out of character to be believed. She looked from her mother to the dog, then back. She shrugged. "He was in the woods at Aunt Bess's. I guess he got a little muddy."

"*A little muddy!*" Frances shrieked. "He's a nightmare! Just look at all those burrs in the poor dog's coat! And what is... oh, for pity's sake! *Feathers!*"

Leigh struggled to keep her face impassive. "He's not *that* bad, Mom." She noted that Jared had surreptitiously crept away from the scene. Mentally challenged, indeed.

The glare Frances turned on her daughter could melt an iceberg. "This dog needs attention," she ordered. "And immediately!"

"I'll get to it," Leigh insisted, withering slightly, despite her resolve. "I just have two or three more stops to make this afternoon—"

"Then I'll do it myself!" Frances said sharply, removing the lead from Leigh's hand. "He can go home with me for the afternoon. That way I can make sure he's groomed *properly*. He'll have to ride there in a carrier, though. I just vacuumed the upholstery in the car this morning."

Jared, who had already begun sweeping the cat litter off the floor, laid his broom aside, magically produced a carrier from a shelf above the cages, and set it down on the floor beside Chewie.

"Thank you, Jared," Frances praised. But when her gaze returned to the floor, her jaws tightened. "I should sweep up that cat litter first, though."

"Oh, no, Mrs. Koslow!" Jared said quickly, snatching the broom to his chest as if it were his first born. "I can sweep up. I'm happy to sweep up. It's my job to sweep up, Mrs. Koslow!"

Frances's lips bent slowly into a smile. "Yes, you're right, Jared. It is your job, isn't it? And you do it very well. My mistake." She turned back to her daughter, and the smile disappeared. "I'll return the dog to you at the park tonight. Same time, same place?"

Leigh nodded. She squatted down to close the door of the carrier, which Chewie had crawled into immediately upon its appearance. He didn't like getting in a carrier at home, but once at the clinic, he would hide in anything. "Have fun, little guy," she whispered. "I owe you one."

Chapter 18

Courtney opened the door of Diana's apartment, took half a step out, and nearly collided with someone.

"Oh," she cried, stepping back inside. "Detective Peterson. I... didn't know you were coming."

Diana's heart skipped a beat. Her apartment was a popular destination today.

"No way you could have," Peterson replied pleasantly, leaning into the doorway. He spotted Diana and gave a nod. "Good afternoon, Ms. Saxton. Would you mind if we came in?"

We? Diana thought to herself, even as she nodded in reply. Peterson stepped through the door, politely wiped his shoes on the welcome mat, and entered. Behind him, much to Diana's dismay, came the Amazonian police woman. The female detective never said much, but she made Diana nervous. Not many people did. It annoyed her.

"I hope you didn't rush down here because of my voice mail," Courtney twittered anxiously. "I'm perfectly fine, as you can see."

"Glad to hear it," Peterson responded. "But I dropped by because it just so happens I need to talk to both of you ladies."

Lovely. Diana applied a fake smile. She had a sneaking suspicion that Peterson was a good deal more intelligent—and hence, more dangerous—than might be assumed from his slight, unimposing appearance. "Come have a seat," she offered, gesturing all three of her visitors to her small living area. She pulled up the zebra-striped desk chair for herself and joined them.

"As I mentioned in the voice mail," Courtney prattled, "I'm only here because I needed help clearing up some issues with Brandon's business. I've rehired Ms. Saxton temporarily until it's settled. Why are you here? Has something happened?"

The detectives didn't answer for a moment. Diana took a cleansing breath. She knew what they were up to. They were about to drop a bombshell, and they were watching for the women's reactions.

"Brandon Lyle's missing gun has been located," Peterson said evenly. "We don't have the ballistics report back yet, but the circumstances in which it has been found are quite curious." He turned to Diana. "Ms. Saxton, you mentioned to me yesterday that you were aware that Mr. Lyle possessed a permit to carry firearms, and that you had been in his presence when he had done so."

Diana shrugged. "I went to the shooting range with him a couple times. But it wasn't like he carried it every day. I told you that."

"Brandon never carried a gun just to carry it!" Courtney interjected, flustered. "He couldn't hit the side of a barn. Where did you find it?"

Detective Peterson's eyes remained disconcertingly on Diana. "At the Ironworks Health Club."

Easy, girl.

Diana shrugged again. "That doesn't surprise me. Brandon was a slob; he left things everywhere."

Courtney sat up. "So Brandon *wasn't* killed with his own gun?"

Diana cast a quick glance at the female detective, and noticed that her eyes were trained on the widow. When Diana looked at Peterson, she found him staring straight back at her. No wonder there were two of them.

"You are a member of the Ironworks Health Club, are you not?" Peterson asked Diana, ignoring Courtney's question.

"I am," she answered calmly. "For the last year or so. I work out there a couple times a week."

"Do you know when Brandon Lyle had last been there?"

"I couldn't say. We hadn't gone together in a while."

"And when were you there last?"

"Yesterday."

"Did you by any chance see Mr. Gil March while you were there?"

"No."

Peterson was watching her intently. Diana didn't flinch.

At last, the detective turned to the widow Lyle. "Were you aware that your husband was a member at the Ironworks?"

"I knew he went to a gym somewhere," Courtney answered, sounding confused. "I didn't pay any attention to where. Why? What's the big deal? I don't know why he would take his handgun to the gym, but if he wasn't shot with it, what does it matter?"

Once again, Peterson ignored the question and turned back to Diana. "Ms. Saxton," he drilled, "have you been inside Mr. Lyle's apartment since you went to look for him the night of the murder?"

"Yes," she answered immediately. "I went back the next day, after I left the office. I had to pick up some of my things from the bedroom."

Diana sensed, rather than saw, Courtney bristle in the armchair to her left. *Miserable hypocrite.* Brandon's wife had been so incensed when she discovered their affair, Diana had actually believed she gave a damn. Turns out all Courtney was incensed about was the injustice of Brandon's being able to charge her with desertion even as he shacked up with an employee. Diana had no sympathy. Courtney should have had the sense to let Brandon cheat first. She would have had to wait what, a week?

"Brandon gave me my own key, you see," Diana finished smoothly.

A flicker of dislike crossed Peterson's pale eyes.

Oops. Too much?

"Detective Peterson," Courtney spat out impatiently, "Do you think Brandon was shot with his own gun or not?"

The detective paused a moment. "We don't know yet, Ms. Lyle," he answered calmly, still looking at Diana. "As I said, the ballistics report isn't back yet. What's curious is that the gun was found not with Mr. Lyle's things, but in a gym bag belonging to Mr. Gil March."

Ah, Diana thought. *There it is.*

"So what?" Courtney responded. "Maybe Brandon loaned it to him. They've been friends forever. What does it matter?"

Diana pretended distress. Her eyes widened; her shoulders drew together. "Oh, dear," she breathed.

"What?" Courtney repeated, glaring at her. "What's the big deal?"

Diana's eyes locked on Peterson's. "I knew there were some... *issues* between them. Brandon was so... agitated. But I really didn't think—"

"Oh, don't be ridiculous!" Courtney scolded, rising to face Diana. "Gil had nothing to do with it, and you know it."

Diana's cheeks flared. She straightened in her chair, meeting Courtney's glare with one of her own. "*Do* I?"

Courtney's face clouded with confusion. "You worked for him!"

Diana wished she could look embarrassed. But it wasn't possible. "Yes," she said firmly. "I worked for him." She cleared her throat. "Among other things."

Brandon Lyle's widow did a double take. For a moment, she just stood there staring, her rosy-lipped mouth hanging open dumbly.

Diana wondered if she had made a tactical error.

"Are you saying," Detective Peterson asked mildly, "That you also had an intimate relationship with Mr. March?"

Diana's gaze stayed on the detective, but she could feel the heat of Courtney's stare like a brush burn. "I am," she confirmed. "But only briefly, while I was still working for him. I broke off the relationship about six months ago, and he fired me."

Courtney made a sort of strangled noise. Evidently, she had started to speak, but then thought better of it. *Perfect.*

"Brandon didn't know, of course," Diana continued. "And Gil didn't know about Brandon. I figured it was better that way. I would hate for myself to be... well, a source of tension between them. They had enough issues as it was."

Detective Peterson sat up straight. "Are you saying that, to your knowledge, neither of the men was aware of your relationship with the other? At least not as of the morning you left Brandon to go to Harrisburg?"

Fished in!

"That's exactly what I'm saying," Diane proffered. "I should think I would know if they did. That could be quite..." she let her voice trail off. She projected a look of profound disturbance.

The room went quiet. Detective Peterson sat back on the couch. He tapped his pen on his notebook thoughtfully. The female detective said nothing.

"Ms. Lyle," he said finally, turning to Courtney, "were you aware of any recent hostilities between your husband and Mr. March?"

Diana looked over to see Brandon's wife tensing with discomfort. Courtney's eyes darted toward her, but Diana turned away. *Don't look at me, idiot!*

"I don't know!" Courtney spat out. "It's not like Brandon and I talked about this stuff! They've known each other since college, and Gil was trying to help him with the business. I've heard Brandon complain that he wasn't helping enough, but that's Brandon for you — he wasn't what you'd call the 'grateful' type."

Her voice rose. "This is all just stupid, anyway! Why can't you people find out who shot my husband and let me know? Is that so much to ask?!"

The idiocy of her question hung in the air a moment. Then Courtney snatched up her bag and made for the door. "If there's nothing else," she snapped, "I'll be going now."

"Ms. Lyle," Detective Peterson called after her, without rising.

"Yes?" she said impatiently.

"I have to ask that you not leave the county. At least not for the next few days. We may need to question you again."

Courtney's lower jaw trembled. Her eyes flashed with a combination of what Diana interpreted to be annoyance, outrage... and fear.

"Freakin' *fabulous!!!*" the widow shouted. And on that note, she left.

Diana startled at the violent slamming of her door. She turned her attention back to the detectives.

"Is there anything else?" she asked politely.

"Not at the moment," Peterson responded. "But the same request applies to you. We need you to stay in town and be available for questioning."

"I can do that," Diana agreed, trying not to look as smug as she was feeling. She had a right to be proud. She had an iron-clad alibi. She had the upper hand on wifey-poo. And the world's most sanctimonious prig was being roasted over an open fire. Slowly.

Delightful.

She felt another gaze upon her, and turned to look at the female detective. The policewoman's body language was impassive. Her stare was blank. But for one brief moment, at the corners of her mouth, Diana could swear she saw the hint of a rather malicious-looking smile.

A shiver slid down her spine.

She was sure she had only imagined it.

The Koslow Animal Hospital wasn't horribly busy. Leigh found her father in the treatment room, bending over a patient. She was surprised to see that the helper holding the patient was her own ten-year-old daughter.

"Allison?" she exclaimed, "what are you doing here?" Frances' earlier statement came back to her, making sense now.

Two heads of dark hair lifted up to look at her. Two pairs of glasses were adjusted with quick wrinkles of the nose.

Birds of a feather.

Leigh grinned. Randall Koslow was graying a bit around the temples, but only a bit. The veterinarian was pushing seventy, but evidently hadn't gotten the memo. He worked as much as he ever worked and refused even to talk about retirement. Steady, plodding, and unflappable, Randall had always been Leigh's rock. Why on earth he had married a woman like Frances was a mystery on par with Stonehenge, but for the sake of Leigh's own existence, she was very glad that he had.

"Somebody dropped this kitty off at the shelter," Allison explained, stroking a scrawny, half-grown gray and white cat that looked like it had crawled out of a trash can. "Aunt Cara took me by there so I could check on the sick kittens, and Angie didn't know what to do. He had a fishhook caught in his paw."

Allison extended one of the cat's front legs to show the grossly swollen digits. "He had it in there a while already," she explained. "But grandpa got it out and gave him some antibiotics. We think he'll be okay."

"You can take him downstairs to Jared, now," Randall instructed, turning from the table to wash his hands. "He'll fix up a cage and keep an eye on him for the next day or two."

Allison smiled broadly. "That's good. All the kitties love Jared." She scooped up the injured cat like a pro, walked past her mother, and headed for the stairs.

Randall dried his hands on a paper towel, crumpled it, and threw it away. "Did you see your mother?" he asked.

"She just left," Leigh answered. "It turns out Chewie was in dire need of a spa treatment."

Randall's lips bent into a subtle, lopsided grin. "I see. Thanks, honey."

"No problem."

He crossed his arms and leaned back against the countertop. "So," he said evenly. "How's everything?"

Leigh cracked a grin. When Frances heard that her daughter had discovered another body, she had immediately driven to Leigh's house to confirm her alibi and assess her need for legal representation. Randall's reaction, two days later, was to ask how everything was.

"Things are fine, Dad," she answered gratefully. "At least they're fine with me."

Randall nodded knowingly. "Cara was here earlier. She looked a little rough."

"I know," Leigh said with a sigh, dropping onto a stool. "I can't say I'd be any calmer if this were happening to Warren. It doesn't look good for Gil, Dad. The woman who's trying to frame him is obviously nutso. And we've had zero luck shoring up his alibi."

"How is the Pack handling it?" he asked.

Leigh looked after her daughter thoughtfully. "Mathias and Lenna seem pretty oblivious. Cara and Gil didn't tell them much, so they don't know their father is a suspect. They know their mother is upset, obviously, but I don't think they've put two and two together yet. Neither has Ethan. But as for Allison... Well, it's hard to know what that girl is thinking."

Or what she's overheard.

Randall's brow furrowed. "I'd say she's thinking a good deal more than most people expect," he suggested. "Don't underestimate her, Leigh. That child has a mind like a steel trap."

Leigh's eyebrows rose. "Had she said anything to you? I mean, about the murder?"

Randall shook his head. "She doesn't talk; you know that. She just asks questions."

"Like what?"

"Like whether or not a woman can be a serial killer."

Leigh swallowed hard. "Why on earth would she ask that?"

Randall shrugged. "She also wanted to know if it was possible to order a bulletproof vest online."

Leigh had no time to respond. Allison skipped up the basement stairs and joined them with a smile. "He took to Jared right away," she announced. "I'm sure the shelter can find a home for him once he's healed; he's such a cutie. Do I have to go now, Mom? Aunt Cara said she'd pick me up a half hour from now."

"Then I'll text your Aunt Cara and spare her the trip," Leigh answered. "You can come home with me."

Allison frowned, but didn't argue.

Leigh thanked her father for treating yet another shelter freebie, grabbed a tube of hairball preventative for Mao Tse, tore her daughter away from a litter of lab puppies due for their first shots, and climbed with her daughter into the van.

Female serial killers?

"Allison," Leigh began, as she pulled the van away from the curb and out onto the aging brick street. "You're not worried about... about that man being found in the woods, are you?"

Leigh stole a quick glance in the rearview mirror. Allison was gazing straight ahead, her face a mask of contemplation.

"Was Brandon Lyle a bad man, Mom?" she asked quietly.

Leigh tensed. She should have waited until Warren came home for this. "Nobody is all bad or all good, Allison," she answered. "But Mr. Lyle did have enemies. Most likely he was killed over money. In any event, it has nothing to do with us. We're all perfectly safe."

Allison paused in thought a moment. "Then why do you keep telling us to stay out of the woods?"

Good question. Leigh ground her teeth. "Well, because sometimes... not often, but sometimes... a criminal will return to the scene of a crime. It's only a very small chance, but until the police have arrested him, it's safer to stay away."

"Why do you say it's a him?"

Leigh resisted the urge to keep looking in the rearview. Not only was traffic terrible, but the Avalon pedestrians were out in force today. Why exactly had she started this conversation?

"I suppose it's possible it could be a woman," she confessed. "I really wish you wouldn't think about it so much, Allison."

"Why not?" The small voice piped up. "It's interesting."

Saints preserve us.

"Hey!" Allison squeaked suddenly, bending down out of Leigh's view. "What's this?"

Leigh checked quickly for vulnerable walkers, bikers, and dogs, then threw a glance over her shoulder to see what Allison was reaching for. "Oh, no!" she groaned, turning back around again. "How did *that* get in here?"

"What is it?" Allison asked again.

"It's some old rawhide thing that Chewie picked up at your Aunt Bess's," Leigh said with disgust. She thought the dog had dropped the treat long before his hosing off, but evidently he had found it again and slipped it into the van when she wasn't looking. Come to think of it, she *had* opened the side door a good while before she and Bess were finished talking.

Allison pulled the filthy thing into her lap. "It doesn't look like a rawhide to me," she said studiously.

"Just put it down, please," Leigh ordered. "God only knows where it's been. Or what dog's mouth it's been in. Please, Allison. Just leave it alone. When we get home, you can toss it in the trash. We don't want Chewie finding it again."

The girl sighed. But, holding the dirty bone carefully with her fingertips, she bent out of view to place it back down on the floor.

They rode along in silence for a few minutes.

"Mom?" Allison asked.

Leigh braced herself.

"You and Dad never said exactly *where* you found the body."

Leigh gulped. "No. No, we didn't."

"Why not?"

Leigh decided to attempt the truth. "Because we didn't want you to dwell on it. We want you to continue to enjoy playing in the woods."

"But you won't let us play in the woods."

"Not now, maybe. But later."

"We could play in part of the woods now, if you told us what part to avoid."

Damned lawyerball genes. "You should avoid it all. The shelter land, your Aunt Bess's yard, and the land behind the church."

"What about Mr. Clem's?"

"You're never allowed to play at Mr. Clem's!" Leigh reminded sharply.

"Oh, I know," Allison said matter of factly. "I was just seeing if you'd rule it out."

Leigh grit her teeth again. "Allison, please. I don't want you kids dwelling on this. It has nothing to do with you, and there's nothing for you to be afraid of. All right?"

Allison didn't answer for a moment. "I'm not afraid, Mom," she said finally, her tone serious. "But if it worries you, I'll quit talking about it."

Leigh opened her mouth to respond, but shut it again. There really was no help for it.

The girl was a Morton woman.

Chapter 19

"Well, Lord love a duck. He's been Francified!" Bess exclaimed.

Leigh ceased petting her aunt's Pekingese mix and looked up. Her mother and Aunt Lydie had at last arrived at the park, an unprecedented ten minutes late. Frances was still fussing with something in the car, but Lydie was walking toward them with Chewie on a lead.

"Oh, no," Leigh breathed.

The corgi was unrecognizable. The mud, burrs, and feathers were gone. So was every drop of natural oil his coat had ever possessed. The dog was so squeaky clean that his thick brindle fur stood fluffed up all over like he'd just put his paw in a light socket, and Frances had completed the transformation by sticking an oversized blue bow on the top of his head. The poor dog was half Beauty's Beast in the ballroom, half golden hamster.

"Oh my," Cara said with a chuckle.

The dog bounded up to Leigh looking thoroughly pleased with himself.

"Haven't passed a mirror lately, have you, boy?" Leigh greeted, glad that her mother's efforts had produced at least one positive result. Cara hadn't laughed in days.

"Frances is coming," Lydie said apologetically, handing over Chewie's lead and redistributing the photos and notebooks. "We got a little tied up collecting our newest conversation starter."

The other women cast a glance at the car, but they could see nothing, since Frances was on the other side of it.

Bess sighed heavily. "What sort of beast did she bring tonight? If this one's bigger than a bread box, Chester's going to need a valium."

Lydie merely smiled. "You'll see. Cara, why don't you and I start out? We don't want to waste any more time. Bess, you can go our way. Leigh, you go the opposite direction—I believe your mother wants to stay near the parking lot tonight."

The women agreed, and the others headed off along the lake trail while Leigh walked toward her mother. When she got around the back of the car, she stopped cold.

Her mother didn't have a dog. Frances was strapping a tow-headed infant into a stroller.

"Mom," Leigh began incredulously. "You *borrowed* a baby?"

Frances's lips pursed. She finished her fastening and straightened. "It's called *sitting*, dear. This is little Maddie Rogalla from down the street. Her mother needed a break, poor thing. Don't you remember what it was like to have little ones and need some time to yourself?"

Leigh considered. Actually, she did not. Her memories from the time between the twins' birth and their first day of preschool comprised a single amorphous blur of sippy cups, dirty diapers, purple dinosaurs, and the wallpaper in her pediatrician's office. Anything else that might have happened during those years had been deleted in real-time, courtesy of sleep deprivation.

"As I hope you recall," Frances continued, "Gil is certain now that when he was walking around the lake he passed a young blond woman pushing two babies in a stroller. That's who we're looking for."

"I remember," Leigh assured.

"It was a double stroller, side-by-side, just like the one you and Warren used to have. He said that's why it drew his attention. The babies were twins also, but both were girls."

Leigh was surprised, for a moment, that Gil would remember what her stroller had looked like. But she supposed she shouldn't be. Both Warren and Gil had been excellent hands-on fathers. The two had probably taken the Pack on many turns around this very lake while she and Cara lay unconscious on their respective couches.

"Now then," Frances ordered. "I'll take the parking lot area, so Maddie and I can stay near the changing facilities. You go the opposite way as the others."

"Will do," Leigh agreed.

The baby gurgled with glee and stretched out a hand toward the corgi. Chewie stuck his nose in her lap and sniffed at her diaper. Leigh winced and pulled the dog away, grateful, as she often was around strangers, that he wasn't any taller.

Pedestrian traffic was heavier this evening, as the weather was clear and less humid than it had been before the rain. Leigh spoke with every dog walker or baby-pusher she saw, but couldn't reach all of the many walkers. Few were certain they had been at the lake three days ago, and none remembered having seen Gil. As the minutes dragged on, her anxiety level rose. None of the Morton women had wanted to voice what they were sure Cara already knew: if the ballistics report proved that the gun found in Gil's bag was the murder weapon, he would almost certainly be arrested.

They had to find a witness to his alibi. They just *had* to.

From the small parking area to her left, Leigh heard a familiar voice laugh out loud. "Chewie! What in hell happened to you?"

Leigh whirled to see her policewoman friend leaning casually against the hood of her dilapidated Ford. "My mother had a little excess nervous energy," Leigh explained, walking closer. "Chewie here took one for the team."

Maura chuckled and scratched the dog's ears. "You're a brave, brave soul, my man."

Chewie licked his lips and sat down on her foot.

Maura was quiet for a moment, and Leigh's anxiety level rose another notch. The detective hadn't intercepted her out here for nothing. Either Maura had information, or she wanted it. And she had made an effort to catch Leigh without the kids around.

"Did something happen, Maura?" Leigh asked.

The policewoman fidgeted. Then she let out a sigh. "I can't tell you anything Peterson wouldn't tell you, Koslow," she explained. "You know that. But there is something I think all of you should know. Whatever else Diana Saxton may be guilty of, her alibi for Lyle's murder is rock solid."

Leigh's brow furrowed. Heat rose in her cheeks. "But she planted the gun! Who else could have? And why would she do that if she wasn't guilty herself?"

"An excellent question," Maura agreed. "Did Gil ever confide his... er... *problems* with Diana Saxton to anyone else before he fired her? Besides Cara, I mean? Did he talk to you about it?"

Leigh shook her head. "Cara didn't even talk to me about it. Gil told her not to. But Warren knew. Gil told him."

Maura's face brightened. "Did he? Excellent. I'll make sure Peterson has a chat with the Future Prez."

Leigh's head was buzzing with thoughts, none of them

comfortable. She cast a glance down the trail, determined not to miss any likely witnesses, but the traffic had thinned. "Surely you can prove that Diana is doing a frame job! Wouldn't the security cameras at the gym have caught her going in and out?"

"All I can say, Koslow," Maura responded, "is that there's a big difference between its being *possible* for someone to plant evidence and proving that they actually did."

Leigh blew out a breath in frustration. "But if she didn't kill Brandon, how did she even *get* the gun? And more importantly, who *did* kill him?"

"Current evidence," Maura answered heavily, "says Gil March."

"But you *know* —"

Maura cut off Leigh's protest with a hand. "Of course I know. But instincts are one thing, and evidence is another." She softened her voice. "I put Peterson on this case for a reason, Koslow. He may not look like the touchy-feely type, but that doesn't mean he's blind to human nature. Peterson gets people. He knows what motivates them, he knows what they're capable of, and next to Gerry and me, he's got one the best bullcrap detectors I've ever seen. He'll get this case sorted out eventually. But what I want you—all of you—to know is this. My gut is telling me that this case isn't what it looks like. It's not linear; it's not clean. There's more than one thing happening here. Do you get what I'm saying?"

Leigh's stomach churned. What Maura was saying was that the police had no idea who had murdered Brandon Lyle. And until they did, everyone involved with him—and his nefarious development business—could be in danger.

"I see," she responded.

"If you could find a witness for Gil that would be great," Maura said, pulling her keys out of her pocket and gently dislodging the corgi from her foot. "But stay away from Diana Saxton. *All* of you." She opened the door of her car, then turned around again. "And, Leigh?"

"Yes?"

"Stay away from Courtney Lyle as well. If she tries to contact you or Cara, let me know right away."

The intensity in her friend's tone made Leigh's pulse rate climb. She nodded wordlessly. Maura started up her car and pulled away, and Leigh turned Chewie back onto the trail. The specter of a homicidal Diana Saxton was bad enough. But what else was going on? How well did Gil really know his old college pal Courtney? Or—worse yet—was Lyle's murder tied to the development deal by more than its location? Maybe Bess had been wrong to discount the entire church full of people Lyle had threatened that night. Given that building's karma, anything was possible. Who was to say that one of the devoted old guard hadn't popped their cork when Lyle started blathering about eminent domain? Or worse still, Lyle's murder could have been random: the act of some indiscriminate, still roaming lunatic...

She started. A woman had just come into view jogging around the bend ahead. A blond woman with two babies in a side-by-side stroller.

Leigh's steps quickened.

She tried to control her excitement as she confirmed that the babies, both less than a year old, were girls. They were dressed in identical yellow sundresses with matching sunflower hats; their mother sported a sleek running outfit and pony tail. Leigh allowed herself a brief surge of jealousy at the young mom's trim, athletic figure. Her own twins had been walking and talking before she'd looked a day under six months pregnant.

"How cute!" Leigh said genuinely, smiling at the little girls. "My twins are ten now, but I used to have a stroller just like this. Well, almost like this. Yours has bigger wheels."

The woman slowed her steps, then stopped. A smile lit up her face. "It's a running stroller," she explained. "Took us forever to find a side-by-side, but it's worth it. We had a tandem one, but—"

"The kid in the back gets bored," Leigh finished, amused at the capacity of any new mom to talk ceaselessly about baby gear. She did remember that much from the lost years. "Tell me about it. The side-by-sides get stuck in doorways, but at least you don't have to switch the kids around every ten minutes to stop the whining. And besides, the wider ones are better to mow other people down with."

The young mom laughed. "Are yours identical?"

Leigh shook her head. "Fraternal. A boy and a girl."

"That's nice."

The women exchanged a smile. Leigh pressed on. "I'm out here tonight for a reason, actually, and I was hoping you could help. My brother-in-law was out walking on this trail Monday night, right about this time. Our family is trying to locate someone who might have seen him here. It's very important."

The woman gave a sympathetic look. "Is he missing?"

"Oh, no. But he's been accused of being somewhere else, and we'd like to clear his name. Were you and the girls out Monday, by any chance?"

"I think so," the woman answered. "Unless... no, it was Tuesday that Ellie had the sniffles. And yesterday it rained. We were here Monday. Is that his picture?"

Leigh's heart thudded in her chest. She held out the picture of Gil that she had been carrying clamped under her arm.

Amazingly, the women's face lit up. An amused smile spread across her face. "Oh, yeah, I remember him! Hard not to notice a man like that, particularly when he takes the time to smile and wave at your babies."

Leigh beamed. It took a good deal of restraint for her not to jump up and down. The woman was telling the truth—she was sure of it. With adults Gil was stiff as granite, but he was surprisingly comfortable around babies. For him to interrupt the walking off of a temper tantrum to coo at two adorable baby girls would be entirely in character.

"You saw him? You're sure?"

The woman nodded. "Absolutely. That was him. I'd thought he'd stepped off a film set. What a hottie!" A sudden flush sprang up in her cheeks. "Oh, but don't tell his wife I said that. Or my husband either, for that matter!"

At this particular moment, Leigh would promise the woman almost anything. "If you're sure," she said carefully, "would be willing to give a statement to the police? I know it's a huge imposition, but it's really very important."

The woman's smiled faded. "The police? What is he accused of doing?"

Leigh steadied herself, then explained the situation as concisely as she could. She figured she might as well be honest; better the woman know what she was getting into now than dash all of their hopes down the road.

"I heard about that man being murdered," the woman remarked when Leigh was finished. "I hate to think of something like that happening so close to here." She cast a protective glance down at her babies, paused a moment, then raised her chin. "But your brother-in-law obviously wasn't involved, so if I come forward, it can only help the police catch the real killer, right?"

Leigh's heart leapt. *Yes!* She held out her pad and pen, her arm practically shaking as she did so. "Absolutely. If you just write down your name and contact information," she said, "someone from the county detective's squad will call you. Probably either a Detective Peterson or Polanski. I can't thank you enough!"

The woman took the pad and started to write. The baby girl on the left had started wailing. Her sister had a blue ribbon, and she wanted it. "Just a second, Zora," the mother crooned without looking up. "We'll get moving soon." She finished writing and handed the pad back to Leigh.

Leigh looked down, saw a legitimate-looking name, phone, and email, and let out her breath with a whoosh. "You have no idea how happy this will make my family," she said sincerely. "We all owe you so much."

The woman smiled. "I don't suppose your dog would consider parting with her bling?"

Leigh glanced over to see the babies engaged in full-blown sibling combat over Chewie's bow, which one of them had unclipped from his head. She laughed. "I really don't think he'll miss it." She gestured toward the corgi, who now lay placidly beside the stroller, licking his toenails.

Licking his toenails?

Leigh looked closer. The dog's nails had not only been neatly trimmed, but each one shone with a lustrous glow. She closed her eyes and shook her head. A lot of people painted their dog's toenails, yes. But only Frances Koslow would use clear polish.

"Your girls are more than welcome to the ribbon," she insisted. "Thank you again."

The woman waved off Leigh's thanks, said goodbye, and jogged away down the trail. Leigh looked in the opposite direction, toward where Cara and Lydie would now be patrolling. She smiled broadly.

Cousin Cara needed a little good news. And she was going to get it just as fast as Leigh's legs could carry it.

Chapter 20

"Whose car is that?" Cara asked with alarm as her van pulled into the gravel drive behind the March's garage. She stopped and let her headlights illuminate it.

"I've never seen it before," Leigh answered, irritated. Her cousin had been deliriously happy for all of about an hour. The women had stayed at the park until dusk, making sure they didn't miss any other possible witnesses—just in case. Then, in true Morton style, they had celebrated by going out for ice cream.

Now, Cara was upset again. "Gil didn't tell me he was expecting anybody," she said tightly.

Leigh surveyed the bright yellow Porsche. Its license plate said "1-BANANA."

"That's a woman's car," Cara said with certainty.

Leigh's pulse sped up. "It's not—"

"No," Cara said vehemently, shaking her head. "It's not Diana's. I know her car. Besides, she could never afford a Porsche. It is a woman's car, though. A woman with a lot of money to burn. And a low-brow sense of humor."

The cousins exchanged a glance. "Courtney Lyle," Leigh suggested.

Cara nodded. "I'd bet money on it."

"We should call Maura," Leigh suggested, pulling out her phone. "She said she wanted to know if Courtney tried to contact either of us—"

Cara's hand flew across the seat to stop her. "Wait a minute," she insisted. "Courtney isn't contacting us—she's contacting Gil. He's known her since they were teenagers, and if he didn't think it was perfectly safe to talk to her, he would never have let her in the house. You can call Maura after we're done."

Leigh's trouble-o-meter dialed up a notch. "Done? Done with what?"

Cara steered the van slowly away from the other car and turned off the engine. Her voice dropped. "Done figuring out exactly what it is that the late Brandon Lyle's wife wants with my husband, of course." She opened her door slowly. "Get out," she ordered, "but don't slam the door. We've got to be quiet."

Cara slipped out of her car door and gently pushed it closed. Leigh did the same, then came around to meet her. "But what if —"

"Shhh!" Cara warned, putting her finger to her lips. She slid open the side door of the van and let the dogs out. "She won't have seen us drive up, because Gil will have put her in the study and closed the door behind them. He wouldn't want to talk to her in the living room with the kids at home. But if we sneak in through the kitchen we can listen through the old serving window. Follow me!"

Cara crept off across the drive on tiptoe. She let Maggie run, but held onto Chewie's lead as she made for the sun porch. Leigh followed mutely, her instincts at war with her better judgment. Surely the phone call to Maura could be delayed by just a few minutes? Leigh hoped so, because she understood completely why her cousin could not, in fact, simply wait and ask her husband about the conversation later. It wasn't that Gil wouldn't *try* to explain, it was that the man had the emotional intelligence of a boiled clam. Even if he could recount every word that Courtney said to him, he could never pick up the nuances. Negotiating with other businessmen was one thing; deconstructing female head games was another.

Cara led Chewie onto the porch and unclipped his lead. The women moved quietly to the sliding doors, and Cara punched her code into the security box. The March's system was so elaborate that Leigh still didn't quite understand it (and tripped it herself on a regular basis), but under the current circumstances she was grateful for its existence. She could also understand, now, why Cara had insisted on putting Bess's camera out by the road. Diana Saxton didn't have a prayer of getting inside the March house to plant the gun, but she could have left it anywhere else on the six-acre property... stuck in a tree, thrown in the creek, laying in the drainage ditch. In which case — God forbid — the Pack could have found it.

Leigh shivered at the thought.

Cara slipped through the sliding doors, ushered Leigh into the room behind her, and silently closed them again. They were standing in the breakfast nook by the kitchen. The study, which used to be the old farmhouse's dining room, was on the other side of a serving window closed off by wooden shutters. Standing close and leaning over the counter, they could hear every word that was said.

"I didn't believe her," Courtney was insisting, her loud voice half-cajoling, half-whine. "I knew you would never sleep with a wench like her, even if she wasn't working for you. But I only know that because I know you. The police don't! They have every reason to believe her story. Brandon sure as hell fell for her."

"I am *not* Brandon," Gil growled.

"I know that," Courtney cooed. "That's why I'm here."

"Why *are* you here?"

There was a long pause. Leigh could feel Cara's tension as the same image undoubtedly swept through both their minds— Courtney sidling her shapely body closer to Gil's.

"To warn you," Courtney said silkily. "Because I don't want anything to happen to you. That woman is evil, Gil. She's a lying, scheming, sociopathic slut, and for whatever reason—although we both know the reason, don't we? You hopelessly loyal thing—she has it in for you. I *wish* she had been the one to kill Brandon, I do, because I'd really like to see her skinny little trash-butt rotting in a prison cell. But I don't think she was."

"So who did?" Gil asked, his voice sounding farther away now.

"I don't know," she answered, her own voice drifting away after his. "I don't even know if she knows. But what's obvious is that she's trying to frame you. She told the detectives that the two of you had an affair, that she dumped you, and that you fired her for it. She also told them that up until the day of the murder, Brandon didn't know you'd had an affair with her, and that *you* didn't know she was shacking up with *him!*"

Cara's lips mouthed a string of vulgarity such as Leigh had never heard before—at least, not from Cara. The other woman's face was beet red and her fists clenched the countertop so tightly her knuckles whitened. Leigh silently encouraged deep breaths.

"Well, that's just fabulous!" Gil fumed, his voice a strangled shout. "You heard her tell the detectives this?"

"I was standing right there!"

"And did you set them straight?"

The pause lasted only a heartbeat. "Of course I did," Courtney soothed. "I told them I'd known you for decades and that you would never cheat on your wife. You *did* know about Brandon and Diana already, didn't you?"

"I suspected," Gil replied gruffly. "But Brandon and I didn't talk about that sort of thing."

"I can see that," Courtney said wryly. "I wonder if he realized he was doing one of your rejects?"

"Diana wouldn't—" Gil was quiet for a moment. Then he muttered a curse. "Who knows what she told him? He was furious with me that night, but there were other reasons... I mean, he'd been acting like a lunatic for days—how the hell should I know what he was thinking?"

There was another pause, then Courtney's tone turned silky again. "Look, Gilsy, I know you didn't ask for any of this. Neither did I. But it's happened and... well, I really do need your help."

Gilsy?

Gil let out a rough exhale. "We've been through this already, Courtney. I'm the number one suspect in Brandon's murder. I can't be poking into his personal business now! I can't help you with the funeral, I can't sort out your finances, and I certainly can't have anything to do with Lyle Development. Can't you understand that?"

"That's not what I'm talking about," Courtney pressed, her voice dropping. "This is different. It's about me."

The room went silent.

"I'm scared, Gil."

Cara made an involuntary movement toward the shutters; Leigh shot out a quick restraining arm.

"Scared of what?" Gil asked tonelessly.

The next pause was nearly unbearable.

"Of a man I met in Chicago," Courtney continued soberly. "Just a month or so ago. I didn't think he was dangerous. Really, I didn't. I thought he was all show. But he was handsome and he was exciting... and he was crazy about me. But now... well, I'm not sure what he is."

"Why are you afraid of him?" Gil asked, his tone gentler now.

Courtney released a long, slow breath. "I may be overreacting. But just a couple days before Brandon died, this man found out that I was married. I thought he knew already... I wasn't keeping it a secret. I just didn't talk about it. But he heard about it from somebody else, and he totally flipped. He never even spoke to me, he just started throwing things around my apartment... and then he walked out. After that I started hearing things from people. About how crazy possessive he was. About how violent he could get. Even about another woman that he..." She paused a moment. "I was terrified. I texted him saying I was going on a shopping trip to New York, but I came back to Pittsburgh instead. I wanted to get some things and lay low for a while—maybe on the West Coast. Brandon wasn't at the condo when I got there, but Diana's crap was everywhere and I sure as hell didn't want to run into her, so I took my stuff and checked into a hotel. The next morning, the police called me on my cell and told me they'd been trying to locate me— that Brandon was dead."

"Did you tell the detectives all this?" Gil asked. There was a pause. Then he spoke again. "Why not? Courtney, do you realize this could open up the whole case?"

"Of course I do!" she fired back, struggling not to shout. "But what if I *am* overreacting, and he had absolutely nothing to do with Brandon's death? If he's not out to get me already, he sure as hell would be after I turned the Pittsburgh police onto him for a murder charge!"

Leigh could hear Courtney's heels clicking on the hardwood floor, could picture her pacing.

"But, still!" Gil argued. "Who is this guy? If he *did*—"

"Even if he did," Courtney retorted hotly, "there's no guarantee the police can prove it! He's so clever; you have no idea. The stories I've heard... and he's never gotten arrested for any of it. If he thought I betrayed him, I'd *never* be safe!"

The heels clicked some more.

"All I can do is wait it out," she finished. "Continue to pretend I really am on that shopping trip—at least until he cools down. He's texted me, finally, and I've texted back. I think we're making peace."

"He could be misleading you," Gil pointed out.

"I know that!" Courtney snapped. Her voice turned whiny again. "But don't you see? It's the only chance I've got to finesse my way out of this. Once his temper cools, I can go back to Chicago and let him break up with me. I played dazzling and seductive to get him; I can just as easily play boring and frumpy to lose him. Then I'll be free of him for good!"

"I don't like it," Gil protested.

"And I don't like being stuck in Pittsburgh!" Courtney exclaimed. "I don't feel safe at the hotel. There are only so many four-stars in town, and they all have only one way in and out. If he knew I was here, he could find me in a heartbeat! Whether he had anything to do with Brandon's murder or not, if he finds out I've been lying to him all this time, that when I told him I was going to New York I actually went home to my husband..." She let out a groan. "Can't you see that telling the police anything about him is only going to make matters worse for me?"

Gil exhaled roughly. "What is it you think I can do?"

Another pause. Courtney's voice became that of a frightened little girl. "Would you let me stay here for a while? I know you've got good security. But even if you didn't, no one in Chicago knows I have any ties to you. It would be the perfect hiding place!"

"Can I listen too, Mom?"

Leigh and Cara jumped a foot, their heads banging together with a clop as they simultaneously whirled to face Cara's twelve-year-old son, who stood lounging casually against the kitchen doorway.

He laughed out loud. "Sorry. Didn't mean to scare you."

"Mathias!" Cara chastised, rubbing her head. "You know you shouldn't sneak up on people like that."

The boy grinned devilishly. "If you say so."

Leigh rubbed her own aching head, wishing she could crawl under the countertop. How did she let Cara talk her into these things?

"So who's the lady?" Mathias asked, opening the cupboard and getting himself a glass of water. "I saw her come in, but Dad made me go upstairs. I suppose he didn't want to be overheard."

Smart aleck.

Leigh kept an eye on Cara's composure, but her cousin was perfectly in control. "She's an old friend of your father's," Cara said placidly. "And it's no concern of yours. Now go back upstairs, please."

"All right," Mathias said with disappointment. "Can I have a cookie first?"

"No."

"But I'm starving!"

"You can have a spinach ball."

The boy winced. "Never mind. G'night, Aunt Leigh."

"Goodnight, Matt," Leigh returned.

He walked out the door and into the hallway. They listened until they heard his footsteps complete the flight of stairs, then Cara turned abruptly to Leigh. "Unbelievable! We've got to go in there and—"

"Cara?" Gil's voice froze them both where they stood. They looked up to see him and a flustered-looking Courtney standing in the doorway to the living room. "I thought I heard the back door just now," he said, throwing them both a hard look.

Leigh attempted an innocent smile.

"Hello, Courtney," Cara said pleasantly. "It's nice to see you again. I wondered whose car that was. It's rather distinctive."

"Yes, I suppose it is," Courtney said thoughtfully. "It's nice to see you too, Cara. And Leigh," she added with a nod.

The air hung thick as tofu.

"Courtney was just leaving," Gil announced, gesturing his guest toward the front door. He spoke to her quietly as he walked her out. "I'll call Ken tonight and see what he says. If it's a go, I'll put you in touch with him. In the meantime, remember what I said."

Courtney's voice was barely above a whisper. "You won't say anything to the police, will you?"

"I'll do what I think is best for everybody," Gil answered stiffly. "Goodnight, Courtney."

The door shut. Gil returned to the kitchen.

Leigh braced herself for an explosion from Cara, but her cousin merely wrapped her arms around her husband's neck and held him tight. "I thought for a moment you might say yes," she confessed when she released him. "I was afraid you'd feel sorry for her."

"You know I'd never let anyone put you or the kids in danger," he said reproachfully, though his gaze was—as always with his wife of fifteen years—adoring. "And you'll be happy to know you didn't miss anything, either. We'd been in the study all of about thirty seconds when you arrived and moved into position."

Cara smirked. "You heard the van on the gravel?"

"Of course," he responded. "But Courtney didn't notice it." His eyes moved to his cousin in law. "Thanks for helping with my alibi, Leigh."

She nodded. "You are going to tell the police about this madman from Chicago, aren't you?" she asked impatiently. Courtney's confession to Gil did seem to fit with the woman's odd behavior on their walk in the rain downtown. Maura had to know ASAP.

Gil's jaws clenched with consternation. "I'll tell them what I know, of course," he responded. "But I'm not sure how much it will help. Courtney wouldn't give me his name — she seems terrified of what would happen if the police contacted him. It was all I could do to get a description out of her — and she would only give me that if I agreed to help her find someplace to stay."

"I don't want her coming back here," Cara said firmly. "I always knew she was a flake, but if I had any idea she was hooked up with mobsters..."

Leigh's own jaws clenched. She wasn't entirely sure Courtney had been telling Gil the truth, but under the circumstances, she didn't need to be sure. The thought of such a person being within a mile of her children made her blood freeze. She could not take any chances. "Do you really think this guy could be... connected?" she asked.

Gil's brow furrowed. "I have no way of knowing. Courtney can be overly dramatic. On the other hand, she's always been attracted to both money and trouble."

"She can't come back here," Cara repeated.

"Of course not," Gil agreed. "I told her that. She knows I won't lift a finger to help her if she comes near any of you again. But we all need to watch out for a man fitting this guy's description — just in case."

Leigh burned the details into her brain as Gil spoke them. *Tall and solidly built. Early fifties, but looks younger. Gray hair, dark eyes. Expensive taste in wardrobe, but more showy than sophisticated.*

She would not forget.

"Where are you suggesting she stay?" Cara asked.

"I have a client from Philadelphia who leases an apartment downtown he rarely uses; I think he'd be willing to accommodate her," Gil answered. "She can make herself invisible enough in a crowd, as long as she watches how she uses her phone and stops driving such an easily recognizable car." He took his own phone from his pocket. "But my first call is going to Peterson."

Gil stepped away to dial a number, and Leigh took her leave. She had a sudden, irrepressible desire to check on the occupants of her own house.

She collected Chewie from the porch and headed down the drive. The distance between the cousins' houses was only a couple hundred yards, and the Marches had lit the whole way with lamp posts shortly after Leigh and Warren moved in. Even in the dark, it was a comfortable stroll Leigh had taken thousands of times. But tonight, every inch of it spooked her.

Her eyes roved the trees and bushes; her ears attuned to any sound that wasn't a passing car, frog, or cricket.

Tall and solidly built.

She chastised herself for the thoughts that swam in her head. She had no reason to act like a child who'd seen a scary movie. Hadn't she suspected that Courtney was mixed up with some bad-news guy in Chicago?

She had. But that was before. Before Courtney had invaded *her* space. Her *children's* space.

Gray hair. Dark eyes.

Leigh stifled a shudder. She clucked to Chewie and started to run. The corgi was game, as always, and by the time they reached her back door his momentum once again outstripped his brakes, making his backside swivel and bump against the house. "You nut," Leigh said fondly, letting him inside and locking the door behind her.

They should keep all the doors locked for a while.

All the time.

She looked into the family room for Warren, but hearing the water running, realized he must be in the shower. She checked to make sure the front door was locked, then started to put out the lights. When she reached the doorway of the dining room, she saw Allison.

The girl was sitting at the computer in her nightgown, quiet as a mouse, so absorbed in the screen that she hadn't seemed to notice her mother's approach. Leigh opened her mouth to remind her daughter that bedtime had long since passed, but the words stopped in her throat.

Allison was looking at pictures of dead things. The bodies of animals in varying states of decay. Road kill. Deer carcasses. She scrolled down and paused on the skeletal remains of a dog. She enlarged the picture and zoomed in on the hindquarters.

"Allison!" Leigh croaked, finding barely enough air in her lungs to form the words. "What on earth are you doing?"

The child startled, then immediately closed the page. "I was just doing some research, Mom," she said meekly, shutting down the whole computer. "I know I shouldn't be up so late, but I couldn't sleep. I'm sorry."

Leigh tried to slow her heart rate. She still could barely talk. "Researching what?"

Allison didn't answer immediately. She slipped past her mother and headed down the hall toward her room. "Just something animal related I'm working on," she said vaguely. "Sorry—I know pictures like that gross you out. I'm going to bed right now, promise. Goodnight!"

The child disappeared.

Leigh stood in the hall, staring after her daughter, her feet frozen to the floor.

A good night, indeed.

Chapter 21

Leigh walked frantically along Carson Street on the South Side, looking in the window of every tattoo parlor, every bar, her pulse throbbing in her ears. Where was she? Where had she gone?

Drunks spilled out of doorways; cars crashed and burst into flames; manhole covers exploded into the air releasing droves of rats who scurried up and onto the pavement around her feet. "Allison!" she screamed. "Allison!"

"What *is* it, Mom?" a lethargic voice drawled.

Leigh whipped her head toward the sound and walked down the trash-strewn alley. Tripping over crumpled beer cans and discarded syringes, she tried to reach the voice, but the refuse deepened until she was wading in it waist high. "Allison!"

"Will you chill?" her daughter said coolly as she emerged from an upright coffin leaning against a downspout. "What are you doing here, anyway?"

"I... I came to save you," Leigh sputtered.

"Save me from what?" protested the girl, who was at least seventeen, but looked thirty five. She was dressed entirely in black leather, though her arms and half her torso were bare, covered only by grotesque, elaborate tattoos of reptile skeletons. Her hair was a solid mass of spiky gel, black tinted with purple, and her lips and fingernails were green. "The dark master treats me well enough," she said with a shrug.

"You have to come home with me!" Leigh pleaded.

The girl considered, tapping her stiletto-heeled boots on pavement that smelled like a urinal. "I don't know," she said with a whine. "Maybe if you'd let me lease a horse..."

"Anything! Anything!"

"Mom? Do you know where my half chaps are?"

Leigh's mind turned cartwheels. She sat straight up in bed, her heart pounding.

Allison stood next to her, creamy-skinned and ten years old, dressed in riding pants and a pink top that said "Mustang Love" in silver glitter. Her hair was in a ponytail. She was shoeless; her socks were covered with blue horse silhouettes.

Leigh blinked, and her mind cleared. It was only a nightmare. *Thank God.*

"Mom!" her son's voice erupted from the doorway. "You didn't throw away my old skateboard, did you?"

The doorbell rang.

Leigh glanced at the clock and swore under her breath. How could she possibly have slept so late? She knew perfectly well that Cara was coming early this morning — the girls had a horseback riding lesson and the boys wanted to spend the time at the park.

"That skateboard had a broken wheel, remember?" she answered her son, jumping hastily out of bed. "You threw it away yourself when we got the new one."

"But I need two for the new trick Matt wants to show me!" Ethan lamented.

"So borrow your sister's," Leigh suggested, throwing on a robe and stumbling to her dresser for a hairbrush. She could hear Warren's voice in the living room; he was letting Cara in.

"But it's *pink!*" Ethan protested, clearly offended. But in the next second he shrugged it off. "Oh, Matt and I can just trade off, I guess. His new ramp is going to be *so* cool!"

"Mom?" Allison piped up calmly. "My half chaps?"

Leigh gave up on her hair, which nothing short of a shower would make a dent in. She had tossed and turned all night, and it showed. "I think you left them in the garage last week. They were pretty dirty, remember?"

Allison's small face broke into a broad smile. "Oh, yeah! Dozer's pee splashed *everywhere.*"

Leigh grimaced. "We'll try to clean them when you get back."

"Okay." The girl scampered off after her brother.

It was only a dream, Leigh reminded herself. She stepped into the bathroom, splashed some water on her face, and brushed her teeth. By the time she deemed herself presentable enough to enter the living room, Cara was ushering the Pack out the door.

"Don't worry about us, Leigh," Cara said cheerily, looking more like her old self than she had since before the murder. "Just finish that project for Gil. He seems really anxious about it." Her eyes twinkled as she spoke, and Leigh was sure her cousin was onto them both. But mercifully, she didn't seem to mind. She was too happy about finding a witness to Gil's alibi—not to mention the discovery of a new and promising alternative suspect.

The plans for the day were discussed, the Pack filed out, and Cara closed the door behind them. Leigh dropped onto her couch, and her lap filled immediately with cat. Mao settled and began to purr, and Leigh stroked her absently. She was frustrated. She and Warren had planned to have a talk with Allison first thing this morning. Now it would have to wait.

"I guess neither one of us slept well last night," Warren commented, straightening his tie in the living room mirror. "If it weren't for Ethan deciding to practice his trombone, I might still be sleeping myself."

Leigh's eyebrows rose. "Ethan was playing trombone?"

Warren chuckled. "Evidently, you had an even worse night than I did."

"It was horrific," Leigh admitted, describing her nightmare. At the end of it, Warren dropped down on the couch beside her. "You know you're making way too much of this," he said sensibly. "Allison wants to be a vet. She's positively brimming with natural curiosity. And with everything that's gone on lately, her thinking about death a little more than usual is perfectly understandable."

"I suppose," Leigh said skeptically.

"However," he continued, "I have to confess that you aren't the only one having creepy dreams. I couldn't stop thinking about Allison asking whether women could be serial killers. I got chased around by women all night."

"What kind of women?"

"The really scary kind," he said soberly. "The ones that look like nice, ordinary, efficient office workers."

"But really they're libidinous skanks who only want to steal you away from your wife so they can get at your money?" Leigh suggested.

"No. Really, they're blue-skinned, white-haired Andorians with antenna ears, and they're firing at me with disrupters."

Leigh groaned. "You seriously dreamed that?"

"I seriously did," he responded. "But at least I know that it was ridiculous. Only a Romulan or a Klingon would use a disrupter." He leaned over and hugged Leigh's shoulders, earning himself a resentful hiss and a swipe from Mao Tse, who hopped off Leigh's lap and stomped away into the kitchen. "That cat has never liked me," Warren bemoaned, standing up. "Don't worry about Allison. She's fine. But we'll have a talk with her tonight anyway—make sure she shares whatever's going on in that warp-speed mind of hers. Okay?"

"Okay," Leigh agreed.

"So, what are you going to do today?" he asked as he grabbed his briefcase.

"I have work to do at the office," she responded. "If I can concentrate. If I can't, I'll probably start investigating the case myself. Tail some suspects, steal some evidence, inject myself in the middle of some high-tension confrontations, thwart the police. You know. The usual."

Warren smiled and kissed her goodbye. "Have a good day, then."

"You too," she returned.

He headed downstairs for the garage, and Leigh got to her feet. She needed a shower and a very large cup of coffee, not necessarily in that order. She watched Warren's car through the window as it pulled out into the driveway and away toward town. She knew that he would indeed worry about her—but he was unlikely to say so. It was one of the reasons she loved him so much.

He had never tried to clip her wings.

Diana looked disdainfully at the selection of shoes Courtney Lyle had left in the back of Brandon's bedroom closet. If any of them were decent, she'd filch them. But they were all a couple years old, and the heels were scuffed. No wonder Courtney had left them in the first place. Same thing with the clothes. Nothing but sweats and hoodies, which no human besides Brandon had probably ever seen Courtney wear. Worthless.

Diana sighed and moved to Brandon's dresser drawers. The whole apartment was a mess—the police had searched it thoroughly, and Courtney had doubtless been through it as well.

What Diana was looking for, she didn't know herself. All she knew was that she'd woken up in a foul mood, and it only stood to get fouler. The work that Courtney was ridiculously overpaying her for would not last long, and her efforts to identify a new job prospect had thus far been fruitless.

This, she blamed on Brandon Lyle. Her hands rifled through his underclothes—he was a boxer man, of course—even as her cheeks flushed with ire at the thought of him. He was such a fake. He had pretended to be so rich, so successful... and by rights, he should have been. His family had money: *big* money, going way back. She had checked that out before she ever signed on. Brandon had the kind of old-money connections that could generally be counted on to keep any single idiot offspring from dragging the family name down into the ranks of the—gasp—middle class in one generation. But somehow, Brandon had managed it.

The man's financial incompetence boggled the mind. Diana pulled out a pair of cufflinks: slightly tarnished, but likely gold. She threw them in her duffel along with the rest of her things and moved on to the next drawer.

Brandon owed her. She had been fooled into thinking that he had money, that he would *always* have money, no matter how much of a moron he was. But she had found out otherwise—and all too late. Lyle Development was in deep doo-doo, so deep that what was left of Brandon's personal fortune would be swallowed up by his creditors in a trice. There was nowhere left for him to turn; he had already torched every single bridge that had connected him to his parents' wide circle of wealthy friends, including his unsympathetic father-in-law.

Diana's hand paused over Brandon's wide selection of ski liners. Of course he had freaked over the Nicholson project; it had been his absolute last chance to turn things around. The night Brandon went to that church meeting, he had been as desperate as he could possibly get. If the Nicholson project failed, not only would Lyle Development go bankrupt, but he himself would be personally destitute... not to mention profoundly humiliated.

Boo hoo.

Diana slammed the drawer closed with a scowl. Who in the world needed sixteen pairs of long underwear? Stupid playboy couldn't even ski!

She left the bedroom and moved to Brandon's desk. No doubt the police had already searched it thoroughly, but still, she had to try. There had to be something of use to her. She deserved it, after the way Brandon had screwed her over. In more ways than one.

She hadn't been stupid; she had prepared for contingencies. All along she'd been constructing a list of benefactors to whose even larger ships she could jump should things with Brandon ever go sour. But now her name would be forever associated with Lyle Development. With *failure*. No one had mentioned the word "fraud" yet, but she wouldn't put it past Brandon, especially at the end. Never mind that she was an administrative assistant and not a financial advisor—the fact was, it looked bad. Nobody who knew anything about Lyle Development would ever want to hire her.

Damn the man.

In a bottom drawer she spotted some address books, including a fraternity alumni roster. She flipped through it, her eyes narrowing as she read the entry for which she sought: Trevor Gil March.

Damn him, too.

She wished they were both dead. Gil's rotting in jail would be some consolation, but to her annoyance, he still hadn't been arrested. How much fake evidence did those idiot detectives need to find? How much more motive did she have to shed light on? Would they get it if she hired a skywriter to blast "Gil March whacked Brandon Lyle" above the Golden Triangle?

She slammed the book shut and threw it back in the drawer. Perhaps there was something left in the apartment that could incriminate the prig. Like nude pictures of herself in Brandon's bed... discovered in Gil's glove compartment?

She laughed out loud. No such pictures existed at the moment, but it would be fun to take some. And how delicious for that saccharine wife of his to be the one who found them...

Diana's grin faded. An image had crept into her head; an image that had, much to her annoyance, kept her tossing and turning all night. A silly thing, really, but disturbing. The female detective, the one who never talked, had in Diana's nightmares been sitting in a chair in the corner of her bedroom, staring at her. Who does that? Just sitting and staring, completely silent, but wearing that secretive, malicious, *knowing* smile...

Diana's shoulders gave a shiver. "It was just a stupid dream!" she told herself, getting to her feet again. But she discarded the cheesecake photo idea. She was in no danger from the police at present; she had covered her tracks well. But there was no point in taking unnecessary risks. Particularly when the odds were—sadly—

that Gil would eventually be cleared anyway.

Her jaws clenched. She hadn't realized until yesterday that the accursed female detective was a friend of Gil's family. It figured he would get special treatment. He'd had family tied up in the land deal, and it was his wife's cousin who found the body—the same one who had been Brandon's contact at the ad agency. A little too coincidental, *n'est ce pas?* And why weren't the police out investigating *her*, pray tell?

Diana's cheeks flared again. *Damn Gil March!* He was going to walk away from this whole mess scot free, while she was left twisting in the wind, jobless, with no payoff, her professional reputation permanently tarnished.

Damn him to hell.

"Well, hello there."

Diana whirled toward the condo's front door. She had been an idiot not to lock it behind her. But it was too late now. The door had been opened, and a man was standing just inside of it.

One of the best-looking men she had ever seen.

"Well," she responded, matching his smooth, seductive macho tone with her own, equally expert femme fatale one. "Hello to you, too. Whoever the hell you are."

The man smiled. Diana drank him in, noting every detail from his thick crop of silvery hair to his strong, square jawline, broad shoulders, washboard stomach, and well-toned everything else. He was dressed in the kind of outfit stores in New York would sell only to certain people and stores in Pittsburgh didn't bother to stock. His features were perfect in the same unnatural Hollywood way that Gil March was perfect, but whereas Gil was sunshine and sailboats, this man was fine wine and fast cars. He studied her with an equal lack of self-consciousness, his dark eyes glinting mischievously.

"I could ask you the same question," he replied, his speech a bewitching blend of the urbane and the irreverent. "This is the home of Brandon Lyle, is it not?"

Diana's heart beat wildly. She knew who the man was, of course. She had known it from the moment she set eyes on him. At best, he had anger management issues. At worst, he could be a murderer.

Whatever.

"It is," she replied. "But if you're looking for Brandon, you're out of luck. Permanently."

The man showed no visible reaction. "So I heard," he admitted. "In fact, I was looking for... his widow. And who might you be?"

Sometimes it was fun to lie. Other times, the truth was even better.

"I would be his mistress," she said silkily. "Otherwise known as his administrative assistant. His widow doesn't live here anymore. Not that she ever did, really."

Courtney should kiss her feet for that one. Why had she said it? She didn't know.

"Do you have any idea where I might find her?" the man asked politely. He had taken no step forward, but remained stationary just inside the door as if, despite having barged into another man's condo uninvited, he felt obliged to follow some unwritten code of propriety.

Diana's eyes drank in his solid form once more. She wondered if he was concealing a weapon. She had no doubt he'd be a better shot than Brandon.

She had no doubt he did a lot of things better than Brandon.

"I don't know where she's staying now," Diana admitted, feigning disinterest. "But I do hear from her occasionally. Any message?"

The man did not respond. He merely smiled at her for a moment, as if assessing her sincerity. Diana knew that she should flinch. But she didn't. Instead she merely shrugged and leaned over to tidy some of the knick-knacks on Brandon's desk, making sure to do so in an enticing—yet ever so innocent—manner.

Everything about this man should scare the crap out of her.

But damn, he was hot.

"It's very important that I find her," the man said finally, his deep, sexy voice caressing her like velvet. "I only just heard of her husband's death on the news. I need to speak with her."

On the news? Diana thought skeptically. *In Chicago?* Brandon's death might have created a stir locally—for all of forty-eight hours—but no way did he rate national coverage. Even in Pittsburgh, the news stories had been maddeningly short on detail. But one could always search online.

Diana considered. This man might be a danger to her; then again, he might not. The "might not" was worth hanging onto.

"What does her husband's death matter to you?" she asked

brazenly.

The man lifted one perfectly shaped eyebrow. He studied her another moment. Then, he surprised her.

"I want to know everything about it," he said flatly.

Diana's lips stretched into a smile. She did love a man who laid it on the line.

"He was shot to death Monday night, near a church where he'd just had a business meeting. The police haven't made an arrest yet."

"Who is suspected?" he pressed.

Diana shook her head. "They're not telling me. But frankly, I think they're spinning their wheels."

"You are a suspect yourself?" he asked, his voice sympathetic.

"I would be, I suppose," she responded. "But I happen to have an alibi."

"And Courtney?"

Diana stiffened. On his lips, the woman's name seemed a purr.

"I would imagine she's a suspect, too," she answered shortly.

The man smiled at her. "Where did it happen exactly? You said a church?"

"The Church of the Horizon, in Franklin Park," she answered honestly. Why the hell shouldn't she? "But he wasn't shot in the church, or even in the parking lot. His car was parked there, but he was shot somewhere back in the woods."

The man frowned. "How far back?"

It was Diana's turn to raise an eyebrow. What *did* this man want? "I don't know, exactly. The police were not inclined to tell me, or the media either for that matter. But if you really want to know, you can stroll down the North Side to Hook, Inc., and ask for Leigh Koslow. She's the one who found his body."

Take that, cousin of Cara!

"What kind of gun was it?"

Diana worked her lower jaw. The man's interest in Brandon Lyle was beginning to vex her. She would much rather discuss herself. "Why don't you call the police and ask them?"

The man seemed taken aback, but only for a second. His dark eyes twinkled suddenly, then raked down her perfectly posed figure.

That's better!

"I'm sorry to bother you," he said insincerely, "but it is extremely important that I find Courtney Lyle. I understand she may be running from the police. But I promise you, I only want to help her."

Diana didn't answer for a moment. She didn't give a rat's behind about Courtney, but she did care—quite a bit—about Mr. Mysterious. Was he a dangerous homicidal maniac... or wasn't he?

He made a sudden movement, and Diana started. He was only reaching for his wallet, but the gesture had shifted his jacket enough to reveal a quick glint of steel.

Well, damn. He was carrying.

Diana's pulse raced. Her face flushed with heat.

The man took a step toward her. He extended a business card.

Diana reached out and took it. It was plain white, with simple black lettering centered in the middle. Just a phone number, email, and name.

Bruce Anjelo.

"If you find out where Courtney is, can you let me know?" he asked, his voice dropping to a husky whisper. "I promise, I'll be grateful."

Diana's heart fluttered. "I do have her phone number," she offered.

The man gave a lopsided smile. "So do I."

He turned and took a step toward the door, then stopped and faced her again. "Does she have any friends in town that you know of? Somebody she might be staying with?"

Diana didn't have a clue. But she didn't want this god of the darkness to walk out of her life just yet, either. She pondered a moment. Then she smiled.

"She does have one college friend in town that I know of. A friend of Brandon's, too. His name is Gil March. Perhaps you've heard of him? He runs a very successful financial consulting firm. He might know where she is."

Or not. Either way, it will be a delightful exchange.

"Thanks for that," he returned. His eyes held hers. "And your name?"

Are you as turned on as I am?

"Diana. Diana Saxton."

"Thank you, Diana," he said smoothly, stepping out the door. "I'll remember that. And you."

I certainly hope so.

"Goodbye, Bruce," she dared.

"Goodbye," he returned.

He shut the door behind him.

Chapter 22

Leigh sat at her desk, fidgeting. She had a sick feeling in her stomach. She had had a sick feeling in her stomach ever since the first mention of Courtney's potentially violent paramour, and it had only gotten sicker when she caught sight of Allison's computer "research." Yet at the same time, she was starving.

Her body had one twisted sense of humor.

"Alice!" she called over the low wall of her semiprivate office. The four founders of Hook, Inc., once co-worker drones at another, giant ad agency which had canned them all simultaneously, had managed to stay good friends even through the firm's early days of near-starvation.

"Ye-ess?" the graphic design head drawled in a sarcastic tone.

"Did we eat all that popcorn Jeff brought in last week?"

"*You* did, yes."

Leigh sighed. She had consumed her hastily packed lunch quite some time ago, but her blood sugar seemed unaware of it.

"Is there anything else?"

"Motria brought in some babka."

"Are you kidding? That's long gone."

"What about Merry's deer jerky?"

Leigh grimaced. Merry's husband was a skilled outdoorsman, but there were rumors of him appropriating road kill. "Pass."

"So go get some of that sugar-free hard candy on Mary Rose's desk."

"That's not food!"

Alice's scowling face appeared over the divider. Though her scowls were always good-natured, you wouldn't know it to look at her. "Go home!" she ordered.

"I still have work to do," Leigh insisted.

"Any trifling thing you might accomplish when you're in a mood like this will be more than cancelled out by the work you're *preventing* me from doing. Now, get the hell out of here and go soothe your nerves with a burger or a candy bar or some damn thing." Alice made a violent shooing motion. "Vamoose!'"

Leigh started to protest, but was interrupted by the ringing of her phone. Alice made one more fierce gesture, then disappeared again. Leigh reached out and picked up the handset. "Hook, Inc. This is Leigh."

"Hey, Leigh. Gerry here."

Leigh's blood pressure kicked up a notch. The voice was friendly and familiar, and by itself no longer constricted every sphincter in her body. Though her relationship with Lieutenant Gerald Frank had begun less than amicably — to say the least — she had long since buried the hatchet with her best friend's husband. For a long time the detectives' courtship had seemed like the stuff of Leigh's nightmares, but when poor Maura had lost her mother and both elderly aunts within a year — the same year during which her two best pals were completely consumed with their newborn twins — Gerry Frank had been her rock. He had supported her through it all, with the utmost love and understanding, and when Maura had at last decided to marry him, Leigh had been the most approving matron of honor in history.

But he never called her at the office.

"Is something wrong?" she asked quickly.

"No, no," he assured. "Nothing that I know of. I'd say it's more of a curiosity. I just came by the house and picked up a phone message from your daughter. She was trying to reach Maura."

Leigh's pulse began to pound. "Allison was calling Maura? Why?"

There was a pause. "I was hoping you might know. Allie didn't sound upset in the message, just her usual calm, cool, intellectual self. But she did say, and I quote, 'it's rather urgent.' I tried to call her back, but no one picked up at your house. And I can't reach Maura either — she must be on a call. I figured you'd want to know."

"Yes," Leigh answered unsteadily. "I certainly would. Thanks so much for calling, Gerry. I'll figure it out."

"No problem, Leigh. And by the way, your pickled beets were awesome."

She smiled faintly. Ordinarily, hearing anyone say that any food she prepared was "awesome" would be cause for celebration, even if said recipe did have only two steps and four ingredients. But at present, her capacity for celebration was limited. She thanked him again and hung up.

Why on earth did Allison want to talk to Maura? What was so "urgent" she couldn't tell her mother about it?

Leigh pulled out her own phone and dialed Cara's cell. "The Pack is fine, Leigh," her cousin said by way of greeting. "Is everything okay with you?"

Leigh let out a breath. "I'm all right," she responded unconvincingly. "What is Allison doing now?"

"I just dropped her off at the clinic," Cara answered. "She had some project she said your dad was helping her with. He told me I could leave her there all afternoon. Do you think you could swing by and pick her up on your way home?"

"Sure," Leigh said hastily. "Listen, what kind of project was she talking about? Did you know that she's been trying to call Maura?"

Cara was silent a moment. "That's odd. Allison never asked to use my phone. She must have called from the house when she was changing out of her riding clothes. As for the project, I have no idea. She was carrying something around in a shoe box. She wouldn't let Lenna look at it—said it might upset her. I didn't think anything about that; Lenna can flip out over a stink bug. What do you think Allison could be up to?"

"I don't know," Leigh responded, grabbing her bag from her file drawer. "But I'm going over to the clinic right now to find out."

"Woohoo!" came a voice from over the wall.

Leigh said goodbye, hung up, gave an obsequious bow to Alice, and departed. She walked down two flights of stairs to street level and headed out through the lobby. A trio of men boarded the elevator as she passed.

Gray hair, dark eyes.

Leigh whipped her head around. As the elevator doors closed, her eyes studied a gray-haired man in a suit and tie.

Tall and solidly built.

He was at most five foot five.

She released a breath and moved on.

She needed to get a grip. Even if the man Courtney was frightened of had pursued his married girlfriend to Pittsburgh, there was no reason for him to be stalking her college classmate's wife's cousin at her place of business! Leigh had enough to worry about with her daughter right now—she did not need to invent gratuitous bogeymen.

She walked out the front door and headed toward the stadium parking lot. Why *did* the specter of Courtney's Chicago man spook her so much? Was she merely projecting her fears onto him, when what really worried her was something else?

She cast an offhand glance back at the Hook building, then froze. A tall, solidly built gray-haired man was striding toward its entrance. A younger woman was approaching at the same time from the opposite direction. He smiled and held open the door for her.

What else had Gil said? Fiftyish? Expensive taste in wardrobe? Leigh continued staring.

The man was wearing jeans and a black and gold Steelers' jersey. He stepped inside after the woman and closed the door.

Stop being ridiculous! Leigh chastised herself. Steelers' jerseys didn't exactly come cheap, but "sophisticated" was pushing it. She was an idiot, and she had to pull herself together.

Whether Courtney's mobster had anything to do with Brandon's murder or not, neither had any connection with Allison's "project" — and that was her number one concern. She turned once more towards her car and began walking rapidly. This time, she did not look back.

Diana Saxton walked into the posh reception room in which she had practically lived for half a year. Little had changed since then, except for the charming throw pillows she had suggested purchasing for the loveseat and armchair. They had been removed and replaced with nothing.

Sanctimonious ass.

"Can I help you?" The sharp eyes of the slight, well-dressed man behind the reception desk widened slightly as he looked at her, but his composure didn't otherwise alter. Diana watched with amusement as his hand moved subtly into position under the lip of the desk near the phone. One button alerted Gil to take a look at the reception-room monitor mounted on his bookcase. The other rang straight to security.

"The one on the left, I think," Diana said with a smile. "The one on the right would be overkill. After all, it's not like I'm armed.

See?" She put her hands in the shallow pockets of her linen suit coat and lifted it, revealing a sleeveless silk tank and no bra.

The man's gaze remained utterly impassive.

Clearly, he was gay.

"What is it you want, Ms. Saxton?" he said flatly.

"I want to see Mr. March, of course," she replied airily. "And if I'm—"

The interior door swung open. The mogul himself stood before her.

"Not mistaken," she finished smugly, "he should be joining us any second now."

"Shall I complete the procedure, Mr. March?" Diana's replacement asked briskly. He was standing now, but keeping one hand on the magic button all the while.

"You can call security if you want," she said lightly. "But then you won't find out why I came here. And you should be curious, given how foolish it was for me to do so."

Gil's cold green eyes smoldered like dry ice. "Nothing you do could ever surprise me, Diana," he said acidly.

They stared at each other for a long moment. Then Gil turned to his new assistant. "Call security on the phone," he ordered. "Tell them to send someone up. But let's not have her thrown out just yet. We might get lucky. She might say something incriminating first."

He swung his office door open wide and gestured Diana inside with mock gallantry. She entered and moved toward his giant mahogany desk. He followed her in, but left the door propped open.

"You have three minutes," he snapped. "What do you want?"

Diana surveyed his perfectly proportioned body and chiseled male bone structure with an uncomfortable mix of lust and loathing. How could anything so beautiful be so... useless?

Well, perhaps not *utterly* useless. Not if she played her cards right.

"All I want," Diana began, keeping her tone even, "is what I was entitled to at the time you unjustly fired me."

Gil's ears emitted steam. Or at least, they would if they could.

"We both know why you were fired," he said coldly. "And I don't owe you a damn thing."

"I beg to differ," Diana replied. "I was fired because I refused to commit adultery with you, which by any legal definition is sexual harassment. I didn't file suit at the time because I wanted to move on, and it so happened that I had already received a standing job offer."

Gil had turned purple again. She had seen him like that once before — when he came out of his hotel shower in a towel to find her lounging nude on his bed.

It was a moment she would never forget.

Never.

"But now," she continued, "I have unfortunately found myself unemployed again. And I would like a reference. Nothing more than I deserve, merely an honest appraisal of my *business* skills, which we both know were exemplary in every way. Is that so much to ask... under the circumstances?"

Her former employer seemed to have difficulty in speaking.

"You know the kind of situation I'm looking for," she continued, allowing herself the slightest of smiles. "I prefer an intimately small corporation, but a highly profitable one, one that stands poised to make full use of my... business acumen. One where the principals work closely together, such that a savvy administrative assistant such as myself would have full opportunity to gain the admiration and... gratitude of her employer. It's all about financial security, after all."

"Get out," Gil growled under his breath.

"I have two minutes left," she returned breezily. "And unfortunately it looks like I'll need them, as you seem disinclined to give me what I deserve."

"Doing that would put me in prison."

Diana caught herself in a snarl. *Stay cool. Make it clear, but inadmissible. Damned prig is probably recording every word.*

She sighed. "I am trying to be reasonable with you, Gil. I certainly think I've been reasonable so far, in not hiring a lawyer and demanding damages. But to be honest, I've been afraid to. Ever since I got closer to Brandon and he told me some things about you. About your... time in Philadelphia."

Gil stiffened.

Paydirt!

"I didn't believe him at first," she pressed. "I didn't think you would ever have been capable of... of something like..." She let her voice trail off.

Gil's cold eyes bore into hers. "Go on," he ordered. "You didn't think I was capable of what?"

Diana's brow furrowed. This wasn't the reaction he was supposed to have. He was supposed to be turning purple again. Or at least a nice shade of puce. What the hell *had* he done in Philadelphia, anyway? Brandon had always insisted he could shake Gil down but good if it ever proved necessary. Leave it to Brandon to get himself whacked without imparting the crucial information. But she hadn't thought she would need it. The mere threat should be sufficient.

"You *know* what," she retorted confidently.

To her astonishment, Gil March burst out laughing. His assistant appeared immediately in the doorway, a uniformed security guard standing behind him.

"What's so funny?!" Diana demanded hotly.

"You don't have a clue what happened in Philadelphia!" Gil proclaimed. "Brandon didn't tell you jack about it. But you know what's really funny? Would you like to hear? *Brandon* didn't know jack about it! He and his buddies got messed up in something illegal, and it's all been so long ago now that the idiot *forgot* I was never a part of it! He didn't even bring it up until the night he died—and I would have set him straight right there and then if he hadn't chosen that moment to take a swing at me!"

Diana felt the blood draining slowly from her face. Gil could be lying. But she knew that he wasn't. *Damnation.* Why, oh why did Brandon Lyle have to be such a friggin' moron?

"Would you like me to escort her out of the building, Mr. March?" the security guard said loudly, stepping forward.

"That won't be necessary," Diana assured, calling on every ounce of her willpower to maintain her composure. "If Brandon misinformed me, then I'm sure I have nothing to fear from Mr. March." She sidled over to the security guard as if he had arrived for her personal protection. "But please do consider my request," she said formally. "All I ask for is a positive job reference. I am an excellent administrative assistant, and my work performance for you was flawless. I am willing to forgive the unfortunate manner in which my employment here was terminated, provided you will offer me the very minimal courtesy of assisting me, in an honest and unbiased manner, to find other suitable employment."

Nicely played.

Diana threw back her shoulders and smiled to herself. Every word she'd said could be played back in court—it wouldn't hurt her. But he had received her message, loud and clear.

Gil's hard eyes locked on hers. He must know she still had the upper hand. The blackmail threat had merely been the cherry on top. A public accusation of sexual harassment could ruin his reputation; if she wanted, she could do worse. Had she not already shown him just how dangerous she could be? The self-righteous bastard was putty in her hands.

"Diana," Gil responded, his deep voice steady. *"Go to hell."*

Chapter 23

Leigh fought the nearly irresistible urge to reach over and grab her buzzing phone. Someone was texting her. But she was driving, it was illegal, and she was two minutes from her destination. When she reached the street by the clinic she pulled off in the first available space, threw the van in park, and practically dove for the device.

The text was from Maura. Her fingers trembled as she opened it. "Call me when you can," it said simply. There was also a voice mail message from her father. "Can you come by the clinic? Allison has something she needs to explain to you."

Leigh leapt out of the van and beat hasty steps to the clinic's basement door. When she passed Maura's beat-up car on the way, her anxiety reached new heights. *Why was Maura here? What the heck was going on?*

She flew through the wash room and kennel room and headed for the stairs; but before she reached them, she heard voices coming from her father's "office." She walked into the back basement corner where his small metal desk sat perpetually buried in papers and where stacks of dog food bags served as furniture. No one in the room was sitting down. Randall, Maura, and Allison were all standing in a huddle at the desk, looking down at something.

"What's going on?!" Leigh demanded breathlessly.

For a moment, no one answered her. Only when she was certain her head would explode did Maura speak. "Nothing to panic about, Koslow," she said smoothly. "At least, I hope it's not. Come and take a look."

The detective stepped back, and Leigh moved forward. The object at which they all stared was a broken bone.

"I don't get it," she said blankly.

"It's the bone Chewie found, Mom," Allison said softly. "The one he left in the van."

Leigh's eyes widened. She leaned in for a closer look. To her eye, the object looked nothing like the gnarled, mud-covered mess she had seen Chewie dragging through the woods. That had looked like a half-chewed, long-forgotten, perfectly harmless hunk of factory-shaped rawhide. Then again, she had never looked at it closely.

When washed off, cleaned up and dried, there really was no doubt. She was looking at an actual bone. From the looks of it, the top half of a femur.

A disturbingly large femur.

"I know you told me to throw it away," Allison said sheepishly. "But I really didn't think it was a rawhide, and I wanted Grandpa to see it."

Leigh grit her teeth in frustration. "But why didn't you tell me?"

Allison cast a quick glance at Randall. "Because I didn't want you to get all upset," she explained. "I know how much it bothers you to think about... bodies and stuff. And I thought, if it was just a deer bone or something, well... you wouldn't have to hear about it."

Leigh's heart began a slippery descent to the pit of her stomach. She looked at her father.

He cleared his throat. "It's the top part of a femur," he said evenly. "I'm no forensic anthropologist; but to me, it looks pretty old. Brittle, with no trace of soft tissue left."

Leigh's heart sloshed on down to her toes. "Anthropologist?" she repeated weakly.

Randall nodded. "Like I said, I'm no expert. But that bone didn't come from a dog or a deer. The shape and angle of the head are wrong."

"That's what I thought," Allison added proudly. "I looked it up."

Leigh turned to her daughter, and a tiny ray of light brightened the otherwise macabre thoughts swimming in her head. So that's what the girl had been doing online!

"The hip joint is different in quadrupeds, even bears," Allison continued. "So I figured we'd better call Aunt Mo."

Leigh's stunned gaze moved toward her friend. The policewoman offered a slight, sympathetic smile. "Don't worry, Koslow," she said calmly. "I can't blame you for this one, since you weren't the one who found it. Technically, Chewie was."

Leigh swallowed. There was no use hoping she was hearing all this wrong. "You think it's..."

"Human remains," Maura finished for her. "More than likely. We'll let the lab tell us for sure. But as your dad says, it looks old.

Are you aware of any family cemeteries out near your Aunt's house? We could be dealing with something as simple as a shallow grave resurfacing from erosion. It happens."

Leigh's breathing began to steady. *An old cemetery.* Of course. That would be where old bones came from, wouldn't it? Why had the mere mention of human remains made her mind jump immediately to murder?

She preferred not to answer that question.

"I don't know, but it's possible," she answered. "I can ask Aunt Bess."

"Do you remember exactly where Chewie found it?" Maura asked.

Leigh shook her head. "We'd been out at the pond, but I only noticed it when we got back closer to the house. He was off leash the whole time—he could have dragged it from anywhere."

"How long a time did he have to dig it up?" Maura asked.

Leigh considered. "Not very long. Maybe twenty minutes. But I saw him periodically without it. I don't think he could have dug very long in any one spot—more likely he just picked it up somewhere."

Maura's brow knitted thoughtfully. "Then it could have been dug up first by some other dog, some other place, and Chewie just stumbled across it."

Leigh nodded. "Sorry," she apologized. "I wish I'd paid more attention."

Maura clapped her friend on the back. It was not a full-strength Polanski backclap—the kind even Warren had to brace himself for. But it nevertheless pitched Leigh forward a good six inches. "Not your fault, Koslow," Maura proclaimed charitably. "You've had a lot on your mind this week, after all."

Leigh's eyebrow arched. She bit back the words she was tempted to say, namely, *who are you and what have you done with Maura Polanski?* She stole a bemused glance at Allison. If Maura's less-than-irate response to opening up yet another case file with the Koslow name in it had anything to do with her daughter's presence—which it undoubtedly did—she owed the child a cookie.

Maura placed the bone carefully into a brown paper bag. "I'll get this down to the lab. It may take a while for a final verdict, but in the meantime I'd like to see if there's any more lying around where this came from." She turned to Leigh. "Do you think if we took Chewie to Bess's now, he might head back to the same spot?"

Leigh considered. A bloodhound, the dog was not. Nor was she convinced that the place where he found the bone would hold any more interest for him now than the places where he had found the dead sparrow, Brandon Lyle's body, or the empty cat food containers that fell out of Bess's recycling bin.

But it was worth a shot. "It's possible," she said dubiously.

"Let's try it, then," Maura suggested. "I need to take a look around the area myself, anyway. And ask Bess about any local gravesites."

"I know of one," Allison's small voice piped up.

The adults all turned to look at her.

"You do?" Leigh asked. "Where?"

"I've never been there," Allison noted. "But I've heard of it. It's somewhere on Mr. Clem's property—that's why we haven't explored it. But Aunt Bess told us once that there were gravestones there from the 1800s. Not a whole cemetery or anything, just like two or three from one family."

"Good memory, Allison," Maura praised. "Thanks. We'll check that out, too." She looked back at Leigh. "Can I meet you—and Chewie—over at Bess's in an hour? That'll give me time to get this bone to the lab."

Leigh nodded mutely. She was proud of her daughter's good memory, too. She just wished the child could have remembered something a little less death related.

Diana's face felt hot. Her entire body felt hot. Not because of the blazing July sun that was currently frying the concrete plaza in front of the high-rent skyscraper that housed Gil March's office. No. Her heat was generated internally.

She hated Gil March with a passion.

He had humiliated her once, and he had suffered for it. But apparently he hadn't suffered enough. Not when he still refused to respect her, to fear her. And he should fear her. Oh yes, he should! Yet instead, he had humiliated her. *Again*. It was not to be tolerated.

It *would not* be tolerated.

She perched her lithe body on the stone rim of the plaza's sterile, artless water fountain. The water looked hot. If she touched it, she was sure it would boil. Just like her blood.

She forced herself to a take deep breaths. Explosion was not her style. She needed to calm down. To think. To *plan*.

Her gaze passed over the pedestrians strolling in front of her — their clothing an appalling mishmash of cheap, tattoo-revealing rags and stuffy business suits. Pittsburgh's "business district" could be walked end to end in less time than it took to polish one's nails — at least, to polish them properly. She needed to get out of this city. To make a fresh start somewhere else, somewhere more exciting, more sophisticated, somewhere much, much bigger...

But not quite yet. First, she must finish her unfinished business.

She made a growling sound under her breath and shifted her hips on the stone. Her gaze scanned over the crowd again — and then stopped short.

It was *him*.

He was dressed differently from this morning: less expensively, less conspicuously. His suit was run of the mill, mimicking an executive trying to impress on a less-than-impressive salary. But this man couldn't help but wear it well. As he stepped from the sidewalk onto the plaza Diana watched no fewer than three younger women turn their heads at him. It occurred to her that she hadn't yet had the pleasure of watching him walk away from her. She would have to fix that. But not just yet.

His dark eyes met hers, and his steps changed course.

A ripple of thrill shot through her.

"Hello again, Bruce," she said invitingly, recrossing her legs. "I see you're following up on my advice."

He paused a step in front of her. "Were you waiting for me?" he said without expression.

Diana laughed. "Don't flatter yourself. I have business in this building that's nothing to do with you. Business that went wretchedly, I might add. I'm resting here to soothe my wounded pride... running into you again is an unexpected treat."

What *was* it about this man that made it so easy for her to tell the truth? The proportion of lies she told him was way below average.

"Any luck locating Courtney?" she dared.

He shook his head slowly. "Not yet. Of course, you could have tipped her off."

Diana frowned. "Why would I do that?"

He stared back at her. "Why, indeed?"

Diana's jaws clenched. She did wish she could get on his good side. Without his knowing she was trying, of course. A man like him could be so... *useful.*

Like a flame igniting in her chest, the idea arose. As it spread through her veins like hot lava, her mouth curved into a smile.

Why not?

"I told you that I don't know where Courtney is staying, and I don't," she said levelly, looking him straight in his devilish eyes. "But if you're putting yourself out to try and help her, you needn't bother. As I learned only this morning, she's well protected."

Diana watched the tell-tale muscle in his jaw. It popped out, right on cue.

"Protected by whom?" he said in a low voice.

She swallowed her annoyance at the man's obvious dedication to Courtney. She was using it, wasn't she?

"Look, Bruce," she explained, "I don't know what's up with you and Courtney, and I have no reason to care about either of you. But I do hate to see a man like you, who can obviously do better, getting jerked around by a woman like her."

Outwardly, he remained impassive. But Diana could feel the ambient air temperature rise a degree.

"I mean, I'll admit," she continued, carefully blending lies with the truth, "I made a play for March. He's married, but he's rich and he's hot. Can you blame me? But Courtney doesn't need him. She's got money of her own. What's the appeal? I mean, hell — you're *way* sexier than he is! And here you are, come to rescue her — her husband's grave not even cold yet — and she's already doing another man!"

Diana refrained from looking Bruce straight in the face. He wore murderous rage extremely well, but still — it was a private moment.

"I'm sorry," she lied, her voice sheepish. "I shouldn't have been so blunt. But that's the way it is. I thought you'd want to know."

Bruce said nothing. He lifted his head and looked up at the top floors of the office building.

Excellent.

"If you still want to find Courtney," she said with a practiced sulk, "he'll know where she is. But he's not going to tell you. He's nothing but a damned bully."

The man started to walk away, toward the building.

Diana rose, enjoying the view. "Bruce?" she said tentatively.

He turned. His face was a mask of stone.

"There's a button hidden on the receptionist's desk, near the phone. It's silent, but it rings straight to security."

His beautiful, masculine lips curved into a smirk. His eyes raked her figure again, from face to toes and back. "Diana," he said, more to himself, seemingly, than to her. "Diana Saxton."

He turned around, strode toward the main doors, and disappeared inside the building.

"What are you doing here?"

Diana whirled, then startled at the unexpected sight of Courtney Lyle, who stood before her dressed to the nines in her usual low-cut, perfectly tailored linen dress and sexy heels. Her concession to looking inconspicuous, apparently, was to wear designer sunglasses and tie a scarf around her head, á la Jackie O. Her voice was tight.

"I could ask you the same question," Diana replied slowly, stalling for inspiration. *Crap!* Why did the woman have to come here, now?

"I'm picking up something from Gil," she answered shortly. "I thought you were working at the office today."

"I finished early," Diana returned. In fact, she had been at the Lyle Development office all of about two hours. The new "business guru" was a pompous idiot who kept telling her she'd done everything wrong, and she'd left him to stew in his own juices for a while.

"Just get it done," Courtney snapped. Without another word, she turned and walked away toward the building.

Diana's pulse quickened. The last thing she needed was for Lover Boy to run into the widow Lyle prematurely. He was on a mission, and she needed for him to finish it. She watched ruefully as Courtney's long legs strutted away from her. Painful as it was for her to admit, she could understand Bruce's near-obsession with a woman *not* young enough to be his daughter. The bubblehead was terribly well-preserved. Diana could only hope to look so good at her age, dammit.

"I saw him," she called out.

The long legs stopped. Courtney spun around and whipped off

her shades. "You saw *who?*"

Diana said the words slowly, watching with pleasure as all color drained from the other woman's face. "Bruce Anjelo."

Courtney's breathing became jagged. After a moment of paralysis, she rushed to Diana's side and grabbed her arm roughly. "Where? Where was he?"

Diana brushed off the arm and nodded her head toward the building. "He just went in."

Courtney's wide eyes scanned the front of the building. "Are you sure? Why? How do you know it was him?"

"How else would I get his name?" Diana answered. "He came by the apartment this morning looking for you. We chatted a bit. Now he's looking for Gil."

"But why?!" Courtney demanded.

Diana shrugged. "As a way to get to you, perhaps."

Courtney's eyes flashed fire. "You're insane. You'd do anything to hurt Gil, wouldn't you?"

Diana shrugged again. "I'm afraid I don't know what you're talking about. I thought that Gil might know where you were staying; I was only trying to accommodate Mr. Anjelo. He seems determined to find and help you, even though you insist on running from him." She faked a dramatic sigh. "I really don't know why you're doing that, by the way. The man's a total hottie. Those muscles, the clothes, that shiny piece—"

"What?!" Courtney exploded. "He had a gun with him? You saw it?"

"Well, I don't think he'd strap on that holster just to carry a can opener," Diana commented. "You're not really afraid of him, are you?"

"Hell yes, I'm afraid of him! And you should be too, you vicious wench!" Courtney turned and stared up at the windows on the top floor. "Gil will know who he is," she said to herself. "He'll call security right away. Then they'll get him."

Diana's brow furrowed. "What do you mean, Gil will know who he is? How could he?"

Courtney paced with short steps, ignoring her. "They'll find the gun; he'll be detained..." She stopped abruptly. "I've got to get out of here!" Without another word to Diana, she turned away from the building and strutted off as fast as her towering heels would carry her.

Diana watched her go, all confidence in her own brilliant plan suddenly flagging. She hadn't expected Bruce to do anything to Gil *now*, here in the building—satisfying as that image was. She figured the Chicagoan would just check him out, get the lay of the land; then take care of him later. Guys like Bruce didn't walk around free if they weren't also crafty.

But she hadn't reckoned on Courtney's bothering to warn Gil about her pursuer, which was an oversight. If Bruce strolled into the office on any pretext, he could be recognized. He could be questioned, even arrested if his gun wasn't legal. Worse yet, he'd lose any chance he might have had to make a good, clean hit and get out of town!

Diana looked to the left and right. She looked at the entrance, at the windows. If security did approach Bruce, what would he do? She was certain she had stirred his bad-boy blood into a full-blown jealous rage. Would he keep his cool and talk his way out of it? Or would he lose it, reach under his jacket, draw his weapon...

She let out a long, slow breath.

What the hell had she started?

Chapter 24

"Go on, Chewie!" Leigh urged, waving her arms. "Go and frolic. Be free!"

The dog gave a little skip, looked up at her happily, panted, and circled her ankles. Then he circled Allison's. Then Bess's.

Then he sat on Maura's foot.

Leigh sighed. "Your lead is off, Chewie. Go play!"

The dog jumped off Maura's foot, came closer, and stared at Leigh expectantly.

"He thinks you're going to feed him," Allison commented.

"He always *hopes* I'm going to feed him," Leigh agreed. "He also knows darn well it isn't dinner time."

Bess chuckled. "Ah well, hope springs eternal."

"Poor Chewie," Allison crooned. The dog immediately switched allegiance and thrust his wet nose against her skinny calf. "He has no idea what we want."

"Hmmm," Bess murmured. "I might have something to help with that." She ambled off toward the back of her house, while the others stood waiting in the back yard. Bess's entire tribe of cats seemed to have gathered along the window ledge of the screened porch to watch them, and the felines were in such near-perfect formation they looked like targets in an arcade game.

Chewie continued staring up at Allison, ignoring the tempting cats completely. He would chase anything that ran from him, as a rule, but he hadn't come within four feet of a cat since his first—and last—encounter with Mao Tse.

"This might spark his memory!" Bess announced, rejoining them with something in her closed hand. Chewie's ears perked immediately. "Take a good whiff, boy!" she urged, holding out the fist. "Now, go get it!" She feigned making a long throw out toward the direction of the pond.

Chewie licked his lips and sat down.

"Go find it!" Bess urged again.

Chewie lay down completely.

Allison giggled. "He knows it's still in your hand, Aunt Bess."

"Well, hell's bells," Bess said with annoyance, opening her hand to show the rest of them the soup bone. "I can't very well give it to him now—he'll be busy for an hour."

"He's not allowed to have bones anyway," Leigh stated.

Bess sighed and walked to her trash can, nearly tripping over the corgi as he dogged her every step. She opened the lid and threw the bone inside. Chewie promptly sat down by the can and proceeded to stare at it.

"Well, this is going nowhere fast," Maura commented with good humor. "An old, dry bone he found a day ago wouldn't seem to be much competition. I think I'll just have a walk around myself."

"Not on my land, you won't!"

The women turned to see Clem, trusty shotgun dangling at his side, approaching them with long, determined strides. In his wake scuttled Anna, who was taking shorter and considerably more numerous strides as she struggled to keep up with him.

"I knowed that copper's car!" the old man fumed.

"Oh, knock that nonsense off!" Bess scolded. "You're on *my* land now, you idiot, and you know perfectly well my note said that Detective Polanski was coming. Now behave yourself before I take that fool shotgun away myself!"

"No need," Anna said sharply, swooping in from behind to twist the gun out of Clem's hand. The man scowled at her, but did not resist as Anna tucked the shotgun securely beneath her own bony arm. "Don't worry, ladies," she said with a sigh. "It's all for show, you know."

Clem stamped his foot. "What's all this about?" he demanded. "Who needs to talk to me?"

"It's about those old gravestones at your place," Bess explained.

Clem looked blank.

"You mean the Crider family's?" Anna asked, stepping forward.

"I couldn't remember the name," Bess answered. "The ones on Clem's back acre, over the hill."

Anna nodded. "Those are the Crider's. Although I'm not sure the names are readable anymore. That was before my grandfather's time, even. Story goes they were tenant farmers who died of diphtheria. What about them?"

"Maybe nothing, Ms. Krull," Maura spoke up.

"It ain't illegal to have folks buried on your property when they died a hundred and umpteen years ago, is it?" Clem fired at the detective.

"No," Maura answered, "as long as those graves are respectfully treated. That's why we're here. We want to make sure that they haven't been vandalized."

"Has something else happened?" Anna asked. She cast a disapproving glance at Bess. "Have there been more young hooligans hanging about?"

Bess's lips twisted. "Sadly, no," she replied. "I've been disappointed about that."

"This is my land we're talking about!" Clem spouted off. He turned to Maura. "If you coppers know somebody's been trespassing, I want to hear about it right now!"

"We don't know," Maura replied. "That's why we want to take a look. Would you mind?"

Clem puffed out his narrow chest. "Ain't *nobody* going on *my* Daddy's land just to—"

His words broke off with a grunt as Anna shot out her free arm and thwacked him across the chest. "Oh, get over yourself, you old fart! It was my Daddy's land before it was your Daddy's land, and don't you ever forget it!" She turned to Maura. "Of course you can take a look. It's just a few minutes' walk this way. Come on. I'll show you."

Leigh struggled to contain a grin. Her Aunt Bess was right. Clem and Anna did bicker like an old married couple.

Anna started walking, and Clem, Maura, and Bess headed out after her. Leigh, who had been keeping a close eye on her daughter throughout Clem's display of machismo, was relieved to note that Allison had not been frightened. If anything, she was amused. "Should we bring Chewie with us, Mom?" the girl asked, nodding her head in the direction of Bess's driveway.

Leigh looked over at her valiant watchdog. He was doing the same thing he'd been doing the entire time the four women were being assaulted by a stranger brandishing a shotgun. He was sitting and staring at the trash can.

She sighed. "Dinner is at six," she reminded him, clipping the lead to his collar and giving it a tug. "Get over it."

There was little talking as the group followed Anna through the thick brush behind Clem's dilapidated dwelling. The ground was no longer soggy with mud, but neither was there any real trail to follow, so the going was slow. Clem hopped about nervously, placing himself between the women and even the slightest piece of property he saw in need of protection: his deer stand, a pile of bullet-pierced cans, an overgrown vegetable garden, the rusted shell of a long-dead lawn mower. When Maura came within a few feet of what looked like an abandoned outhouse, he literally cringed with angst.

Leigh was grateful that the shotgun was no longer in his hands. She hung on to Chewie's lead herself, watching to see if anything in particular sparked the dog's interest. She knew he hadn't been on Clem's property yesterday... but still. If stray dogs — or people — had raided the gravesites, other remains could be scattered anywhere. She suppressed a shudder. If she had her way, Allison wouldn't be with them at all, but she was hard pressed to think up a good reason why the ten year old couldn't investigate a centuries-old gravesite in broad daylight in the company of two relatives and a police detective. Leigh's smart-mouthed aunt had called her "Frances" twice this week — she'd be damned if she'd risk going for three.

"It's not much farther," Anna called back finally. "Just on the other side of this rise." Leigh couldn't help but be embarrassed at how clumsily she herself moved through the brush relative to the three oldest travelers in the group. Allison was thin enough to slip through anything, but Leigh's childhood trail-blazing days were long behind her, and she knew her now-suburban self would have struggled even if Chewie hadn't been entangling her legs the entire way. When at last she caught up with the others, her only consolation was noting that it was not she, but city-girl Maura Polanski, who brought up the absolute rear. "Next time we'll rent mules," she quipped as the policewoman joined them.

"Oh dear," Anna said with a sigh, kneeling down next to one of several odd-sized pieces of light-colored stone. "These markers are falling apart, aren't they?" She reached up and whacked Clem carelessly on the shin. "Why haven't you been keeping an eye on this place?"

"It ain't my job, woman!" Clem fired back. "Ain't nobody paying me upkeep!"

"Show a little respect!" Anna rebuked, as she gathered the pieces of stone and attempted to match them up like a puzzle. "This was one of the children, I think," she explained, laying the pieces down again close together. "But you can't read the writing anymore. Now this one..." She paused to brush away some weeds and debris from a stone lying flat on the ground. "This was the mother. You can barely see the writing on it. And there was one more..." she hunted in the brush nearby to unearth another, much smaller stone. "This was the baby. I remember that. Sad, isn't it? For them all to have died at once. But such things happened all the time, back then."

They were all quiet for a moment. Then Bess, Leigh, and Allison bent down and began to assist Anna in pulling up more weeds around the stones. Leigh noted that the trees around them were relatively young; back then, this area had probably been a grassy knoll cleared for farming. Clem stood by awkwardly, his resentful gaze hovering over the gun that lay close to Anna's side. Maura walked the length of the plot slowly, her brow furrowed, stooping down here and there to examine the ground. Chewie had lain down in the leaves to rest his short legs. If anything, the dog looked bored.

"Well, thank you both," Maura announced, giving a nod to Clem and Anna. I appreciate your showing us this. But other than being untended for a while, these graves do seem to be intact. No vandalism here."

"What made you think they might have been vandalized?" Anna asked.

Maura cleared her throat. "We haven't verified anything yet," she explained in her best detective voice, "but this dog picked up a bone fragment somewhere near Bess's house, and there's a chance it could be human remains."

Clem and Anna paled. "*Another* murder?" Anna asked in a whisper. "Or do you mean that the man's body wasn't—"

Maura held up a hand. "No, no. I assure you that Brandon Lyle's body was properly disposed of by the authorities. There's no reason to assume any tie between the two. The bone Chewie found was old; and it was only a fragment. We still aren't even sure it was human. But since if it was, the most likely source was an old gravesite, I thought we should check this one out. Are you aware of any other graves nearby? I mean, besides the church cemetery?"

Clem remained standing silently with his mouth open. Anna

shook her head slowly. "I never heard of any besides this one. From as far back as I know, people used the church."

"Well," Maura said assuringly, "We'll figure it out. I don't expect any trouble, but just to be on the safe side, if you happen to see any people wandering around your property who shouldn't be here, I'd appreciate it if you'd give the police a call."

Anna dipped her chin and looked at the ground; Clem shook himself and shut his mouth with a snap. Leigh suspected that green aliens could descend on their roofs and spit toxic slime before either one of them would call the police, and she suspected Maura knew that, too. But it never hurt to ask.

"You getting off my land now?" Clem croaked.

"Will do," Maura responded cheerfully. "We're done here."

The group turned to head back, but Leigh startled as her peripheral vision caught Clem bending stealthily to make a reach for his shotgun. Before she could make a sound, however, Anna had nabbed it again. "Behave yourself, you old goat!" the woman hissed, getting to her feet.

"I just want to *hold* it, you fork-tongued harpy," Clem muttered back.

Leigh thought that she had been the only one to catch this little drama, but when she caught the hint of a grin on Allison's face, she knew otherwise. The child never missed a thing.

The group parted ways with Anna and Clem behind his shack, and as they neared Bess's house again Allison approached her mother and Maura with an earnest expression. "Mom, couldn't we take Chewie on the trail to the pond now? I'm sure if we walked the same way you and Aunt Bess did, and let him off his lead there, he would go back to where he found the bone. He'll remember then, I know he will."

Leigh bit her lip. Taking Chewie closer to where they had been when she first saw him with the bone was the obvious next step. She just didn't want to do it. "What do you think?" she asked Maura.

The detective shrugged. "I wouldn't count on much help from the pooch," she replied. "But I don't see how it could hurt either, as long as you guys stay on the trail. I still need to have a look around myself, anyway."

Leigh's jaws clenched. She didn't want Allison or any of the children anywhere near where she'd found Brandon Lyle's body, not even if there were a hundred police officers with them. She knew it was irrational, but she didn't care.

"All right, then. But I think I should run Allison home first," she suggested brightly, trying not to notice as her daughter's eager, hopeful face dissolved into misery.

"Over my dead body!" Bess piped up suddenly from ahead. Leigh hadn't thought her aunt was listening, but now the older woman turned, hands on hips, and glowered at her niece like a drill instructor. "Pardon my choice of words," she began, "but I do believe this child discovered the artifact, *and* alerted the authorities to it. Why on earth shouldn't she be allowed to try and figure out where it came from? This is practically an archeological expedition. It's *educational*, for crying out loud!"

Leigh's cheeks reddened. "I just don't think, given everything that's happened—"

"I'll be right here, Koslow," Maura added.

"Don't make me say it," Bess threatened in a sing-song.

"Then don't!" Leigh retorted, her whole face burning. She was beaten, and they both knew it.

Bess extended a hand to Allison, and the two skipped ahead as Leigh swore under her breath.

Not turning into her mother was proving a serious pain in the ass.

Chapter 25

Diana paced by the fountain. She fretted. She hated fretting.

But what could she do? The building's hallways were riddled with security cameras, and she wasn't supposed to be there. She hadn't come so far just to get herself into trouble now.

But she *had* to know what was happening!

Inspiration struck. There was an upscale hair salon on the second floor. If by some fluke she were caught on camera, she could say she was inquiring about an appointment. In fact, she *would* inquire about an appointment. Mr. King-of-the-World March didn't control the whole building, did he?

She put her feet in motion. She cleared the front doors and turned quickly toward the elevators, just in case the guard at the desk had been told to watch out for her. But oddly, there was no guard at the desk. Instead, the uniformed officer was standing in the center of the lobby, his phone to his ear.

Within seconds, all turned to chaos. White lights flashed near the exits; security guards appeared from nowhere to guard them. People attempting to leave were detained. The elevator in front of Diana opened, and as soon as its large group of occupants disembarked, she slipped in behind them and hit the close button. With only an inch to go she heard a voice calling—no doubt to her. But it was faint enough she could claim she had missed it. "Ma'am! I'll have to ask you to stay here for the—"

The elevator sped swiftly to the second floor. Diana disembarked, being careful to make steady progress toward the salon, even as she took in her surroundings. She passed by the emergency stairs, a box above which had begun to blink white, emitting an intermittent buzz. She heard footsteps pounding in the stairwell, men's voices yelling.

She stopped. Anyone would be curious, wouldn't they? She leaned in to peer through the narrow window. The solid back of a uniformed security guard flew by her field of vision and went stomping off down the stairs. "Stop him!" the man bellowed.

Diana popped open the door. She stuck her head in the stairwell. She could hear feet pounding furiously, but she could see nothing. Wrenching the shoe off one foot, she stepped inside, wedged the door open with her heel, and crept out to peer over the railing.

It happened in a flash. Bruce was flying down the stairs like a madman with the security guard hot in pursuit. He had a good lead, but Diana could see that another guard was waiting below to block him at the street level exit.

Don't interfere, Diana! Her rational brain ordered, treating her to the image of grainy black and white video being played to a testy jury in the county courthouse down the street. *And now, ladies and gentleman, you can clearly see the defendant render the guard unconscious by bashing him over the head with her cellular phone...*

As it happened, there was no time for her to act. Nor any need.

With the momentum of a freight train, Bruce parlayed his arrival on the ground floor landing into a full body blow that smashed the seemingly unprepared guard back into — and from the sounds of it, entirely through — the fire exit. Whether the guard had ever managed to draw a weapon, Diana couldn't see. She knew only that for a moment sunlight had spilled freely onto the landing, that guard number one had somehow stumbled over guard number two, and that Bruce was out the door and gone before either of the incompetents could get back to their feet again.

The sound of other doors opening echoed down from above, and she pulled quickly away from the stair rail, collected her shoe, and slipped back into the hall. "What's going on?" a trio of dazed-looking office workers asked her from the elevator lobby. "Why are all the lights flashing?" "It's not a fire alarm, is it?"

Diana shook her head. "I don't think so," she said with confused empathy, as one innocent bystander to another. "I was just on my way to the salon and I heard a bunch of yelling in the stairwell. Some men ran down and outside, but I don't know why."

The workers looked at each other and shrugged. Diana shrugged also, and continued down the hall.

He got away, she assured herself, her entire body flushing at the thought. She wished she could have seen the whole thing. The man was like an action film star...

"What are *you* doing here?!" A familiar voice raged.

Diana's teeth clenched. How many times had she heard that line today?

She offered Gil, who must have just emerged from the same stairwell himself, only the briefest of backwards glances — and continued walking. He was thoroughly disheveled, dripping with sweat, and seriously pumped with adrenaline, and at any time prior to this morning would have set her female hormones into a tizzy. But since then, she had met a *real* man.

"I'm making a hair appointment," she threw over her shoulder offhandedly. "Do you mind?"

Heavy footsteps pounded; Gil reappeared in front of her.

"You tipped him off," he said with a growl. His green eyes burned with anger; his chest heaved, still struggling to recoup lost breath. "He knew what Chad was doing the second he went for the button. Otherwise, we would have had him!"

Diana reached up a hand and swept a stray strand of bang from her forehead. "I really do need a trim," she replied.

Leigh, Maura, Allison, and Bess had not yet reached Bess's backyard when the sound of slamming car doors and shouting boys reached their ears. Allison gave a jump and ran on ahead.

"Oh, right!" Bess remarked. "In all the excitement, I completely forgot. Mathias left his ball glove somewhere — Cara asked if she could bring him over to look for it."

Leigh stifled a groan. It had been a long walk on a hot day, she was sweaty, and her legs were crisscrossed with scratches from thorn bushes that only she ever seemed to walk into. But all that was nothing compared to the fact that now she would have to worry about not just Allison, but all *four* kids getting an unhealthy dose of the macabre. Even if Bess's house weren't so close to a crime scene, tracking down the source of aged human remains hardly seemed an ideal pastime for a summer afternoon. She would have to try and divert the children's attention to something a little more wholesome. Like watching mindless television...

Fat chance of that. She emerged from the edge of the woods to see the Pack already converged in a tight huddle, with Allison gesticulating excitedly. Leigh realized with a sinking feeling that the other kids, unlike herself, had probably been party to Allison's suspicions about the bone all along. In which case, Leigh had about as much chance of distracting their interest now as she did of Chewie refusing food.

"Was your grandpa certain it was a human bone, Allison?" Cara asked intently as Leigh and Maura caught up to the others.

"No, nobody's certain," Maura answered. "But until we know for sure one way or the other, I thought I'd do a quick check of the area. Make sure there's nothing more to be found."

"Can we help?" Ethan offered.

"We were going to take Chewie on the trail to the pond," Allison informed.

"We can search the whole woods!" came the take-charge voice of the twelve year old who was so clearly Gil's son. "We can split it up into sectors, just like the real search parties do. We can assign a formation, and walk in straight lines — "

Leigh fought a strong urge to bundle the four of them into Bess's cellar and turn the key. "I don't think — "

"Koslow," Maura interrupted. "Will you chill out? I got this."

The policewoman cleared her throat. Loudly. "All right, troops. Listen up! This isn't fun and games — this is serious police business. I can deputize you all for certain limited duties, but you've got to follow the rules. First one is: The only mammals wandering around in these woods today are going to be Chewie and me. You guys can walk *on the trail* as far as that big oak tree right before you get to the pond. No one's allowed off the trail — you can't be crashing around in the bushes getting the dog all riled up. Your job is to keep an eye on him — and if he stops anywhere and starts digging, you let *me* know. Don't go interfering with him yourself. Second rule is: Don't forget the first rule, or you will feel the Wrath of Polanski. Got it?"

Lenna and Allison stifled giggles. Leigh had no idea what the "Wrath of Polanski" was, but the not-so-ominous threat had kept the Pack in line ever since kindergarten.

"Got it!" Ethan and Mathias said cheerfully.

"Mom?" Lenna's soft voice quivered, "The bone *was* old, right?"

"Yes, honey. There's nothing to be afraid of," Cara answered. Then she sighed with resignation. "But you don't have to go if you don't want to. I can stay here at the house with you."

Lenna's cornflower blue eyes lit up with alarm. "Oh, no!" she said quickly. "I *want* to go!"

Cara threw her cousin a sideways look. Melanie's all-too-stereotypical feminine timidity was a constant source of aggravation to her strong-willed mother, but lately, there had been signs of hope. Just last week a boy in Lenna's gym class had told her that she threw like a girl, and instead of tearing up in embarrassment, she had turned around and yelled at him to stuff it. Cara couldn't have been more pleased if her daughter had gotten detention.

"All right, then," Maura ordered. "Fall in!"

Leigh watched as the Pack immediately hopped onto the trail in single file. They all adored their Aunt Mo, who had begun drilling them in pseudo-military formations as soon as they'd gotten too big for horsy rides on her back—which, incidentally, was some time after they had gotten too big for horsy rides on their father's back. As much as Maura enjoyed the Pack, however, she had never shown any interest in kids of her own. Between the four of them and Gerry's two, who were now in college, Maura's standard response to the question was, "I have enough kids."

"Leigh," she said, "You can go ahead and let Chewie off lead now. Maybe we'll get lucky."

Leigh did as she was instructed, but made no response, as she suspected her idea of luck was different from Maura's. She hoped quite fervently they would find nothing at all.

Bess had taken the lead on the trail, and Leigh and Cara brought up the rear. After they had progressed about a third of the way to the pond with the most exciting thing happening being Lenna's panic over a wasp, Leigh began to feel more optimistic. The corgi was having a fabulous time, which was no surprise, seeing as how there was nothing he loved better—besides dinner, of course—than being surrounded by attentive humans. But making himself useful was not on the agenda. He got under people's feet, ran circles around their shins, and came closer every time someone shooed him away. He hadn't strayed more than six feet from the trail since they left the house. But then suddenly, without warning, he stopped short. His giant ears perked high and twitched from side to side like antennas.

The travelers all stopped with him. Chewie stood frozen a moment more, then bounded off toward a thick section of plant life that surrounded a fallen tree. When he reached it he stopped and whined, then began to pace, all the while peering more deeply into the underbrush. "Aunt Mo!" Allison called in a loud whisper. "He's found something!"

Chewie whined again. He paced some more. Then, with a sudden explosion of nerve, he charged straight forward into the foliage.

He emerged again, with a yelp, three seconds later. It took another two seconds for everyone present to know exactly why.

"Ugh!" Leigh groaned.

"Oh, Lord," Bess exclaimed.

"SKUNK!!!" Ethan and Mathias shouted.

Lenna squealed like a banshee.

"Back to the house!" Cara ordered. "No one touch him!"

An embarrassed and chastened Chewie, his nose wrinkling and whole face grimacing with distaste, made a beeline for Leigh's legs. "You walked right into that one, my man," she commented, picking up her feet alternately to keep the dog from sitting on her shoes as she attempted to clip his lead back on without touching any wet fur. The stench was so bad her own eyes watered, and as soon as he was attached she held the lead out from her side and started moving him towards the house. "Aunt Bess," she said, feeling as if she could taste the vile spray in her own mouth, "Do you —"

"I'm on it, kiddo," Bess answered briskly, passing by her. "He's not the first dog to meet a skunk in these woods, and I dare say he won't be the last. I've got everything for the recipe up at the house — just give me a minute to throw it together."

She hustled forward to join the Pack, who were already well on their way to the house, shepherded by a determined Cara.

Leigh watched the children moving steadily away toward safety, then turned an affectionate eye toward her dog. "Taking one for the team yet again, eh boy?" she whispered. "Just between you and me... *you done good.*"

Chewie sneezed.

Leigh's aunt proved a tower of efficiency. Within minutes four eager children had donned hazmat suits of plastic rain ponchos and latex gloves and were standing ready with a giant batch of Bess's special recipe, a garden hose, one tube of eye ointment, and six towels. Chewie's "treatment" was begun.

After a few minutes Maura emerged from the woods and joined Leigh in leaning against Bess's woodpile.

"See anything?" Leigh asked.

The detective shook her head. "I saw tracks that could have been Chewie's here and there, but no freshly dug holes, and no more bones lying about. But that's to be expected. Locating the original source would have been a long shot, even with the dog."

Leigh was relieved — and disturbed — at the same time.

"So, what if the lab report does confirm it's human?" she asked.

"Then we bring out a real search team," Maura responded. "And I'll see if I can get a cadaver dog. Those K-9 units are amazing; if there are any more human remains out here, they'll find them."

Bess, who had noticed Maura's reappearance and made quick strides in their direction, caught her last words. "Ooh!" she exclaimed. "I'd love to see some police dogs in action!"

"Bess," Maura said, straightening. "You wouldn't happen to know anything about a camouflaged, motion-activated camera that's hidden on the edge of your property by the pond, would you?"

The older woman's eyes glinted mischievously. "I might. Provided it's not illegal, of course."

"And might you know what's been happening by the pond lately?"

Bess's face changed to a pout. "Not a blasted thing, Detective," she said bitterly. "Maybe the criminal returning to the scene of the crime was too much to hope for, but still! I know the news reports just said 'wooded area behind the church,' but you'd think *somebody* would come sniffing around the pond, wouldn't you? Yet all I've caught were a couple of does and a groundhog!"

Maura's phone buzzed, and she pulled it from her pocket and looked at it. Her brow furrowed. "I've got to take this," she said brusquely, moving off toward the drive.

"Did Maura find anything?" Cara asked, walking up. But before anyone could answer, her own phone beeped with a text. At the sight of it, her face paled. She immediately stepped aside and dialed a number. "Gil? What's going on?"

Leigh watched as her daughter, who had probably been loitering within earshot all along, now surreptitiously drifted after the women and their phones. "Allison!" Leigh chastised. "*No.*"

"Spoil sport," muttered Bess, returning to dog duty.

As soon as Leigh was left alone, Allison approached, her face set with determination. "Mom?" she began.

"Yes?" Leigh answered nervously.

"I've been thinking about what Aunt Mo said... about the two things not being related. You know, Brandon Lyle's murder and Chewie finding that bone. You don't really believe that, do you?"

Leigh felt an urge to fidget. She suppressed it. "I haven't thought about it."

Allison's brow furrowed. "How can you not think about it?"

Leigh fidgeted. Why couldn't the girl obsess over something a little more normal for her age? Like baking brownies? "What am I, a detective?" she said dismissively. "It's not our business to think about it, Allison. Particularly yours."

Allison looked frustrated. "But, Mom, the two things *have* to be related! I mean, coincidences that big don't just happen. Two bodies in four days, found so close together? Remember when I was trying to find a four-toed salamander in our backyard, and Grandpa started telling me about statistics and probability, and he said that—"

"Aunt Bess!" Cara's sharp voice caused everyone to stop and look at her. She offered a conciliatory smile, but no one was fooled. She stepped quickly to Bess's side. "Would you mind if Leigh and I left the Pack with you until they finish up with Chewie?" she asked. "We need to go somewhere—but we won't be long."

"Of course," Bess answered, collecting Allison and redirecting her toward the deskunking area. "They can stay as long as you like. But what—"

Her question went unanswered as Cara grabbed Leigh's elbow and hustled her toward the vans. "We should drive separately," she instructed.

"I assume you've heard from Gil?" Maura asked when the women reached the driveway.

"Yes," Cara answered. "We're meeting him at the house; the kids are staying here for now."

Maura nodded. "I'm going to go see Peterson up at the station." She looked over her shoulder at Leigh. "Let me know what's going on with you, all right?"

Leigh had no time to respond. The detective was already in her car and driving off.

"Cara—" Leigh began.

"Just drive!" her cousin ordered, all fake equanimity gone. "I'll explain when we get there!"

Chapter 26

Cara's "explanation" left much to be desired. All Leigh knew by the time she and Cara walked into the farmhouse—where Gil, Lydie, and Frances all stood rigidly in the living room waiting for them—was that Courtney's "mafia man" was loose in Pittsburgh and had shown up at Gil's office. The women's faces were ashen and Frances was clearly in need of a valium.

Cara greeted her husband as if he'd been through a military battle. "Are you sure you're okay?" she pressed, checking him over herself to make sure.

"I told you, I'm perfectly fine," he insisted. "Nobody got hurt. One of the guards got the wind knocked out of him, that's all."

"But what was this man *doing* there?" Cara insisted.

Gil ran a hand through his rumpled hair. Leigh couldn't remember ever seeing him so disheveled. Outside of a gym, the closest he came to breaking a sweat was driving his golf cart with the top down.

"I told you, he's trying to find Courtney," Gil explained. "How he connected her with me, I don't know. But I have my suspicions."

"Diana Saxton," Cara said sharply.

"Probably," Gil agreed.

"Do you even know where this Courtney woman is?" Lydie asked. Frances said nothing. Her eyes were wide as saucers. Leigh knew the signs. At any moment her mother would morph from passive panic into active panic—at which point the orders would begin. Frances' brain was clicking all the details into place even as they spoke.

"Not right now, I don't," Gil answered. "She was supposed to come by my office this afternoon, to meet an associate of mine and pick up his keys. She never came, and she isn't returning my calls. In fact, her phone seems to be shut off entirely. I'm guessing she realized this man had followed her to Pittsburgh and now she's on the run again."

"So, he is dangerous," Leigh said stupidly.

Gil looked at her. "Courtney certainly seems to think so. But we still don't know exactly *who* he is. She refused to give me a name. We've got him on the security tapes, but it's no easy feat to ID a man when all you have to go on is that he's from Chicago." His voice grew edgier. "I think Diana knows who he is; and I think she put him on to me. But I can't prove it. She admitted to the police that she ran into him this morning at Brandon's apartment, that he was looking for Courtney. But she insists she didn't tell him anything."

Cara referred to Diana with a distinctly unladylike term. "She *always* tells just enough of the truth not to get caught!"

"But why would he go after Gil?" Leigh insisted, trying, in her own mind, to minimize her irrational fear of the man. Every criminal on the planet was not out to get her family. Really, they weren't. "Brandon is dead — all he wants now is to find Courtney, right?"

Gil's eyes flickered with something Leigh really did not want to see. She suspected he didn't want to say it, either.

"Diana believes I wronged her, and she wants revenge," he said levelly. "She proved that again when she came to see me earlier today." He paused a moment, looking at his wife. "You're always telling me I can't read people, and I know I'm not that good at it. But I was up at the reception desk when this guy walked in, and he never even said a word. He just looked at me. Just stood there looking at me, and after about three seconds, Chad hit the security button. The guy saw Chad's hand move, and he bolted. He never even asked where Courtney was."

"Why did Chad hit the button?" Cara asked, sounding as if she knew the answer already.

"Because Chad *can* read people," Gil replied. "I could tell the guy was mad about something — anybody could see that. And we both knew who he was, from the description Courtney gave me. But Chad said he hit the button because..."

Frances wavered a little on her feet. Both Lydie and Leigh jumped in, prepared to take an arm, but Frances gave herself a shake and pushed them away. "Because *why*?" she demanded.

Gil put an arm around Cara. "Because Chad thought he looked like... well, that he looked like he wanted to kill me."

Cara repeated the unladylike term she'd used earlier. "Diana!" she raged. "She told that man something, something she *knew* would set him against you! Either that you had intentionally hidden Courtney from him, or that you had done something to hurt her, or that you and she—"

Cara swore a little more. "Oh, Diana *would* think of *that!* And it would work, too!"

Gil cleared his throat. "The bottom line is, if this man is pursuing me, I'm not going to take any chances about putting the rest of you in danger. So what I—"

"What we're going to do is this," Sergeant Frances interrupted, meticulously adjusting her sleeves from three-quarters length to just above the elbow. Leigh and Lydie stepped back. The transformation was complete. "You and Cara are going to pack up your family's things and move into Lydie's house. Leigh, you and Warren will do the same and come to our house. This Courtney person evidently knows about the farm already, and she could return, which means she could lead this man here. But she has no connection with our houses in West View, and neither will he. It *isn't* overreacting," she stressed, looking at her daughter. "It's common sense. Now, let's everyone get moving. Chop, chop!"

Gil's eyes pleaded with Cara's for understanding. "I called your mother because I thought it would be a good idea to get you and the kids away as soon as possible," he explained. "We have a top-notch security system here, and I could hire guards, but I would hate for the kids to go through that, to feel unsafe in their own home. And the fact is, a man like him would have no trouble figuring out where I live, even without Courtney to lead him. And if he wanted to make trouble—"

"We'll go," Cara answered quickly. "But only if you come with us." She looked at Leigh. "And you guys, too. In this case, our houses are too close together for comfort."

"Sure," came a deep voice behind Leigh. As familiar as it was, she still jumped a foot. But when Warren's arms came around her she leaned against his tall frame gratefully. "We can camp out in West View for a day or two, no problem. I've been looking for an excuse not to mow the lawn. And maybe, if we're good, Frances will make my favorite sausage casserole."

Leigh's mother beamed.

The men exchanged a look, and Leigh's teeth gritted. Once again, clearly, she had been the last one to get the memo.

Her instinctive impulse to resist a mandatory evacuation order —
purely on principle—flared up right on cue, but it was a pathetic
little impulse, at best. *Had* she seen Courtney's mafia man outside
her own office earlier? Maybe, maybe not. Either way, the mere
possibility had scared the crap out of her. Having such a man in the
same city as her children was bad enough—the thought of his
coming to their home, with intent to harm, made her physically ill.
Nobody messed with her babies.

She imagined the Pack playing happily at Bess's, fussing over
Chewie, trying to talk Bess into making her famous cinnamon chili
dogs. All but Allison, whom she pictured looking wistfully into the
woods, wishing they could all walk back to the pond again...

"You start getting everyone's things together, and I'll meet you in
West View," she told Warren, breaking away from the group and
pulling her van keys from her pocket. "I'm going to fetch the Pack."

Leigh pulled into Bess's driveway, hopped out of the van, and
cringed as she looked beneath the vehicle, fearing she was bound to
see something either leaking out, banged in, or hanging off. She had
taken the private road a bit too fast and forgotten to dodge the
potholes.

She had other things on her mind.

Seeing nothing obviously damaged, she straightened and headed
for the house. She didn't plan to tell the Pack anything except that
they were all having dinner in West View tonight. She would let
their fathers explain the rest of it. Trusting herself not to seem
frightened would be pushing it. Particularly with Allison's sharp
brown eyes watching her every move...

Coincidences that big don't just happen.

Of course they did. Coincidences happened every day. No one
else thought that Chewie's bone had anything to do with the
murder of Brandon Lyle. She certainly didn't.

Never mind that the mere thought of the Pack being out here, in
the very place where Chewie had found that bone, bothered her so
much that she had nearly taken out her transmission getting back to
them.

She was nervous about Courtney's criminal boyfriend
threatening Gil. That was all. Wasn't that enough?

Her hand punched Bess's doorbell.

There was silence.

Leigh took in a shaky breath and held it. She looked over her shoulder at Bess's car. It was parked in the garage, as always. There was no one outside. No shouting boys. No squealing girls. No dogs barking.

"Bess?" she called, letting out the breath in a croak. There was no response. She put her hand on the door and turned the knob.

A cat mewed at her plaintively as the door swung open. Many more cats looked up at her, with varying degrees of disinterest, as she stepped inside. Everything looked perfectly ordinary, perfectly in place. The television was on, but the sound was muted. There was not a soul in sight.

"Ethan?" she called up the stairs. "Allison? Are you guys here?"

Silence.

Leigh pulled her cell phone out of her pocket and dialed her Aunt Bess. They had to be around here some—

From its position on the coffee table, her aunt's phone chimed "The Entertainer." Leigh swore out loud and hung up.

She had to think. So Bess had left the house with the kids and both dogs, doors unlocked, television still on, no phone. Most likely, they had all gone on a walk. That's what they always did at Bess's, didn't they?

A walk to the pond.

Leigh shoved the idea from her mind. *No.* The kids knew they weren't allowed to do that now, and Bess would never let them. As much of a nut as Bess could be, she was a perfectly trustworthy babysitter. Maura had told them all to stay out of the area until further notice, and Bess would never go against a direct police order.

Or would she?

No. By herself, maybe. But not when she had the Pack.

Leigh felt an unpleasant tightening in her chest. So where *were* they?

She cast another glance around the living room, and the television screen caught her eye. It didn't look normal. The colors were flat; there was too little motion. She took a closer look.

Her blood froze in her veins.

She wasn't watching television. She was watching Bess's motion-activated camera at the pond. And some motion was happening right now.

Dirt was flying. It was an odd angle; the source of the movement wasn't in the frame. But moist dirt was hitting the muddy bank of the pond, one clump at a time. As Leigh watched, the tip of a shovel came in and out of view, as someone — clearly a human — dug a hole just off camera.

Her heart pounded in her chest. Bess and the children could not be out at the pond, digging. That was crazy. It was someone else.

Who?

Leigh leaned in closer to the monitor, wishing desperately to pan the camera, just a little. But it was no use. Whoever was wielding the shovel remained just out of sight.

Digging what?

Her heart beat faster.

Coincidences that big don't just happen.

Could Chewie have found the bone right there, beside the pond? Of course he could have. She and Bess had been busy talking and camouflaging the camera. They hadn't paid the least attention to him.

She forced herself to take a breath. But Chewie had found an *old* bone. Old! What could old bones possibly have to do with Brandon Lyle? Or with some mobster from Chicago? The digger was most likely some random adventurer, goofing off with a new metal detector. It had nothing to do with her. The kids and Bess were nowhere near...

Another shovelful of dirt hit the bank. In the midst of this one fell something else. Something firmer.

Something shaped like another piece of bone.

Leigh stomach heaved. It was true. She wasn't imagining it. She wasn't imagining any of it.

She pulled her phone from her pocket again, her fingers trembling as she struggled to push the quick code that would connect her to the help she needed.

The kids *wouldn't* go to the pond. They wouldn't. Not even Allison. Not even Bess.

Unless they, too, had been standing here, watching the monitor, when suddenly the screen flickered on...

"Koslow? What's up?"

"Maura!" Leigh cried, holding the phone to her head with one hand even as she tore through the house and out the back door. "Send police to the pond! I can see someone on the monitor digging out there—and the kids and Bess are out there, too! There *are* bones buried there—it's real... Please *hurry!*"

Maura said something back to her, but Leigh did not know what. At a casual walk, it took about ten minutes to reach the pond. She had no idea how long it would take at a run, or how far ahead of her the Pack might already be.

She shoved her phone in her pocket and set off to find out.

She didn't know whether to be silent or to scream. A thousand scenarios ran through her head, each requiring a different plan of action. If she called out, she might be able to stop the kids before they got there. But if they were already there, in the clutches of God only knew who, it would be safer for them all if she could approach undetected...

Her ears strained for the sounds of children and dogs, feet thrashing through old leaves, carefree laughter, even cranky grade-school bickering... but there was nothing. The only sound was that of her own heavy breathing and the stomping of her feet as they pounded on bare ground, brush, and thorn bushes alike.

She had to get there fast. She just had to.

The pond drew nearer. There was still no sight nor sound of the Pack. Fearfully, Leigh slowed her steps. They must have reached the pond already. She could not explode onto the scene like a maniac, unarmed and completely helpless. She had to think.

She stuck tight to the trail, careful now to step only on bare ground. Her lungs were struggling for air, but she tried her best to keep her breathing quiet. The pounding of her heart, she could do nothing about.

Silence. It was so brutally silent. If the Pack, Bess, and both dogs were at the pond ahead of her, surely they would be making *some* sounds. Unless...

Stop that!

Leigh crept forward as rapidly as she dared. One more twist of the trail ahead, and the pond's banks would be in view.

The police would be here soon. Maura would send the nearest unit, no matter where she herself happened to be. Leigh had only to stall the person somehow—and that she was determined to do.

Whomever she was about to encounter had almost certainly murdered before... were they not digging up an unmarked grave mere yards from where another man was shot to death just days ago?

Coincidences that big don't just happen.

The thought struck her like a blow. Brandon Lyle hadn't been just any businessman, had he? He had been the one, very determined man who on the day he died had informed an entire churchful of people that he fully intended, by fair means or foul, to bulldoze the very ground in which those rotting bones lay secretly buried...

Of course. She should have fit the pieces together before, not been so deceived by her preconceptions. Maura had been halfway there, but the detective hadn't known what her Aunt Bess knew...

Leigh blinked back furiously at tears that squeezed out the corners of her eyes. *Allison.* The girl had less information than any of them, yet she had been able to intuit so much more.

Leigh reached the bend of the trail, and the foliage thinned. She stopped herself awkwardly, her chest heaving for breath, her body thrown off balance. Her eyes roved the banks of the pond.

A figure stood before her. One figure alone, holding a shovel. One slim, petite figure who would almost certainly appear harmless, were it not for the presence of the handgun that lay ready on the ground by her side, within inches of her right hand.

Leigh's eyes widened. Her heart stopped. But it was too late to be quiet. The figure had already seen her.

The woman's eyes looked squarely into Leigh's. Her head gave a nod.

It was Anna Krull.

Chapter 27

"Stay there," the woman said without expression. "Don't come any closer."

Leigh shook her head. There was no risk of that. Her eyes surveyed all that she could see around the pond, and her heart leapt as she realized that they were alone.

"I was looking for the kids," Leigh said, her voice sounding like gravel.

"They're not here," came the response. Anna's affect was flat; her face utterly without expression. She lifted the shovel high and thrust it down in the hole like a spear. The head caught in the mud; the handle stuck straight up.

"Damn tractor," she muttered. "Stupid bones stayed put for fifty years. What moron thought they could drive a tractor on the bank of a pond after a solid day of rain? Look at those ruts! Broke everything to bits, churned it up. Not so you could see any of it, but your pup wasn't fooled." She rested her arm on the shovel's handle and sighed. "I'm sorry you're here. I thought your little search team had quit for the day. I could have waited until after dark, but I figured bringing a light out here would be even more foolish." She glanced back down at the hole. "Oh well. What's done is done."

Satisfied that the children were nowhere near, Leigh weighed her risk in turning tail and running. But before she could act, Anna reached down and swooped up the handgun. Leigh swallowed. She had seen before how spryly the older woman could move, but the scene before her was still surreal. Leigh was standing in the middle of a beautiful woods, in late afternoon on a hot summer's day, with a white-haired woman in her mid seventies who weighed less than a hundred pounds. A part of her refused to be afraid—told her it was all ridiculous. But another part knew better.

To Leigh's surprise, Anna chuckled. "I know what you're thinking, young lady," she said wryly. "You're thinking that a little slip of a thing like me couldn't possibly hurt anybody. And I wouldn't, of course. Not ordinarily. But desperate situations call for desperate measures."

Leigh's already overstressed brain attempted math. Fifty years ago, Anna Krull would only have been in her twenties. "I'm sure it was self defense," Leigh offered weakly. "Or an accident?"

Anna smiled. "How charitable of you, dear. But I'm afraid not. The bastard had it coming, simple as that."

"Your husband?" Leigh croaked.

Anna smirked. "He *wishes* he'd got to Brazil. He did succeed in cleaning out our joint account, and there were other women. But sadly, his plans to travel met a bit of a snag."

Leigh's blood ran cold as Anna stroked the muzzle of the handgun lovingly with her mud splashed, bony fingers.

"I got some of my money back," Anna continued, her voice proud. "Eventually. Had to pay a passel of lawyers to find it and then wait seven years until he was declared legally dead, but it was worth it."

Leigh had a fleeting image of a sun-tanned model on a South American beach. "The postcard?"

Anna chuckled. "Nice touch, don't you think? Coming up with a good story is one thing, but it's the juicy details that keep tongues wagging."

The faintest of human sounds drifted through the trees. It was far away, but to Leigh's ear it sounded like the high-pitched squeal of a young girl.

Lenna. No, no, *no!* Where were the police?

"You can just leave it," Leigh said, running her mouth as she tried to think. "No one will know whose body it is."

Anna's lips twisted. "Now, that's foolish. It's my property. I have a husband I hated who went missing fifty years ago. It's the teeth that give it away, as I understand. So I thought, if I couldn't dig up the whole thing, maybe I could find his skull." She reached out with her left hand and rotated the shovel in the hole a bit. "But it's a moot point now."

"No, it's not," Leigh insisted. She strained her ears, but heard nothing further. "You could make up some explanation. No one's going to put a woman your age in jail!"

Anna frowned. "You know, people are stupid that way. That's what made this so damned easy in the first place. Oliver knew how well I could shoot; he just didn't think I had the guts. And that idiot"—she tossed her head carelessly toward a spot farther along the bank—"was no more scared of me than he would have been a toddler in a tutu. Ridiculous."

Leigh's stomach took another heave. *Brandon.* This harmless little old lady had killed Brandon, too.

"Came to my house that night, threatening me!" Anna bellowed. "I would have gone on to bed and left him banging all night, if he hadn't started in about eminent domain." Her voice dropped. "I'd heard that term before. I know what happens. Damned government comes in and *takes* your land, and you don't have a say. All to build some fool shopping center or some other fool thing. Well, that wasn't happening to me. I wasn't going to prison for putting Oliver out of my misery and I sure as hell wasn't going into any old folks home after that SOB bulldozed my life away for pennies on the dollar!"

Anna fiddled with the gun and flipped something. Leigh didn't know squat about guns, and didn't want to, but she had heard of a safety and she figured the development wasn't good.

"No one thinks a woman my age is capable of defending herself," Anna continued, watching Leigh steadily. "If a *man* had told that Lyle idiot that he was afraid to let him in the house, but would be happy to meet him up at a church—never mind that it was night and no one was even there—do you think Lyle would have bought such a fool story?"

Leigh assumed the question was rhetorical. Another sound—the shout of a young boy—made her heart leap up into her throat. *No, Ethan.* Don't come any closer!

Anna huffed out a breath. "Hell, no. But when a hysterical little old lady tells him that, he thinks he's getting everything he wants. Even when that little old lady doesn't drive up to the church at all, but calls to him from a dark woods and tells him to follow her flashlight!"

Anna shook her head. "Cocksure, that's what he was. I told him then that I'd rather die than sell—but he didn't believe me. He didn't believe I'd rather kill him than sell, either. Not even when he saw my thirty-eight! I don't believe he thought I knew what to do with it. Well, he found out otherwise. Funny he should fall so near where I carted Oliver. But then, there's a certain justice to that. They were both handsome, charming scum."

Another child's shout echoed through the trees. Leigh's heart couldn't beat any faster. Where were the police? Had she really been here as long as it seemed... or had it only been a minute or two?

"I don't want the kids to see this," Leigh blurted. "They don't know anything; they can't hurt you. You can walk away right now."

"Do you think I could shoot *you* from here?" Anna asked calmly, aiming the handgun with both hands.

An unwelcome image flashed across Leigh's vision. The waxen face of Brandon Lyle, frozen in death. Frozen not with an expression of fear... but of pure, unadulterated shock.

"I do," Leigh answered honestly. "Absolutely."

Anna smiled and lowered the gun. "Why, thank you, my dear. How heartening. Now, I think it's time you turned around and went back."

Leigh stared at her in confusion. The children's shouts and squeals seemed louder. How close were they? How far could a handgun shoot?

Another sound met her ears—this one from the opposite direction. A car door slamming?

Yes!

But Anna heard it too. Her brow creased. "You knew I was out here, didn't you? How did you know?"

Leigh's mind raced. Honesty? "I saw you on my Aunt Bess's camera, up at the house."

Anna's eyes widened. Her voice rose. "Bess put one of those things out here? She didn't tell me that! Where?"

Leigh gestured toward the clump of brush concealing the equipment. Anna stepped back a pace, then swore.

"I always liked your aunt," she said gruffly. "But I do wish she weren't such a damned busybody." She raised the handgun again. More noises, clearly audible now, met their ears from the direction of the church. Anna scowled. "Go on!" she yelled at Leigh angrily. "Turn around and run back where you came from. Quick!"

Leigh's feet seemed mired in the mud. She wanted to believe that Anna didn't intend to kill her, too, that the older woman would be willing to take a chance on Leigh's keeping her secret. But she could not forget how Brandon Lyle had died.

Shot in the back.

The older woman aimed the gun at her once more. "I said, *run!*"

Leigh thought quickly. She could no more charge forward, hoping to tackle the older woman before she could shoot, than she could sprout wings and fly. More than likely Leigh would trip on a root, fall flat on her face, and wind up with a bullet between her eyes. Her best shot at protecting the children was to warn them before they got any closer. So if the woman told her to run, then run she would.

But she'd be damned if she'd make an easy target.

Anna's finger moved on the trigger.

Leigh turned and ran.

She sprinted in a zigzag motion, making her path as erratic and unpredictable as possible. The girl-squeal met her ears again, and her efforts redoubled. *This way, that way, this way, forward...*

She tensed for the expected shot, the shot that she was determined would miss her. She would escape Anna's range, meet the children and Bess wherever they were, hustle them all safely inside...

She could do it. She knew she could. How far could a thirty-eight fire?

The sound came like an electric jolt, rattling her skull and sending sparks of fire down her arms and legs and through her every, already shot nerve.

Yet nothing hurt. Her arms and legs kept moving. Her body seemed functional.

The shot had missed.

She stopped her zigzagging motion and raced for the house as the crow flies. She was out of range now. She had to be. Anna hadn't chased her, had she?

Leigh was sure she could hear the shouts of grown men somewhere behind her in the distance. But she kept running. When at last she neared the house, she could see someone coming toward her on the trail.

She no longer heard the children's voices. Where were they? Only one figure approached.

It was Aunt Bess.

Leigh closed the distance between them in a trice, tried to stop, and stumbled at the other woman's feet.

"Aunt Bess," she breathed. "The Pack! We've got to get them inside!"

"They're inside already; they're safe," Bess said quickly, her face as pale and anguished as Leigh had ever seen it. "Are *you* all right?"

"I—" Leigh considered. She had heard of people not realizing they'd been shot, but she didn't think she was one of them. She took another look down to make sure, and alarm spiked as she saw blood smeared everywhere—both on her arms and legs. But a quick swipe of her hands soon confirmed it—there were no bullet holes. Only a heck of a lot of scratches.

"We have to get inside," Leigh panted, trying to rise. "She shot at me... she may be following..."

"No, kiddo," Bess said soberly, her hands on her niece's shoulders. "Anna won't be coming here. I saw it on the monitor. She wasn't even aiming at you."

Leigh looked up.

Bess's eyes teared. "Anna shot herself."

Chapter 28

Leigh took another long, savoring drag of decaf. It was late. Very late. Ethan and Allison were tucked upstairs in Frances' sewing room, theoretically asleep, with Chewie snoring on the floor between them. Mathias and Lenna were with Lydie in her house next door. Everyone else in the family, plus Maura, was gathered in the Koslow's living room decompressing over hot drinks and warm apple pie. Everyone except Gil, Leigh noted. He had been present a moment ago, but must have slipped away.

"Are you sure Allison is asleep?" Leigh asked her husband, who had just returned from his third child reconnaissance trip up the stairs.

"As sure as I can be without poking her and waking her up," Warren answered. He returned to Leigh's side, where she sat on the couch with her swollen, smarting legs propped up on her father's favorite ottoman. Warren had been hovering at her side, quite uncharacteristically, all evening.

She was rather enjoying it.

"I can't believe Allison is upset that she didn't guess about Anna," Leigh commented with a sigh. "How on earth could she? None of us did."

"I'm the one who should feel responsible," Bess said ruefully. "I knew the woman was a strange bird, but I never would have thought—"

"Don't you dare blame yourself, Bess," Maura said firmly. "She fooled everybody. Peterson and I both interviewed her, and we missed the signs. Maybe if you'd known her back then, when she was still married, you'd have had a clearer picture. But Anna was right about one thing. People do tend to underestimate the elderly. Especially women."

"I still don't see," Randall said calmly from his leather armchair in the corner, "why Allison was asking about female serial killers, if she didn't suspect Anna."

Over in the loveseat, Cara let out a sigh. "Leigh and I figured that out," she offered. "Allison overheard us talking one morning in the kitchen, when I was worrying about Diana doing something to frame Gil. I'm not sure exactly what we said, but what Allison *heard* was that some woman was out to get Gil, and she assumed it was the same person who had killed Brandon."

"She was surprised we weren't doing more to protect her uncle," Leigh said.

"Ah," Randall noted. "The bulletproof vest."

"Exactly," Leigh confirmed. "I do believe she would have ordered one herself, if she had a credit card."

"I just wish she would have told us what she was thinking," Warren said.

Leigh sighed. "Well, I suppose we were asking for that, the way we tiptoed around the whole subject of murder. She could see how uptight I was, and the way I flipped out over those pictures on the internet..."

Warren smiled sadly. "So she was protecting our delicate sensibilities."

Leigh nodded. "Speaking of which," she turned to Bess, "thank you again for keeping the Pack out of the fray tonight. I'm sorry you had to see what you did."

Bess shuddered. "So am I, believe me. And when I recover, I plan to be plenty miffed at you for thinking I would let those children go anywhere near that pond."

"I know," Leigh apologized, "I'm sorry. But once I saw the monitor, I could barely think straight."

Bess had, as it turned out, left a note for Leigh and Cara in the kitchen, telling them that she and the Pack were headed over the hill — the opposite direction from the pond — to nose around some of the abandoned houses Lyle had left in his wake. When they returned to the house, Bess had let the kids play in the yard while she presumably went inside to see Leigh, but instead got an eyeful on the monitor, tuning in just as Anna stepped back into the frame with the gun pointed off camera. But rather than turn to jelly when her neighbor turned the gun on herself and pulled the trigger, Bess had unplugged the monitor, locked the kids up inside, grabbed her phone to call the police, and then run out after Leigh herself.

"You were amazing, Aunt Bess," Cara agreed. "We all owe you so much." She shuddered herself. "I hate to think of what might have happened if the Pack had seen what you saw."

Bess took another swig of her herbal tea, which Leigh was pretty sure Randall had supplemented with his secret stash from the basement. Her father didn't drink a drop himself, but living with Frances required certain talents in the pharmaceutical department. "Don't worry about me, kiddos," Bess responded. "I'll be jus–sst fine."

Leigh and Cara exchanged a glance. It was a good thing Bess would be staying at Lydie's tonight.

"Maura?" Gil's voice came from the dining room doorway, where he stood holding his phone. "That call I just took was from Courtney."

The detective straightened in her chair. "Where is she?"

"Back in Chicago," he answered, coming and joining his wife on the loveseat. "She wanted me to find out if she's in any trouble here. For leaving the county, that is."

Maura let out a snort. "That woman has far worse to worry about than Peterson — but I'd advise her to call him, pronto. Has she been in contact with the boyfriend?"

Gil nodded. "She was hanging out in an airport bar, waiting for a flight to Nevada, when the evening news reports broke. She turned her phone back on, and he texted her. Long story short, they agreed to meet in the airport parking lot. After they talked, she switched her ticket for a flight to Chicago, and he drove back in his car."

"So they're back together?" Cara asked incredulously.

Gil released a tired breath. "I wouldn't say that, no. She confessed what she'd suspected him of, apologized for running, claimed she still wanted to be with him. But she doesn't have any intention of continuing to see him. This business with Brandon really did terrify her. And although he obviously didn't murder her husband, she's not at all sure he's never murdered anybody else."

"He might not *let* her go," Maura said soberly.

Surprisingly, Gil smiled. "Funny thing about that. Apparently the only reason this guy came to Pittsburgh was because he looked up Lyle online and found out he'd just been murdered. He thought Courtney did it."

Leigh's jaw dropped. "So she could be with *him?*"

"What an ego!" Cara exclaimed.

"Indeed," Gil agreed. "He thought that's why she was running scared. He figured she was only being coy and evasive in her texts with him because she was afraid of the police getting her phone records. What he wanted to do was catch up with her in person."

"To tell her how proud he was?" Cara asked.

"Evidently," Gil continued. "But apparently he wasn't too impressed once he learned the truth. Courtney thinks *that* disappointment has already accomplished her next goal — to disenchant him of her charms."

Maura stood with a groan. "So many crimes. So few charges to be filed."

"What?" Leigh asked, surprised. "What about the boyfriend?"

The detective exhaled. "I wouldn't hold my breath, Koslow. Gil's office is in a public building. The guy didn't force his way in, and a good lawyer could argue that the security guards had no right to forcibly detain him. He might get charged with simple assault for the guard he plowed over, but the DA's office isn't likely to knock themselves out pursuing that, considering the effort it would take to extradite the man, whoever he is. We still don't have a name on him."

"The important thing is," Frances proclaimed, "whatever his name or occupation, he poses no threat to this family."

"No," Gil agreed. "No worries, there." He squirmed awkwardly a moment, then faced his wife. "Diana Saxton did tell him that Courtney and I were... having an affair. Just to make trouble for me."

Cara jerked upright, but Gil hastened to soothe her. "It's all right. Courtney denied it, and he believed her. In fact, she said he seemed rather... amused by Diana's ploy."

Cara's eyes narrowed. She turned to Maura. "And Diana? Please do *not* tell me there are no charges that can be slapped on her!"

Maura's lips twisted. "Peterson will talk to the DA. But don't get your hopes up. The ballistics report on the gun came back negative, of course. It wasn't the murder weapon. So even if we could prove that she took the gun from Brandon's apartment and Gil's gym bag from his car, and left them both in the health club — which so far we can't — none of it was actual crime scene evidence. Peterson's tried to nail her for the bomb threat, but it looks like she used a disposable phone; he's got nothing to go on. There might be something related to interfering with an official investigation, but even that's iffy. Fact is, she had nothing whatsoever to do with Brandon's murder. She's just been screwing with all of us for the fun of it."

Cara's face turned dangerously red.

The room turned so quiet Leigh could hear Chewie's snores through the ceiling. Bess let out a hiccup. The mantle clock ticked.

Finally, Cara's unpleasant color diffused. She took a long, deep breath. "Well, I'm done thinking about her," she proclaimed, slapping her thighs. "No more negative energy—that's done. The wench will trip herself up eventually. Somehow, someway, she'll get what's coming to her."

Leigh watched as a tiny spark of determination lit up both of Maura's baby blue eyes.

"Yes," the detective said evenly. "I do believe she will."

Epilogue

Two weeks later

Diana Saxton sat back in her zebra-striped desk chair and sighed.

The job that wifey-poo had paid her so generously to accomplish was done at last—no thanks to the snippy business guru and his sniveling accountant friend. Two worse whiners, the world had never seen. She could have done the work in five days if it weren't for their anal-retentive badgering. As it was, she'd had to work every hour of the two weeks Courtney had already paid her for.

And she still hadn't found a new target.

With all the fuss over Brandon's murder, she wasn't at all sure how she was going to. The once promising Lyle Development, Inc. was no more—or at least it would be no more, once the bankruptcy lawyers got through with it. The undeveloped properties Brandon had bought would be auctioned off to the highest bidder, with the proceeds going straight to his creditors. She had thought the Nicholson project might be revived, since the primary holdout, a.k.a., Brandon's murderer, had conveniently bought herself a one-way ticket to hell. But *no*, wouldn't you know it! The old bat had left all her property to another old bat—that relative of Gil's, no less—and old bat #2 wouldn't grant access if hell did freeze over. All those now-worthless plots of Brandon's would be divided back up and sold to more insignificant little people to put more insignificant little houses on.

"Insignificant" didn't interest her.

Neither did "little."

She pulled a file from her drawer and addressed a ragged nail. She couldn't stand this town much longer. She had been quite good, lately, and the strain was getting to her. She had cooperated with the police—been ever so helpful, ever so innocently unsuspecting of their motives. They couldn't make a single charge on her stick, and they knew it. She was free to leave town, now. The dance had reached its end.

She sighed once more.

It was funny how things worked out. She'd never had a clue who'd killed Brandon. She had thought—when she bothered to think about it—that it was probably some nefarious business contact from the past. Someone he'd tried to steal from, someone he'd tried to blackmail. Regrettably, Brandon had not been in the habit of telling her his secrets.

But she did know one thing for certain. Brandon Lyle would not have been pleased at the nature of his demise. Being shot by a disgruntled business associate was one thing. A vicious attack by a jealous lover—all the better. But being shot in the back by a crazy little old lady with a vintage 1950s Smith & Wesson thirty-eight?

OMG! The man would *die*.

Diana chuckled at her own joke. It was quite comical, really. And to think that the murderer got caught red-handed, out digging up *another* grave, by the same woman who had found Brandon's body! What was it with Gil's in-laws, anyway? Diana had never actually met Cara's cousin Leigh, but she had to admit she was curious. That chick had some seriously weird karma going on.

Diana tossed her nail file back in the drawer, and her eyes caught sight of something interesting. A white business card lay in the tray, just under her purple highlighter. She reached in and pulled it out.

Bruce Anjelo.

She smiled as the image replayed in her mind of his stunning body blow to the security guard. He had a stunning body, period. She had thought of it often.

She tapped the card gently across her lips. Courtney and he were history; she was certain of that. Though wifey-poo had barely said two words to her in weeks, she knew that Courtney was in the process of leasing a new apartment in San Francisco, that she was no longer in hiding, and that she had been in an exceptionally foul mood.

Excellent.

Diana looked again at the writing on the card. Bruce Anjelo, assuming that was his real name, might very well be a criminal. He could even be a murderer; she didn't really know. But there were other things about him she did know. She knew that he was hot. She knew that he was rich. She knew that he could handle himself on the street. And, though she hadn't previously considered it an asset in a man, she knew that he wasn't an idiot.

All she needed to know, now, was whether he needed an administrative assistant.

Her lips drew into a smile. She had always believed you reaped what you sowed in life. She had gotten screwed twice now, through no fault of her own. But this time, she was picking her sugar daddy right.

She picked up the phone and dialed the number.

This time, she would get *exactly* what was coming to her.

About the Author

Edie Claire enjoys creating works of mystery, romantic suspense, YA romance, comedy, and soon to come—women's fiction. She has worked as a veterinarian, a childbirth educator, and a medical/technical writer; when she is not writing novels, she may be found doing volunteer work, raising her three children, or cleaning up after an undisclosed number of pets.

To find out more about her books and plays, please visit her website (**www.edieclaire.com**) or Facebook page (**www.Facebook.com /EdieClaire**) If you'd like to be notified when new books are released, feel free to sign up for her newsletter on the website. Edie always enjoys hearing from readers via email (**edieclaire@juno.com**). Thanks so much for reading!

Books & Plays by Edie Claire

Leigh Koslow Mysteries
Never Buried
Never Sorry
Never Preach Past Noon
Never Kissed Goodnight
Never Tease a Siamese
Never Con a Corgi

Classic Romantic Suspense
Long Time Coming
Meant To Be
Borrowed Time

YA Romance
Wraith

Comedic Stage Plays
Scary Drama I
See You in Bells

24526730R00129

Made in the USA
Charleston, SC
30 November 2013